I0554000

APOCALYPSE
Cape Breton Island

MIKE SENCZYSZAK

ISBN: 978-1-7751373-0-6

ISBN: 978-1-7751373-1-3 (E-book)

www.senczyszak.com

Book jacket design by R. L. Weeks

*For Melina
and Natasha.*

MIKE SENCZYSZAK

FORWARD

This novel is a stream of consciousness piece.

'Apocalypse – Cape Breton Island' is a work of fiction, although the natural beauty of Cape Breton Island is fact. Locations, establishments, persons and events referred to in this book are not meant to represent reality; rather they are a blend of the author's imagination and fictional embellishment.

MIKE SENCZYSZAK

"I have travelled around the globe. I have seen the Canadian and American Rockies, the Andes, the Alps and the Highlands of Scotland, but for simple beauty, Cape Breton outrivals them all."

Alexander Graham Bell

MIKE SENCZYSZAK

CHAPTER 1

THE BEGINNING OF THE END

The snipers are gone, or dead, one of the two. I haven't heard a shot or sensed their presence in days. I'm not sure if that's a good thing or not. If they're dead on the island, if no one's left to make sure survivors don't cross the waters, I don't know if there's any worth finding out the truth.

I sling my binoculars and straighten up. A hundred feet before me, splayed on a rock face, is Hans, dead, decaying, providing a well-needed feast for the sea-bearing gulls, monstrous birds that dwarf the inland gull population. Hans is the name I've given the poor sod, who in better days, before he took a bullet to the cranium, looked to be a tall, blonde-haired Swede, golden mane like Fabio, a physique to match. He wore army fatigues, a Swiss backpack on his shoulders, pump-action shotgun slung across his back. I can only assume he pushed his luck, pinning his hopes on a one-man dingy as his transport, the kind you buy at Canadian Tire; maximum capacity two adults, but in reality one dwarf—unless sinking is your intent. By my speculation, he'd waited until after dark, when any remaining lights on the island dimmed. He crouched and bided his time, not daring to light a smoke or check his watch for fear the tiny glow would expose his intention. Hans was alone, no vehicle I could see, no backup, no stash of supplies other than the backpack, one I've long since ransacked and discarded. Within in it he had the staples; canned food, ammunition, Bowie knife, flashlight, First Aid Kit, lighter, and a carton of cigarettes. I'm not a smoker, at least I wasn't, but lung cancer is no longer a concern of mine. Hell, I could be in stage four, cancer metastasized beyond all hope, and it wouldn't make a fucking difference. My days, our days, humankind's days, are numbered.

At least that's what I figure.

The putrid goop of pink brain tissue has long since turned black, a fly-fest. Hans is decomposing, and not in a good way. The birds have turned what remains of his head and neck into a banquet, a free-for-all, snippets of his vertebrae glistening like ivory, even from this distance. Every now and again the wind off the Straight dies down, and I get a whiff of reality. I can't shake the feeling, watching his corpse, smelling his rot, visualizing his soul, lost in oblivion. Who was he? What were his intentions? Why did he survive the sickness only to be splattered by a high-powered lead equalizer?

As I fumble out a smoke, I glance at the lighter, another of Han's possessions, a shiny Toronto Maple Leafs logo emblazoned on the front. Hans was a Leaf fan. Too bad he'd never see them win a Stanley Cup. Not because he was dead—because the Leafs were dead. Hockey was dead. Society was dead.

I light my smoke, peering across the water, scanning for movement, but I know there will not be any. I glance to my right, the Causeway jammed to the hilt with abandoned tractor-trailers, barbed wire, and booby traps, a stoic reminder that mainlanders were no longer welcome on the island.

The initial pull on the cigarette causes a slight dizziness followed by a welcomed comfort. I'm a smoker now, thanks to Hans. I suppose if he'd had some weed or coke, I might be a junky. Who gives a shit, old age is not a concern. Not anymore.

A seal's head pokes out of the water fifty metres out. A second head appears. What do they know of man's demise? Do they care? I set my cigarette down and reach for my binoculars. Something is moving on the island.

Goddammit, I'm not fucking alone.

I flatten, shielding myself behind the boulder, the one with bullet marks, likely from the last poor soul who sought refuge in this exact spot. Could the snipers be back? Shit. It may have been a large animal. Bears aren't unheard of in Cape Breton, neither are coyotes. Hell, I imagine the wild dog population has seen a resurgence. There's no longer an endangered species list, other than humanity. I'm the endangered one.

Had to be an animal. Maybe a deer. I raise my head and angle the binoculars, scanning, panning, as I've done every day for the past two weeks. Nothing. But I can't risk it. It won't be tonight. I don't want to end up like poor Hans, rotting away, providing a heavenly feast for scavengers; I'm not going out that way.

Reaching for my cigarette, I take a final pull and stand, careful to keep myself concealed. I grab my pack and turn.

"Later Hans."

In seconds, I'm down the embankment. Another day on the mainland won't kill me, at least I hope not. Any motherfuckers who survived the sickness are not my friends, nor am I theirs. This much I've come to realize in a short time. It's the way of the world now.

As I approach my vehicle, I scan for movement, an ambush, always wary of letting my guard down. I press the remote and the RV's lights flash, giving me the all clear. It's time to head back inland, towards Guysborough, away from the dangers of the Causeway, back into hiding.

CHAPTER 2

I awaken with a jolt. Not so unusual these days, I sleep poorly. Let me clarify–I sleep only when exhaustion has consumed me, and even then, I wake every twenty minutes. My senses have never been so keen, on overdrive, every second, even when sleep has taken me. But this time I sit bolt upright ten minutes into my first wave, my eyes adjusting to the blackness, my hand fumbling for the comfort of my rifle.

Voices.

From outside, voices are whispering. I stand and move stealth-like toward the rear of the RV, my heart pounding, the blood pulsating in my ears. I consider screaming, hollering, a primal urge invoking my inner warrior. I always contemplate the warrior's cry, letting them know I'm bat-shit crazy, dangerous, unpredictable.

But I quell the urge.

Silence, stealth, preparedness has let me survive this long. Plenty of guns and ammunition hasn't hurt.

I freeze.

The bastards are trying to pry open my storage compartments. As I move towards the front, navigating the cramped quarters, I sling my rifle and crouch the final few feet towards the driver's seat.

A muted clang comes from the rear, followed by silence. They're trying their best not to disturb my slumber.

Nice try, but not today shit-birds.

Staying low, I slip into the driver's seat, laying my rifle across my lap, peering out the window. Blackness, the moon is behind clouds, nothing blocks my escape. The smart ones, the rogues as I call them, plan ahead and block you in if they get the opportunity. That's not to say they haven't rigged my tires with deflation devices. I've seen that move, that's always a possibility.

Crack.

They've opened another compartment.

I hear whispering, a quarrel between at least two, maybe three.

Bastards.

I check my breathing, rein in my focus, and turn on the ignition. The RV, a virtual Hilton on wheels, lights up like a goddamn Christmas float. I can hear shit filling their drawers as I slam the behemoth into drive.

They scream, stifled war cries from a band of startled hobbits.

The side window shatters, but no gunshots. That's a bonus. The RV barrels forward, gravel peppering the undercarriage, the headlights illuminating a hundred metres ahead. No roadblocks, no one lying in wait, just the morning fog hanging low over the surrounding fields. After a minute I slow the beast down, kill the lights, and stop.

I'm out the door, rifle at the ready, moving towards the rear of the RV, my eyes transfixed, my ears straining. No movement, no sound of vehicles, only a rumble of thunder off in the distance. They had to have been on foot the entire way; I would have heard a car within two hundred feet. A Prius would have made no difference; I have the ears of a bat in the apocalypse. Instinct has a funny way of doing things.

I pull out my flashlight and examine my vehicle in tow, a black Ford Explorer, Platinum Edition. The tires are intact; all looks okay. I glance back to the roadway, no movement. The RV's tires show no signs of deflation, no tampering, and only one of the storage doors is damaged. They got my spare gas cans, the pricks. But it could have been much worse. And I have spares in the Explorer.

A noise.

I kill the light and freeze, pivoting at the waist, raising the rifle to my shoulder. They've followed, clever girls. I can't see shit, but I know they're advancing, slinking in the shadows, gaining ground, forming an ambush.

I fire.

Like a sonic boom, I pierce the tranquil night sky. A flock of birds erupt into a frenzy, awakened from their slumber. Everyone within twenty kilometres knows I'm here, knows I mean business. Keep on coming fuckers. Come get some.

Nothing.

The first raindrop falls, and within seconds, I'm drenched. I slam the pried compartment door into place and climb back into the RV. Rain delay. It'll rain all day now. I peel off my wet shirt, grab a smoke, and slip behind the wheel. I look to the photograph pinned to the sun visor above the passenger seat.

"You always loved the rain."

I light the cigarette and take a long haul, staring out into the darkness, listening to the drops pelting off the roof.

"Guess we'll do a little sightseeing today after all."

CHAPTER 3

NINE WEEKS EARLIER

Fucking hell. I'm still alive.

My eyes adjust to the sunlight entering through the cracks in the blinds. I've never felt this ill in my life. Like the old joke, I'd have to be dead three days to feel better. The taste of puke and bile is overwhelming, but a weeklong bender will do that. I have little recollection of recent days, only hazy memories, images, sounds, vomit.

I thought I'd be dead by now.

I sit up, not particularly concerned I'm naked, dried puke encrusted in my hair, urine-soaked sheets beneath my skin.

At least I didn't shit myself.

Rolling over, I hang my feet off the side of the bed, waiting for the wave of nausea to pass. I've barely eaten in a week, my body lean, my beer gut blasted into infamy, replaced by a six-pack. There's a first time for everything. I manage a weak smile—at least I still find myself funny.

My stomach cramps and my smile sours.

The apartment resembles an episode of *Hoarders*—'Alcoholics Edition', spurred on by weeks of self-imposed solitary confinement. Stumbling for the bathroom, I navigate an assortment of discarded beer cans and rye bottles, pausing to absorb a gut-wrenching full-body spasm. I drop to my knees, dry heaving, expecting to see a lung, but only spit and bile remain, the tank empty. I crawl the rest of the way on my hands and knees and climb aboard a toilet bowl caked with shit and dried blood.

I remember knocking, pounding.

People, yelling, arguing, banging on doors.

Maybe I had the stereo cranked, maybe I took a shit in the elevator or pissed off the balcony, I have no recollection. Anything's possible. After a month-long stupor, all at my liver's expense, I have little memory of time or events. Nonstop drinking, and that bastard of an organ survived the onslaught. That wasn't our deal.

I remember sirens.

At all hours. And the electricity going out. I recall warm beer and shots of rye by candlelight.

My business done I flush. The poop's gone, but the caked blood has found a home, at least until I can find some industrial strength cleanser. I stand, steadying myself with one hand on the towel rack. Clarity is slow in coming, but I know one thing–I'm a filthy mess. Not even the dog would recognize me, not that I have one anymore. He died soon after her. Canine heartbreak, the mutt just stopped eating. She was his world.

I turn on the taps.

I spoke with someone, a few days ago.

My cell phone kept ringing; I thought it was the landlord or cops with threats of eviction. I ignored it. I must have answered at some point because the calls stopped. Or my phone died, one of the two.

The water is ice cold, the power still off. No matter, I survived this far, a cold shower won't kill me–unfortunately.

I climb into the tub as the spray hits, my body absorbing the initial shock, days of filth peeling off me, the drain resembling the infamous scene from *Psycho*. Minutes later I'm dry, donning the last of my clean clothes, standing in the middle of the apartment, lost and alone. I always got the blues after a binge-drinking weekend, but not like this. This was fatal.

My mind falls to her, it always does. What would she think of the place now? Five months and it's fallen apart. All of it. Our lives, our future, gone.

I need a fucking drink.

But I'm dry. This much I know. Last night I polished off the last bottles of wedding wine, wine Rene and her bridesmaids made from scratch, under the watchful eye of her father, a connoisseur. The stuff was three years old, turned a vile amber hue, no longer fit for human consumption. We kept the bottles as mementos, the labels depicting a photo of the two of us in front of the 'Welcome to Cape Breton' sign taken at the Canso Causeway in Nova Scotia, moments after she agreed to be my wife.

The happiest I'd ever been.

I drank every last bottle of vinegar memories; each dead soldier placed carefully back atop the mantle, sentries guarding Rene's urn.

I'm one step away from mouthwash and hand-sanitizer.

My name is Jack, and I'm a raging drunk.

I step to the door, unlocking the array of deadbolts and peer out into the hallway. The neighbouring door is ajar. Further up

I see a figure, lying motionless, half in, half out of a doorway. The person isn't drunk or passed out as far as I can tell; I'm the only piss-tank on this floor. This dude wasn't moving, nor did it look like he'd moved in a while. I step out. At the far end of the hall, scrawled across the stairwell doors, the word 'repent' in black spray paint.

What the fuck?

I move forward, scanning for signs of life, movement, sounds. There's nothing except the musky smell of stale air and the intermittent wail of a car alarm off in the distance. I crouch down beside the figure, the torso twisted, contorted as if in some agonal misery.

It's a person I don't know, in his fifties maybe, dead as a sack of shit.

Dead.

Right here in the fucking hallway. And ripe, he's been here a while, two or three days.

No one came. An upscale apartment complex and no one came.

What the fuck is going on?

CHAPTER 4

The beauty is lost on me. The mountains of Cape Breton rise in the distance, hovering above the ocean mist like some desolate remnant of a forgotten time.

Time.

It's lost all meaning. In a matter of months, time became irrelevant. How man once gambled his present on an uncertain future, sacrificing family for advancement, money and power, only to be wiped out in a cataclysmic blur. Too few paused to appreciate the moment, to smell the Starbucks, to be grateful. Now, time factors not. For those of us left, clocks, calendars, day planners, all useless relics of a lost world. A world gone in a viral flash. Our time on earth was limited, finite; no one knew when, no one knew how, but each hoped for another year, another sunrise. How times have changed. I figure I have a year, and that's if I survive the survivors, and myself. The sickness has not retreated, perhaps hibernating, waiting, evolving, down but not out. I survived the first wave, but other killers lie in wait—dysentery, the plague, a plethora of Mother Nature's natural born annihilators. Take your pick.

My eyes move from the distant mountains, off toward the west, a few kilometres from my location. The trail of smoke is still there, rising silently into the still morning air. Not unusual, until you consider the location—the outskirts of Antigonish, the small Nova Scotia community that sprawls forever, the last populated stretch before the Causeway. Smoke is a sign of life, survivors. Allowing others to see your fire is either a careless move, or a cocky one.

Weeks back I learned the hard way. The highway bypass was a parking lot of death, and considering there was no other passage to the Causeway other than the old Trans Canada route, I had no other options. I used the cover of darkness, but the rogues still had me in their sights. The RV endured a few gunshots, a Molotov cocktail, an ill-fated roadblock, but all for naught. Both the late hour and the size of my rig caught them with their pants down, wanking into a sock. When they didn't follow, I knew they had a camp, a home base, one with food and supplies, generators, gas, a crew. You don't leave a setup like that unprotected on a gamble, especially on a big sumbitch like my rig. I figured they had to have been scavengers or hunters, maybe both. Either way, it was clear there was no going back the way I came—unless hell got a lot hotter ahead. But it makes no difference. I got nowhere else to be. Not anymore.

I stand from my seat and grab the binoculars. The view from atop the RV gives me a three-hundred-and-sixty-degree advantage. I take no chances. When you're this close, you don't give an inch, letting your guard down is what they wait for. Impatience is an ambush's best friend. I'm not letting those assholes ruin our plans.

A bird cries from overhead, drawing my gaze towards the island. Emerald green pines line the ridge of the mountains, jagged guardians of the valleys beneath.

"Tomorrow night," I say aloud.

I stiffen, the sound of my voice snapping me back into reality. It's gotten so I don't know if I'm speaking aloud or not anymore, an early sign of dementia perhaps. If it is, so be it. It's not as if I'm having any debates on politics or creationism anytime soon, not unless schizophrenia runs in my DNA.

I sling my rifle and strike a pose, feet apart, hands on my hips, suddenly cognizant of my predicament. Jack, humanity's last bastion of hope. I'm fucking Mad Max up here, solitary survivor, warrior, future of humankind. My gaze falls due west.

If only there were someone to admire the view.

I sigh, a distant part of me, a dissolving remnant of who I once was, recalls the wonder and joy of the unbridled nature around me. God's work. I close my eyes, allowing my senses to define the moment, the salty ocean air in my lungs, the gentle breeze on my skin, the squawk of gulls overhead.

A bullet pierces the air conditioning unit.

Sniper.

I drop, prone.

Time to go.

CHAPTER 5

"Anyone in?" I lean my ear against the door to apartment twenty-one.

Barking from within. Not a committed bark, not the usual boisterous greeting I'm accustomed to hearing. Misty the lab was dying.

"It's Jack Mr. Tudyk, you alright?"

The bark fades to a whimper. Several of the doors along the hallway are damaged, some refortified. This door was intact. I fumble a key ring from my pocket.

The lock clicks and the door opens a crack, a security chain inside, still intact.

"Mr. Tudyk? Misty, it's me."

I shoulder the door, it gives.

The place is dimly lit. Misty looks up at me from the corridor trying to stand, but unable. She looks like shit, her black fur matted, her breathing laboured. I step towards her and kneel, patting her head. Watery eyes look up at me with recognition.

"You'll be okay girl, I'll get you some water."

I manoeuvre through the abandoned apartment, the stench thickening as I approach the kitchen.

Old man Tudyk sits at the breakfast nook, putrefied, solid, his head slumped forward, hands on the table, like he's waiting for waffles. He's been dead a while, days by the looks of things. A nest of Misty's fur is clumped beside him; she's been keeping guard over her master, without food or water, not leaving his side.

"Jesus."

But he's got nothing to do with this. I fill a dish with water, calling for Misty but she doesn't come. She's too weak, and I go to her. Misty raises her head, looking at the dish, but doesn't drink. Her heart beats quickly, her panting strained. I kneel beside her, debating if I should tilt her head and force the water down, but I decide not to. She's too far along that Rainbow Bridge to turn back. I sit down, my back against the closet door and lower her head onto my lap. She is spent. Her cloudy eyes gaze up at mine, and she licks my hand. Her tail jerks, almost a wag, but not quite.

I caress her head and massage her ears, watching her chest move in and out, each breath more laboured, more irregular, her eyes closed now.

"You're a good girl Misty."

Her ear twitches at the sound of my voice.

Minutes later, she is dead.

I sit, unmoving, petting her.

I don't know what it is about animals, how we can feel more for their loss than a human's. I'd only known them a year, but I suddenly felt death. Why now? Why not the dead guy in the hallway? And why the dog and not the old man? He was a person, a friend, a human being, left to die alone.

Pets love without restraint. Misty held on, never giving up, even after her master's death. Animals don't abandon, and yet we treat them like possessions, trading in the old for the new when things get inconvenient.

Well done girl.

A wave of nausea hits me. Not alcohol withdrawal, not this time, it's the cold despair of realization.

He came looking for me. He must have. Looking for help. But I didn't respond. I was busy, wallowing in self-pity, self-medicating, the centre of my universe imploding, not giving a shit about anything or anyone else. I could have helped them.

I could have saved them.

I stand, my knees popping like firecrackers. Carrying the dog into the kitchen, I lower her onto the old man's lap. The stench is horrid, but I ignore it. I place his bloated purple hand on the dog's head.

And I leave them.

My mind spins in opposite directions as I rummage through the apartment. I try to focus on what I need to accomplish, on survival, priorities, but my thoughts drift.

Tudyk lived alone; his wife died years back, I never knew her. I struck up a conversation with him when I saw him carrying a gun case into the building. It turns out he was from Ukraine, immigrated to Canada in the sixties, joined the army and fought in Vietnam. He was an avid hunter, until poor eyesight got the better of him.

He had a shitload of guns, always adding to his collection, worried the Government was clamping down, introducing gun registries, preparing for an outright ban. This is Canada after all, no need for guns in a land of hockey sticks and good manners. A lot of the older generation thought that way.

Tudyk remembered what it was like living under the thumb of the Soviets. How after Ukraine declared independence in the nineties, they gave up their nuclear weapons on the condition the Americans and Brits would step in if Mother Russia ever invaded. And he remembered how the U.S. and Great Britain promptly abandoned their promise when Crimea was taken. He bought more guns, more ammo after that.

I learned a lot over a plate of kielbasa and a bottle of rye.

He had restricted weapons. He'd show me when he'd had one too many. A Kalashnikov with extended magazines was his favourite. Tudyk was smart, and responsible, old-world responsible, he kept things locked up solid. In Canada, that type of weaponry is rare, hard to come by legally, harder illegally, and worth a fortune on the street. Tudyk was no fool.

I need those guns now.

I pause my search and step back into the kitchen. The key ring still hung off his trouser belt loop. I lean in, removing the keys, trying not to notice his bloated purple hue, how his hands had ballooned to a cartoonish size, his wedding band no longer visible, consumed by sausage-sized fingers. Tudyk carried these keys everywhere. Why should death be any different?

I find the key.

The safe.

The Cadillac of all gun safes. A cruise missile could hit the apartment, and the armory would survive, wouldn't even be warm. Without a key, I'd never get in there, not with a pair of pliers and a blowtorch. I step towards the bedroom, then stop. I turn and remove a bottle of rye from his liquor cabinet. No visit ended without a toast, whether it was ten in the morning or ten at night, it made no difference. We toasted to our familys' health; *Nazdorovya* meant *to a long life*. He always had two shots, one for Rene and I, the other for his wife. He always teared up after the second shot.

Evidently, the toast didn't work for her.

Or him.

I pour two shots into coffee mugs and place one in front of the old man. I raise mine.

"Nazdorovya," I say, downing my shot.

And turn for the bedroom.

CHAPTER 6

Goddamn snipers.

They picked the wrong jersey. The Great One was a playmaker, not a sniper, no wonder they miss. But this was close. Another foot and I was JFK, with no one around to absorb the chunks of brain and skull.

The sound of revving engines rises in the distance. They're coming for me, but I have time. I roll and drop to the ground.

The first sniper I encountered was in New Brunswick, walking along the side of the road wearing the number ninety-nine L.A. Kings jersey. I thought little of it, it is still Canada after all, until a shot pierced the rear wheel-well of the RV. Then in Amherst, I spotted a second one, perched atop an overpass, this one looked to be wearing an original Oilers jersey. I couldn't make out the number, but I didn't have to.

I dash for the Explorer, detaching the tow-bar and cables, then back into the RV. Cranking the ignition, I jam her into drive and pull the rig left, stopping dead centre of the roadway. At thirty-two feet the sucker's big enough to block both lanes, they won't be able to manoeuvre past. I grab my duffle bag, my rifle, and the photograph from the visor.

"Time to go."

I run to the Explorer, opening the rear hatch as the engines grow louder. She's stocked and ready to go; my bug-out vehicle. Stuffing my items inside, I remove a small red gas can, unscrewing the cap as I head back to the RV.

I douse the dashboard and seats, the smell of accelerant reminding me of my childhood, pumping gas for my dad's tractor, the aroma pleasurable to this day. I drop the container and step out, removing a cigarette. A cloud of dust rises in the distance, two cars, maybe an ATV by my guess. I light my cigarette, inhale, then flick it into the cab.

The RV lights up like jet-fueled charcoal barbeque.

Inferno nation.

"Assholes to assholes," I say aloud, watching as the fire spreads, devouring the RV from within.

Then I'm in the Explorer, buckling up, checking the rear-view. The first vehicle appears over the crest of the hill, a kilometre back. It looks like a black Hummer. Nice choice, but it won't catch a Ford. I smile to myself, wondering how in the hell I find humour in moments like these. I slam the gas pedal, the tires kicking up gravel and dirt in a cloud of controlled panic, like the Road Runner, leaving the coyote in a lurch. Seconds later, I'm up to one-sixty.

I hear the explosion.

No racing engines after that, just the hum of the Ford. They won't get around, not easily. And they won't get my shit either. None of it. Fuck them.

I slow to one-twenty, keeping watch in the rear-view, making sure all's clear. Taking a left onto a side road I scoped out earlier, I drop my speed to keep the road dust to a minimum, just in case they're following. I have two escape routes if they do, and my new four-wheel-drive home can improvise if things get dicey.

I pull over and stop on the crest of a hill, a clear view east and west from this vantage point. From the west, thick black smoke fills the sky. I cut the engine and climb out, lighting a cigarette, one I'll have time to savour, like the first cigarette of the day, or the one after a big meal, a well-earned reward.

All is quiet; not even birds disturb the tranquility as I hop up on the hood and pull Rene's photo from my pocket.

There's no more delaying. No more waiting for the perfect moment or the safest time. No such thing anymore. They'll come looking, and if not them, others. Rogues don't care, there's no sense of logic in their actions, no patterns, despite being connected somehow, like the snipers. They communicate, signal one another over distances, I don't know how, but they do. Two-way radios perhaps, satellite, I haven't quite figured that one out yet. But the more you look like you got your shit together, the bigger a target you become. If I'd stayed drunk, drove past them on a six-volt Rascal, case of empties on the back, Hamilton Tiger-Cat flag flapping in the breeze, they wouldn't have looked at me twice. No threat, nothing to loot, no interest.

But the RV and the tow vehicle were too good to ignore. I imagine they're extra pissed right about now.

Plumes of smoke rise west of me, the fire visible for kilometres in every direction. There's no fire department to put it out, not anymore. While I'm sorry to see her go, I'm glad she went out in style, on her own terms, no maggots looting the shit out of her.

I replace the photograph and stare at the smoke trails swirling up from my cigarette. Tonight we start the final part of our journey. We retrace our steps, you and me. Heaven help anyone who gets in our way. And that includes you God, you fucker.

CHAPTER 7

"Any chance of a lift?"

I'd not heard a voice in days. I step into the sunlight holding a five-gallon water jug over my shoulder. My newly acquired Ford Explorer sits parked next to the loading doors, the hatch hanging open, stuffed to the hilt. I drop the bottle into the back.

Before me stands the remnants of humanity. He wears a Wonder Woman costume. Not a cheap Halloween knockoff, this is the real deal—Hollywood quality, complete with knee-high boots, bustier, cape, tiara. Only this dude isn't built like Lynda Carter, hell not even Jimmy Carter, this guy's got the body of Wolowitz from the *Big Bang Theory*, and an Adam's apple you'd see from space. And besides the fact he was bleeding from the forehead like a third-rate UFC fighter, he was high as hell.

"Not interested." I motion to the parking lot across the street. "Look around. You can have any ride you want."

He wipes the blood from his eye with his cape and turns, glancing behind him, as if expecting company. "Ass, gas or grass, no free rides, I hear ya. I got drugs, patches, good ones, see." He raises the Lycra covering his left shoulder revealing three small patches affixed to his skin.

"I got a shitload. What do you say, just drop me off a couple miles? Ten patches. That'll keep you high a week. Deal?"

I close the hatch. Blood trickles down the side of his face, dripping off his chin. His head swivels back and forth on his pencil-thin neck, like an over-caffeinated barn owl.

"I'm not an Uber." I remove my keys and reach for the door handle. "You'll want to get that looked at," I say, pointing to his forehead.

Transvestite Wonder Woman steps closer, his pipe-cleaner legs wobbling, unable to support his emaciated frame. Powdered residue encrusts his nostrils; this creature hasn't slept in a week. He wipes his face again, the cape saturated in blood.

"Just get me the fuck out of here—please."

Voices call out from the distance, hooting, hollering, like a redneck mating call.

Wonder Woman's eyes bug out; he clasps his hands together, pleading. "Please, here it's yours, all of it. Just give me a ride."

He removes a metal tin from his boot and holds it out.

I shake my head. "Not interested."

Two figures emerge from the alleyway, one tall, one obese, both carrying baseball bats.

Wonder Woman yelps. He moves past me, reaching for the rear door handle but I'm in the car in a flash, door locks engaged. I start the engine and put the car into drive, adjusting the rear-view, ignoring the pleas and banging. The dudes are running now, the hooting and catcalls increasing to a fevered pitch.

Wonder Woman plasters his face at my window, inches from my own, panicked, bloody, staring at me through micron-sized pupils, pounding and screaming to unlock the door. I stare back, cold, unfeeling, a part of me wanting to lower the window and tell him to climb inside his invisible plane, the one right fucking behind him. I resist the urge.

I mouth the words 'run' and hit the accelerator.

A block ahead I pull over and stop, lowering my window to clear off the blood. I want to look back, but I won't. I want to imagine Ms. Gadot got away, that good prevails, but fairy tales are for the naïve. Label me a coward, selfish, phobic—it doesn't matter. Survival takes precedence. I'm not risking my life, not for a strung-out transvestite who was going to die anyways. It was just a matter of time. Getting injured, wounded, breaking a limb, is a death sentence; Emergency Rooms are now closed. Compassion is for fools, losers, the doomed. Wonder Woman was all three.

Sorry, but that's the way of the world.

I hear a piercing scream, then silence. I hit my left turn blinker, out of habit, and pull away.

CHAPTER 8

The moon is gone. Clouds will stay the night now. A warm breeze blows from the south, rippling the waters of the Straight. The nights are surreal these days, with no electrical grid, and no one left to care, the darkness is infinite. Like it once was.

Before me, Cape Breton Island lies in wait, a dark mass of mountains and valleys, isolated, foreboding, alluring. A kilometre of strong, cold current separates me from my destination.

I lower the last of my supplies into the dory, a fifteen footer, flat-bottomed, seen better days, but sturdy and watertight. I glance over to my vehicle, bidding her a silent adieu. Giving up the safety of four wheels is a risk, like leaving behind an old friend, a faithful servant, but the time has come, and with luck, I'll find her replacement on the island.

Waves crash against the rocky base of the Causeway in the distance. I scan its length, from mainland to island. I'd thought the Causeway was the safer option. Crossing by water was dangerous, leaving you exposed too long, whether by propeller or paddle. A motor would get you across faster, but you might as well shoot off a flare in the process, the snipers on the island would spot you faster than fatty on a donut. A paddle or trolling motor was better, but by my estimation, it would take at least twenty minutes to cross. Silent, but you'd be exposed too long, an easy target, for even the worst shot.

Three weeks back I did a test run on the Causeway, to explore my options. I set out with limited supplies, no intention of making the entire trip, rather a scouting mission to scope out the terrain, the dangers, the unknowns. I wasn't disappointed. Back when things went bad, the Islanders didn't mess around.

Word had it they used tractors and excavators to dump cars, trucks, buses, one on top of another, bumper to bumper, the entire length of the Causeway, along with barbed wire and other assorted deterrents. That's two kilometres of impassable road. Not by vehicle anyhow. Why they didn't use dynamite is anyone's guess, but I'd imagine they wanted to leave their options open, should the cavalry arrive. The fools.

Aside from vehicular traffic, they also looked after rogues on foot too. I found that out quick enough. Under cover of night, I ventured forth, climbing over vehicles, squeezing under buses, crawling on my hands and knees in the darkness, praying I didn't impale myself. But it wasn't just the rusted metal carcasses to be wary of. Half a kilometre in I came across the first stretch of razor wire. It was everywhere. Where they got it from I don't know, the nearest major army base was in New Brunswick, five hundred kilometres away. I sliced my right palm open before I knew what was happening. That was the first setback. I regrouped, bandaged myself up, considered aborting the mission, but despite intuition, I forged ahead. It was then I had to stop and risk turning on my flashlight because something wasn't right.

And that's when I saw it.

Bodies.

Eight, in advance stages of decomposition. A few were impaled, booby-traps by the looks of things. I climbed atop an overturned Aerostar to get a better look. The others, the remaining corpses weren't impaled, but they were dead just the same. Some curled up, fetal style, like they died of starvation or sickness. An ambush perhaps.

I kept moving until I felt my left-hand burning, stinging. I stifled a scream and chanced turning on my flashlight again. Acid. Fuckers used chemicals, likely some good ole Cape

Breton home-brewed concoction. I wiped my hand down with gauze, wondering just how potent this stuff must have been when it was deployed.

Whatever it was, it had worked. No one got through.

Both my hands incapacitated, the test run was a failure. My biggest fear was ambush or sniper, how foolish I'd been. The Causeway was a write-off, the Straight was my only option.

I lower my rifle into the dory and sigh, curtailing wandering memories, looking across the water to my destination.

Grabbing the boat's bow, I wade out knee-deep into the water, pulling myself inside. Above my head a gull squawks, an island sentry, curious and watchful. With humanity gone, perhaps gulls are the sole inhabitants, sole beneficiaries, nature's spies, the island lookouts. Or maybe, a beacon of hope.

I scan my surroundings. The shore awaiting my arrival looks quiet and still, no lights, no movement. Aside from the gull, it's just me, my dory and a rough stretch of water. I reach back and turn on the trolling motor, the whirr of the propeller quiet, comforting; I made the right choice. Paddling against the current would be risky, a strong wind could drag me too far north, where the shoreline was too steep, too rocky to make landfall. I'd be lucky to get ashore with my life, never mind my cargo. Most of this shit I can lose, even the guns, but one thing I'd go down with the ship for, one thing I won't risk. That's the reason I'm here, on the water, chancing fate, fulfilling a promise.

The motor is slow but steady, with any luck I'll be across in fifteen minutes. The marine battery should have enough charge to last, and if not, the quick-charger at my feet will do as a backup. Either way, I'll need the charger to boost my next vehicle, a dual-purpose necessity, heavy, but worth lugging along, one final time.

A stiff breeze caresses my face and cold droplets saturate my clothing as water chops at the sides of the boat. Behind me, the mainland dissipates, succumbing to the darkness of water and sky. My life, what's left of it, lies ahead. Redemption or death awaits; my fate in the island's hands.

I adjust the angle of the motor, fighting a current that wants to pull me north, out towards open water. That would not be good. The ocean is not my friend, not tonight. I need the island. We need the island.

As I watch the mountains rise before me, I feel a sense of home, of purpose.

"Welcome to Cape Breton," I say aloud.

Approaching the midway mark, I look to the entrance point of the island, the old swing bridge, a moveable section of the Causeway that allowed boats to pass through, the dividing line between the island and the mainland.

A sound is coming from somewhere.

Music.

What the fuck?

I turn off the motor and listen.

A solitary violin plays, the melody echoing across the water. My ears strain to make out the direction, the source, but it's impossible. The music is everywhere and nowhere, as if descending from the heavens and rising from the depths. The sound is alluring, mesmerizing, surreal.

I soon realize I'm drifting out to open water. I turn on the motor.

The music fades, and I steer the boat hard right, my eyes scanning the shoreline for movement, light, anything that might account for the unexpected development. But all is still and quiet, leaving me to wonder if my sanity is the culprit. Perhaps the cumulated stress of waiting, surviving day-to-day, has overridden my coping capabilities, how could it not? What else could explain the siren's call? I've been out here every night for two weeks and not heard a sound. Why now? Why tonight?

Ask not for whom the violin tolls.

A gull swoops down within a few feet of the boat, snapping me back from the brink. The bird is following me, keeping a watchful eye on those who approach. I look back towards the mainland and see a low-hanging fog creeping along the shoreline, an earthly cloud materializing from nowhere. The weather's turned, fast. How odd.

Nearing the shore, I angle the dory towards a narrow outcropping of rocks, not ideal, but I don't have time to find the perfect spot. I cut the motor and lower myself into the water, hanging onto the sides until my feet find the rocky bottom. The water is cold, but I work quickly, pulling the boat towards shore, careful to watch my footing. Once I reach the bank, I heave the stern out of the water, far enough on land the waves won't drag her back out, at least not until I've unloaded my supplies. After that, she's free to roam, her mission complete.

I begin unpacking my supplies, then freeze.

The siren's call. The mournful music emanates again. I cock my head towards the open water, straining to hear, trying to pinpoint a direction.

And then I realize it's coming from the swing bridge.

The entrance to the island.

CHAPTER 9

She descends from above, basked in an ambient glow, ethereal, enigmatic.

"Wake up now, everyone is dead. The time has come for you to go. Listen to my words. Do not dream of day's past, but look to the future, to the time left, to your destiny. For all humankind is ill, shedding its mortal coil, vanquishing earthly existence. Death will consume, without fire, without brimstone, without remorse. Do not question why, do not despair, accept the coming. I left this earth as part of the greater will, spared the pain and sorrow of the great cleansing, but not spared the knowledge and depth of humanity's grief, of your grief. I come to you now, not as a savior, but as a conduit to the new realm.

Humanity is facing its end. Those who live will perish as is the Divine will. I tell you this not to cause you further sorrow, but to reaffirm your path. Our love is eternal; our souls connected by a beam of light, a light that exists in all realms. What we had remains. Look within yourself, find the light, seek solace in the knowledge we are one.

Your peril consumes my being, more so than the fate of all humankind. I am selfish in this regard, a sin for which I must account. Gather your things, leave at once. Take only what you require. Trust no one. Travel at night, stay hidden by day. Head east, to our island. Enemies will reveal themselves; those who remain have witnessed the Rapture, the death of all they once knew. They will try to stop you. Do not allow them. Their souls cannot be saved.

Journey to where we merged as one. Where our love was without limits, absolute. Release my light into the waters, and I will travel to the great ocean. We will be together again.

Fail, and our paths will diverge. The light will extinguish.

Know that I cannot follow, I cannot protect you, but I will appear when the time is right.

I love you."

CHAPTER 10

ON ISLAND TIME

My eyes won't open. I don't want them to. Closed I can still see her, feel her, embrace her presence. If I try, if I concentrate, the dream may continue. I so want it to, but the moment is fleeting, out of reach, vanished in an instant.

She is gone.

The message is unchanged. The first time she appeared I felt I was in the presence of God, me, last of the great pretenders, blemished and tainted, basking in a spiritual glow. But my dreams changed. I dream of strangers now, people I've never met, places unfamiliar. As Rene fades, her presence is replaced by confusion, the cruelty of existence, echoes of lost souls and distant places, rife with the ghosts of humanity's past.

I no longer want to dream.

Sunlight peers through a crack in the blinds. The room is sparse, a bed and nightstand, nothing more, the television and anything else of value long since looted or destroyed. As I sit up, gathering my bearings, I wonder if I'm asleep, still reliving a serial nightmare, but I'm not. I have little recollection of how I got here, or where here even is. My guess is I'm holed up in a motel near the Causeway, the Highland, or maybe the Travellers Inn, two bargain basement lodgings for frugal tourists. On the nightstand is my Glock, along with my watch and a set of car keys. I rise from the bed, my head pounding, examining the keys. Ford keys. What is it with me and Fords in the apocalypse? I look to my right, the door fortified, a broken chair braced against the knob, my rifle standing at attention alongside it. At least I had my wits about me before I checked out.

I don't know what time it is, or what day for that matter. I'd stripped down to my underwear before I passed out; no doubt the fever was back. My throat is dry and I grab a bottle of water from the table and chug it down, scanning the room, hoping to trigger my memory. I sit back down, my mind sorting through lost images and distorted thoughts; landing ashore, the music, the swing bridge, but the rest is dark.

I stop.

Where is the urn?

Fighting the urge to vomit, I roll across the bed and fall to the floor, searching until I find the urn inside the backpack, wrapped in a towel. Relieved, I guzzle down the rest of the water, the liquid warm, tasting of plastic, but I don't care. My stomach rumbles, a familiar feeling, one I've grown accustomed to. How long has it been since I've eaten, a day, a week?

I pick up the car keys, looking at them as if they were the missing piece of the puzzle, the conduit to unlocking the mystery of recent past. Images flash through my brain, memories, scattered and disjointed, rise to the surface.

I remember prowling through allies, checking parking lots, forcing doors, scavenging.

I went on a supply run.

I remember a Tim Hortons Restaurant—an actual Tim's, sitting at a table, surrounded by broken glass and pilfered memories, imagining the smell of brewed coffee, maple glazed donuts, and breakfast sandwiches. There is a Tim Hortons in Port Hawkesbury, a five-minute drive from the Causeway. Snippets of recall come quicker now, like a garden hose un-kinked, a trickle erupting into a flow. It's as if I'm a spectator, watching my decline into madness from afar, a fly on the shit-house wall, an impartial observer, a ghost.

Fever.

It had to be the fever, mixed with the little blue pills, a precarious combination. Illness, delusion and pharmaceuticals, a post-apocalyptic cocktail, shaken, not stirred. How I avoided being seen, ambushed, is a miracle. But maybe instinct trumps insanity.

The sickness has taken hold. I'm sure of it.

I knew it was only a matter of time, but this last setback, this lapse in memory, is unlike the others. I've had episodes before, but even drunk for a week I had better recall of incidents and events, of waking up and passing out again. My diagnosis has changed, progressed. There's more I don't remember than I do, and that's a dangerous way to live, considering everyone else is already dead.

I step to the window and pull back the custard yellow curtains. The sign says Highland Motel, I'm in a room at the back, overlooking the mainland. At least my delusional self was clever enough to avoid a room off the highway. Any traffic passing by would be tempted to stop and check things out, especially if there's a vehicle looking like it doesn't belong.

I wonder where the fuck I parked the car?

By my watch, it's noon on Tuesday. I crossed the Straight Sunday, two days lost. I pace the room and ponder the implications of my hiatus. Outside, ominous clouds look to be overtaking the sun, rain on its way, but just as well, I hate the fucking sunshine. I'm at home in the rain, miserable, depressing weather is my friend, what I prefer, what I deserve.

I remove the urn from the towel and sit back down on the edge of the bed, securing it between my thighs. A half-eaten can of creamed corn sits on the carpet at my feet, flies lighting on the leftovers.

"You don't talk like that. That's not your voice," I say aloud. "You're fading."

I try to recall the dream, shutting my eyes, searching for a clue, a prompt, anything.

"Am I going mad?"

The urn doesn't reply. My callused fingers caress the copper casing as if rubbing a magic lamp, expecting a miracle. But the time for miracles has passed.

"When the time is right," I whisper.

I set the urn down and reach for my cigarettes, noticing the beer can I used as an ashtray, overturned on the carpet. It looks like I smoked an entire pack, the acrid smell of stale tobacco competing with the room's natural stench of mold and mildew. I pick up the can and set it on the table. I light my cigarette and prop a pillow behind my head, lying back down.

Rene's ashes kept me up at night.

Keep them, spread them, entomb them, she never specified. A traditional burial was always out of the question, waste of money she said, taxing an already overburdened planet. We talked long into the night, sometimes reminiscing about past indiscretions and intimate moments, sometimes planning her death. There is no greater sorrow than watching your loved-one fade, knowing their journey is ending, listening to talk of final days and last wishes. Each word, each thought, tears at the soul and scars the heart, wounds that do not heal. Rene faced the unknown with courage and selflessness, never wavering, always more concerned for those left behind than herself. Her world was ending, her light dimming, yet she blamed no one, not God, or religion, not fate.

I blame all of them. Fuckers.

Some choose to display their loved one's ashes on the mantle, while others scatter them at a preordained location. A few spread them surreptitiously, they refer to it as wildcat scattering, spreading remains illegally, on private property without permission. Disney World in Florida was a favourite, the Haunted Mansion ride a popular dumping ground for the eccentric deceased Mouseketeer. Not very sanitary, and a bit morbid, but a grim grinning reality. A more recent entry into the not-to-be-undone bizarre tributes to the departed, was having your loved one's ashes packed into professional grade fireworks and shot up into the heavens. Prices started at a grand per minute.

Rene would cross over and take me with her, if I so much as picked up a brochure.

The cigarette ash drops onto my shirt. I look down, realizing I hadn't taken a drag. I butt it out.

Rene loved the island. Her eyes would widen when we spoke of it; even towards the end, her childlike wonder never waned. Cancer lost that fight. Her spirit kicked its ass until her final breath.

Reaching for my pill container, I pop the lid and tap two into my hand, staring at them, debating whether I should. After a moment, I replace them. The longer I stay put, the greater the risk. I'm in new territory now, an island, one that's proving to be as enigmatic as the one in the television series *Lost*; a show Rene introduced me to, the show I lost my binge-watching cherry to.

No one knows what happened in Cape Breton the final days. Rumour had it the island was clean, those few who were infected segregated, moved to different locations, some to Fort Louisbourg on the eastern coast, a historic site; living out their final days in eighteenth-century comforts, stone walls and straw mattresses. Not a nice way to go.

But they were only rumours. The survivors defended the island, the Causeway, shorelines, anywhere desperate infiltrators might make landfall. But I can only imagine those who didn't succumb, eventually consumed one other.

Or perhaps not.

Maybe this is a sanctuary, civilization's last stop on the road to purgatory. Perhaps Cape Breton, the most beautiful island on earth, home to Alexander Graham Bell, John Cabot and Dave and Morley, survived the plague.

Maybe.

I reach for my rifle and move to the window. I hear a car outside. I'm not alone.

CHAPTER 11

A part of my brain clicks and fires. I saw them. In Port Hawkesbury, yesterday morning. I was there to pillage the remains of the plaza, the Canadian Tire, the Sobeys, when I saw the convoy of vehicles approaching, cresting the top of the road, up past the Tim Hortons and the burned down Subway. I was on foot, my Ford Flex ditched behind the strip mall.

The NSLC store was pillaged, but I scoured around until I found a decent supply. No Alexander Keith's India Pale Ale, no surprise there, but enough discarded bottles and cans to create a decent mixed pack. Three bottles of Australian Shiraz were overlooked, and a half bottle of vodka, all happily received. The vodka was someone's traveller, but forgotten. My win.

Sobeys was equally pillaged, canned goods, non-perishables absent, but more than enough left to sustain my body weight for a while. I lucked upon a case of beef jerky in the storeroom, along with tins of canned corn. Score.

It was exiting Sobeys' loading doors with my haul when I heard the vehicles. I was a good two hundred metres from the car so I dropped what I had and took cover. If they cornered me, I'd have been finished.

A convoy of three vehicles passed by, the first, a black BMW 7-series, followed by matching Cadillac Escalades, red. My ears strained to make out where they had gone, their direction, my mind visualizing them continuing straight, off towards Highway 4 on a scenic jaunt to visit Rita's Tea Room, or Sydney, anywhere other than the plaza I just happened to be looting.

And to my disappointment, they did not.

I swallowed hard when the cars appeared in the alleyway—a head-on collision course with me. Flattening myself against the perimeter fence, I considered scaling it, but I'd be seen. I crouched and thought small. Be tiny, insignificant, blend in, you're good at that, they won't see you, why would they?

The Beamer passed by, windows tinted black, soulless. A moment later the Cadillacs passed, windows down, Jimmy Buffett's Margaritaville playing on the stereo.

If they find the Flex, I'm fucked. I don't move. Not yet.

And then the memory is gone.

Just gone.

CHAPTER 12

They're cars all right. And they've pulled into the lot. What the fuck are the odds?

The BMW and an Escalade stop on the asphalt driveway, two rooms down from mine. A dude in baggy blue jeans exits the Cadillac and steps to the BMW. He's painfully thin, limbs like skeleton appendages and a mop of hair that hasn't seen a shampoo bottle in weeks. He wears a revolver on his waist, questionable choice for the apocalypse, but hey, maybe he was a *Walking Dead* fan. The BMW's window lowers, and thin Rick Grimes leans in. A hand emerges from the car with a roll of toilet paper. Grimes takes the roll, I hear him laugh. He turns, and I drop, fearing he'd spot me.

"Bathroom break. You're gettin' two-ply, damn you special."

I peek out. Grimes is pulling someone from the rear of the Escalade. They're coming to use the washroom. My fucking washroom? I glance over my room and snatch the Glock off the night table. Things are about to get real. I move back to the window, but Grimes is out of sight.

"Don't fuck around." His voice is louder, but I can't see him. I adjust the curtain, trying to get a view without exposing myself.

He reappears with her.

At first glance, you'd mistake her for a boy. That was the intent. I'd not seen a female since things went bad, no kids either. They died off first, another example of God's fuck the world attitude. But this girl was young, even in oversized jeans and a hoody, she looked to be no more than eighteen. A kid. And her eyes bled terror.

My heart races as their footsteps approach. All I can think of is how fate has a way of fucking with you when you least want to get fucked. I look to the bathroom door wondering how big the window is, but I won't have time. They'll know something's up when the door doesn't give. They'll know it's barricaded, know someone's hunkered down inside. I tuck the Glock into my pants and grip my rifle with both hands. Moving to the far wall, I take up a position and wait for the boot to hit.

There's a smash, wood splintering, but it's from the room next to mine. Grimes hoofed the door. I move to the wall, pressing my ear flat against the mildew stained drywall.

"Five minutes or I come in and wipe that sweet ass myself."

A door closes. I'll be okay, as long as she does her business, in five minutes or less, and they leave. No reason it shouldn't play out that way. It's not my problem, not my concern. Grimes whistles a tune, one that vaguely reminds me of a Barenaked Lady's song, the title escapes me.

I hear a muffled bang from the back.

Pushing the bathroom door open I step inside and listen, placing my ear to the wall. She's trying the window. Judging by mine, it's big enough, but there's no way she'll have time.

There's movement within. A clang.

Grimes is pacing in the other room.

"Wipe front to back now," he thumps the door and resumes whistling—'If I Had a Million Dollars', I remember the tune now, he's musical, for a bandy-legged scumbag.

I hear a crack and the thud of porcelain.

"Bitch!"

Grimes is in.

"Fucking bitch!"

He's running out the front door. She made it, somehow. I move to the front.

"Fucked off out the window," Grimes yells, his thin frame flashes by. The door of the BMW opens, and the driver climbs out.

It just got darker outside, he's that fucking big. The man wears army pants and a black under-armour tank top, his bald head gleaming like it's topped with three coats of varnish.

Big John Stud slides his Oakley's to his forehead and turns. I drop.

"Where you at bitch?" Grimes' voice is up an octave, resonating from somewhere in behind the building.

"She ain't back here!"

Footsteps in the unit next door. And then a scream.

"Don't touch me!"

Back to the window. The big dude appears, holding the girl by the arm. Grimes runs into frame, flustered, out of breath.

"Where the fuck was she?"

The quiet calm of the big man is unsettling, like a Tony Montana, only the super-sized version, not a guy you fuck with, not someone you disappoint.

"You check behind the door?" asks the big man.

"Fucking bitch," Grimes steps forward as if to backhand her, but stops. "Sorry Bull." Grimes slinks back.

Bull, did I hear that right? A fitting name. Bull releases the girl.

"Take her."

Grimes grabs her by the arm.

"There's a car around the side," he says. "I think it…"

He's cut off, mid-sentence.

"I don't give a fuck about a car. Do I look like I give a fuck about a car?"

Even from this distance, I can tell he doesn't give a fuck about a car. My car.

The girl pulls away from Grimes and lunges towards the door, my door. I flatten myself against the wall, staring as the doorknob turns in furious desperation.

Grimes is on her.

"Where the fuck you going? Bitch, you had your chance to take a shit."

I pull the blind and peek out. He has her in an arm bar, she struggles, and he slams her face hard into the window.

Our eyes meet.

Hers and mine. For a second. And in that moment, her desperation turns to hope.

And then she's gone.

I slump back against the wall, the rifle clasped in my hands. I hear voices, two or three talking over one another, shouting, the girl yelling, something about the bald-headed prick inserting something into his anus.

A voice says 'dope her.'

There's a slam of a car door, and everything goes quiet. Someone else approaches, another player, someone I'd not yet seen.

I force myself to peer through the curtain.

The girl is on her knees. Grimes and Bull are on either side of her, the newcomer stands before them, obstructed from my view.

"Have we not treated you well?"

His voice is calm, flat.

"Have I not protected you, kept you fed and watered, safe, comfortable? Do you think I do that for everyone?"

I get a side glimpse of this person as he hands something to the giant bald-headed prick. A uniform. He's dressed in a uniform, like a military officer.

"I told you, you don't behave, you don't play nice, I don't play nice."

Bull pulls the girl to her feet with one arm, like he's landed a marlin.

"Please, I'm done, I promise," her voice is frail, weathered, beaten. The fight gone.

"Promise?" The sarcasm is palpable.

I slink down to the floor, no longer wanting to watch. Car doors open and close, engines start. I shut everything out, focus on me, survival, doing whatever it is I have to do, whatever it is I've done to get me this far.

Then they're gone.

I lay the rifle down and clasp my hands together, my entire body shaking. Silence envelops the room. Nothing stirs, no sounds, just the beating of my heart.

I should have done something.

She'll give me up. She's a desperate kid, trying to avoid being raped or killed. It's her right to survive. But I don't give a fuck, not anymore. If they come, they die, I die, we all die. It's a fucking apocalypse, get over it, we're all heading south.

I sit, content to wait for the inevitable, not planning, not caring, not giving a goddamn fuck.

But no one comes.

I wait for darkness to consume the day, like it's consumed my soul.

With the sun's descent comes the quiet and stillness of night; extended silence—silence to drown out the voices in my head.

The pleas of a desperate child.

CHAPTER 13

How does a person without a soul manage to sleep?

Australian Shiraz and a little blue pill.

Waiting out daylight takes a toll, but moving before the darkness of the island is absolute, is risky. You don't realize how dark the night is until the world stops and life, human life, ends. Then you begin to comprehend the larger questions, what life means, spirituality, mortality, finality. All that shit.

Curled up on the dank sheets, I lay awake for hours, replaying the scene in my head; a scene in which I am the star, a despicable cowardice scum of a leading man, my finest moment, on repeat for all eternity. Eventually I clocked out and fell asleep, my mind's pause button hit. The only trouble is, if the era of VCR's taught us anything, it's that keeping things on pause doesn't work. Something breaks.

I dreamed of the mainland. I was back in the RV, but things were different.

They were watching. Eyes upon me, scrutinizing me, judging me, waiting for the nod. But the nod for what? I was prey, frozen, unable to move, escape not an option. The feeling was unlike anything I'd ever experienced. I'd always heard about night terrors, but never understood the depth of their grasp. Beside me sat a figure, unrecognizable, cloaked in a swirling fog, disguised and terrifying. I remember squinting, like Mister Magoo, trying to see who or what it was, but I couldn't see past the swirling vortex. As my terror grew, the paralysis held. I sensed dread, an evil from another realm, not earthly, not spirit, but something in between. Perhaps the reaper, perhaps worse.

Headlights illuminated the darkness.

An army of jersey-wearing snipers stood facing the RV, aglow in the headlamps, standing separate, dead eyes watching me, calculating, waiting. Beside me, the vortex was gone. I watched as the snipers raised their rifles in unison, the precision unsettling, a firing squad, only with high-powered lead equalizers, any single shot capable of sending my skull into orbit. I felt the spread of warmth in my pants, and I knew this was the end.

The headlights extinguished, the snipers dissolved into darkness.

I was no longer paralyzed, no longer seated behind the wheel. A sliver of moonlight cast elongated shadows over the grassy terrain, and I realized I was standing outside.

And I felt her presence. I looked, and she was there.

The girl I abandoned.

No longer in disguise, she wore a yellow sundress, her hair long, auburn, cascading down her neck in rivers of spun gold. Piercing eyes, tree frog green, stared through me. She sensed my fear, my shame.

She smiled.

"I am Allie."

Frozen, not with fear, but guilt, I remained silent. She read my thoughts, my desire for redemption, an opportunity to rewind.

A do-over.

There was no judgement in her emerald eyes. As she

approached, my gaze was drawn to the gold chain and pendant that hung from her neck. The tiniest glow of amber light emanated from the heart-shaped pendant.

"Who are you?" I asked.

And she was gone.

I looked around, realizing I was standing outside the Highland Motel, staring at the entrance to the room beside my own.

Room twenty-one.

CHAPTER 14

I awaken with a jolt to complete darkness. According to my watch, it's past midnight. I sit up, my mind racing, straining to recover a fading dream. What was it she'd said? Allie?

And then I hear it. Breathing. Shallow. Someone is in the room with me. I stand, my hand fumbling for a light but I find only my lighter. Backing up towards the wall, I try to determine where the sound is coming from. It's here, in the room, in the darkness with me.

"Who's there?"

I flick the lighter.

A figure stands across from the bed, facing into the corner—an unsettling image, reminiscent of *The Blair Witch Project*.

Am I still dreaming?

I can hear breathing–and a heartbeat.

How can I hear a heartbeat from across the room?

I release the lighter, sparing my thumb a third-degree burn, holding my breath, listening. I relight it.

She stands in front of me.

The girl.

Eyes black, void of life, the tree frog green no longer. I gasp, frozen, like my dream, watching as a pale-skinned arm reaches out, her index finger extending, as if pointing to something. I look to the adjoining wall, to the room she was in.

"Fuck." I drop the lighter, stumbling backwards. I reach around in the darkness, removing my industrial-sized flashlight from the backpack.

The beam illuminates the room with a funnel of light.

She's gone.

How could that be?

I check the room, the washroom, behind the door. Nothing. The window is intact. She couldn't have left.

I step back into the bedroom, examining the still barricaded front door. No one got in or out.

Lighting a candle, I sit back down on the bed.

Madness. It must be. A dream bleeding into another dream, bleeding into reality. Like the film *American Werewolf in London*, a gimmick that became overused, played out in film after film, show after show. That has to be it. The wine, the little blue pills, the sickness, heavy on the guilt. I dreamt it.

I grab the wine bottle and drink, regaining composure with liquefied courage. Let's not lose it just yet. We've got plans, goals, much to accomplish before I succumb to madness. I hold out the bottle in a mock toast.

"Keep me sane a little longer Rene."

The bottle drops from my hand, but I don't notice. I grab the flashlight and angle the beam towards the washroom. There is a noise, a sound from the other side of the wall, coming from the next room. I stand and listen, doubting my senses, convincing myself I'm delusional. The door's been kicked in for hours, probably an animal, raccoon or squirrel, nothing worthy of panic. I press my ear to the wall, but the only sound I hear is my heartbeat.

No more sounds. I glance at my watch. Time to leave.

CHAPTER 15

I set the backpack on the front seat. All in all the Flex is a decent choice, roomy, stylish, in a retro 1950's California orange-truck sort of way, fitting for a post-world landscape. The crimson red body and white roof make a statement; if I could add anything, perhaps a pair of customized plates, something like *SURVIVOR*, would complete the package.

Leaving under cover of darkness is the right decision. I've been here days, and I'm only a kilometre from the mainland, the heart of the island waiting, unexplored.

I tried disabling the Flex's running lights, but I was short on time, and I didn't want to fuck anything up. No headlights are handy for staying inconspicuous, but the highway would be risky to navigate in the dark, especially without moonlight. My eyes aren't what they used to be; headlights were a must.

I climb into the driver's seat. Nothing is moving in either direction, at least nothing I can spot. A breeze wisps through the open window, the ocean air thick, reminding me of how close I am to the mainland. I've been careless, holed up here far too long. Staying put is asking for confrontation. I can fault the sickness, my onset of post-apocalyptic dementia, the little blue pills, but in reality, there's just me to blame. If I want to survive, at least the next part of the journey, hell, if I want to survive the night, I have to be smarter.

I put the car into drive, then pause.

My eyes fall to the room next to mine, room twenty-one, the door ajar. I can't shake the feeling, the sudden draw to that room, or what lay inside. It's like a premonition, as if something is beckoning me, like the dog that senses an earthquake and barks for no reason, something you can't see but you sense. A part of me feels like I should alert someone of something, but who, and of what?

I take my foot off the brake and pull away.

I stop, turn off the ignition and grab the flashlight.

I move to the entrance and peer in. The room is identical to mine, no surprise there, but the bed is in pieces, the headboard demolished, as are the dresser and side tables. Someone went rock-star mental in this one, and well before Grimes and Bull showed up. I step inside, maneuvering my way across the floor, towards the bathroom. My heartbeat quickens, my mind replaying the dream in my head. I place my hand on the bathroom door, pushing it open.

The toilet bowl is in pieces, the tank lid missing. Curtains flap in the breeze, the window frame cracked, the glass punched out. Mould covers the decrepit tub, the shower nozzle broken, dangling from the wall. Nothing unusual, no furry friends, no roosting owls. Satisfied my spider senses misled me, I turn to leave when I stop. My eye catches sight of something shiny on the floor, behind the door. I reach down, brushing aside splintered pieces of porcelain and glass.

It's a heart-shaped pendant, on a gold chain.

My heart skips a beat. It actually fucking skips a beat. Arrhythmia. Great, another ailment to add to my growing list. *"I'm coming to join you Elizabeth,"* my mind's eye recounts a scene from the 70's sitcom *Sanford and Son*, Redd Fox clutching his chest, feigning a heart attack.

Only this was real.

I squint under the flashlight beam, my eyes struggling with the contrast of light and dark. I can just make out a tiny inscription on the back.

For Allie, love you always, Dad.

Some refer to it as a sensory overload, a sudden brain circuitry malfunction, a complete unadulterated mind fuck. But when you're hit with it, hit with an intellectual impossibility, a sudden realization that challenges your entire belief system, everything stops. Some people can't handle it, the reality too disturbing, the moment too intense for coping skills. Blood leaves their head, rushing to protect the more vulnerable parts of the body, and persons faint. Some, depending on the danger level of the situation, piss themselves or shit their pants, another way the body protects itself, by expelling urine and feces. A ruptured bowel spilling fecal matter into the body is lethal, not even Dr. McCoy and his Tricorder could save you. That's why people soil themselves when faced with a life and death threat. It's natural. Then there's me. I freeze, solid. Breathing stops, eyes fixate; it's as if my soul has evaporated, left the physical body at that moment.

Breathe fuck-head.

Breathe.

If I'm asleep and dreaming this, I'm already dead. No CPAP machine in the world would have jump-started me, not this time.

I was holding Allie's pendant.

How is that possible?

I straighten up, clasping the pendant, my thoughts swirling. I search my mind for clues, hints, something I missed, an explanation for the impossible. But I have nothing.

I turn to leave, and the flashlight beam exposes something else. On the bathroom mirror, above the sink, written in soap, a single word.

Manor.

Fuck me.

CHAPTER 16

Leaving home wasn't as bad as I'd expected. The roads were difficult to navigate within city limits, but the highway was passable, except for the thoroughfares where major roads intersected one another. Those were death traps; people who got caught there deserted their cars and walked, or died. I imagine the police abandoned the cause, shit, everyone has family at home. I saw evidence of the military, it looked like their main function, at least initially, was to barricade the main arteries, force people to stay put or try their luck on the side roads. Contain the threat.

You shall not pass.

It was just past Montreal when I picked up the RV. Thankfully, the TransCanada highway extension bypassed the downtown area; it would have been massive chaos otherwise. It looked like the military did their best blocking access to the highway, most barricades still in place, now guarding corpse cars, a series of eternal parking lots. The parallel arteries were a suicide mission, left at a standstill, likely precipitating riots, beatings, killings.

I recall earlier trips out east, the stress of getting through Montreal, the traffic and congestion, the ongoing construction. The fucked-up signs were a visual overload, you'd think you were passing through downtown Hong Kong, except the signs you were deciphering at a hundred and thirty kilometres an hour were in French—Nord, Sud, Est, Ouest, arrows pointing in every direction. Trying to navigate through, making sure you didn't miss the only exit to the Maritimes was enough to make Vin Diesel pull over and cry. If you missed the ramp, welcome to downtown Montreal, population two million. Good luck finding your way back.

The new extension bypassed all that shit. It was a long time coming, considering it was the only thoroughfare to the east coast. You'd think construction would have been a priority, but I guess the days of Bud the Spud heading west with a truckload of Prince Edward Island potatoes were dwindling. And hell, maybe they knew, anticipated the great cleansing, no more drivers meant no more construction. No need for it.

I kept a lookout for signs of life, passing through towns, farmland, industrial areas, but I found only death. The lack of bodies in the open led me to believe the dying had time to seek shelter, privacy, a familiar place to live out their final days. Like a sick cat that crawls into a tight space to die. I saw little evidence of death on the streets, the occasional burned-out car, rancid smoky skeletons trapped inside the metal carcass, entombed for an eternity in a Jeep Liberty. I saw two bodies hanging from an overpass near Trois-Rivières, giant spray-painted letters proclaiming *Death Lives Here*, a warning to travellers heading east—or west, it didn't fucking matter which direction you went, or what side of the road you travelled, traffic rules were no longer a thing. If I were heading west in the eastbound lanes, I'd have missed the graffiti, but not the bodies. Hell, maybe the other side of the bridge had the bilingual translation. Regardless, either direction, either lanes, you wouldn't miss the rotting corpses swaying in the breeze. A part of me wondered just how long a body could hang before the head popped clean off. Couldn't be more than a couple of weeks. But what the hell did I know?

The sickness, the plague, whatever the official diagnosis, came on quick. The few still alive appeared to be fine, physically, but that's from a distance. Other than Wonder Woman, I've averted close contact, except for the odd jersey I saw along the highway. I didn't understand the connection then, and it makes even less sense now. How these crazed bastards, a thousand kilometres apart, mimicked one another, dressed alike, I didn't have a clue. Communication was out since day one, at least from my experience, no landlines, no cell service, no jabber on CB radio or shortwave. GPS systems were still working, both in the RV and on my phone, but they won't last. Satellites, from what I gather, will continue in their orbits for now, but without adjustments from technicians, they'll slide off course, and that'll be the end. I figure a month or two, tops. Not that it does much good down here. I know where I'm headed, and if the main road's jammed, back roads are a last resort.

The snipers concerned me. There was no logical explanation for their behaviour, and it scared the shit out of me. What was their purpose, their motivation? What was the common thread?

The only saving grace is that they've been bad shots. All of them. But it only takes one to ruin your day.

Stumbling across the RV was a bonus. The rig was brand new, not plated. Filling the tanks was a challenge, my syphoning skills rusty, but I managed not to poison myself or set myself ablaze. Driving the rig took a bit of getting used to; the biggest vehicle I'd driven was a sixteen foot U-Haul. I'd have never made it through Montreal in the behemoth, too many choke points, it was a challenge getting through by car. But I was confident once I cleared the capital of La Belle Province, the big cities behind me, the remainder of the trek would be less turbulent. Quebec City I wouldn't get close to, and I'd be avoiding St. John and Fredericton altogether, the biggest city left was Halifax, and I had no reason to stop there.

I left a bigger footprint and drew more attention in the RV, but the benefits outweighed the drawbacks. She was impossible to miss, especially at night, she lit up like an Ice Road Trucker. I ran into an impasse at Rivière-du-Loup, the last cut-off before heading south into New Brunswick, a transport truck flipped on its side. There was no way around, except on foot. Lucky for me it wasn't a trap, I'd have been fucked if it were, no chance of escape. I lost considerable time, not that I was on a schedule, but I backtracked and found a parallel artery, one that was accessible. Thanks to Global Positioning Systems, and all those dead scientists.

I stopped soon after crossing into New Brunswick, found a quiet back road and pulled in for a rest. It was a couple of hours before dawn, but I was spent, my mind shutting down, my eyes failing. Dozing at the wheel and crashing the big sumbitch would not be ideal. Autopilot wasn't an option. Driverless cars didn't quite evolve into reality, not in my lifetime, other than the bullshit story of the old cunt who sued Winnebago because he mistook cruise control for autopilot. That never happened, just a load of urban legend bull crap.

Falling asleep at the wheel was not an option.

I laid down in the back and dreamt of old man Tudyk. I was back in his apartment, only he wasn't dead. He was sitting in the same spot, at the breakfast nook, cleaning his Kalashnikov with a rag and a bottle of rye. I watched him, but he didn't seem to notice, like I was invisible, a ghost. He was humming a tune I didn't recognize, and when I looked over, Misty was growling, her fur standing up, teeth exposed. Tudyk hushed her without looking up. Misty stifled her growl, continuing to stare in my direction, not with recognition, but with fear. It's then I noticed the gun safe.

It was in the kitchen where the fridge should be. I took a step closer, watching as Tudyk poured a shot into his rag and continued polishing his gun with forty proof whiskey. There was a number scrawled on the front of the safe in crimson red paint.

Twenty-one.

His apartment number.

The number started to bleed, viscous fluid trickling down the sides of the vault, pooling on the kitchen floor. Misty backed up, like she was seeing this too. She let out a low, guttural growl, primal.

Tudyk hushed her again, but this time his voice sounded peculiar, distorted. I turned to look.

He was purple, decomposed, bloated hands, dead like I remembered him. Only he wasn't. His head turned slowly, on a pivot, looking in my direction. Soulless dead eyes, pale white, no pupils, widened in recognition. He smiled a morose grin that stretched and contorted his misshapen face.

And then I was awake, staring at the RV's ceiling.

The sound of a vehicle woke me. I sat up, my mind setting aside the horror of the dream, trying to figure out where the fuck I was.

In the RV, pulled over, New Brunswick.

A pickup truck, no lights, drove past the window. A second vehicle was idling on the opposite side of the RV. They were boxing me in. I stood up and moved towards the living area, middle of the rig. The pickup sat idling across from where I stood, not five feet away, the driver's window down. I could hear voices. Without hesitating, I grabbed a firework from the overhead compartment, a huge professional grade Roman candle. I slid open the window, lit the fuse, and pointed the fucker into the pickup.

Like a cannon, Disney calibre fireballs ejected into the cab, my arm jerking backward with each shot, the kickback comparable to firing a forty-four magnum.

The result was instantaneous. The driver hit the gas, the truck lurched forward into the culvert, and flipped onto its side. I dropped the cannon out the window, stars continuing to erupt, skimming off the roadway, lighting up the night like a hillbilly fourth of July.

I climbed behind the wheel, turned on the ignition and hit the gas, not slowing until the 'Welcome to New Brunswick' sign was a hundred kilometres in the rear-view.

No one followed.

I bypassed the Visitor's Centre, maybe next trip.

CHAPTER 17

I toss my cigarette as I approach the roundabout. The cut-off to Highway 105 is just ahead, the remaining two exits leading back towards the Causeway and Port Hawkesbury, both places I've been and have no intention of revisiting. It's a fifty-minute drive to the eastern jaunt of the Cabot Trail, the exit to our remote hideaway, secluded, even by island standards. The waning moon lights the roadway, casting patches of diffused light over the surrounding trees and forgotten road signs. Soon the mountains will appear. The road ahead is clear, only the occasional abandoned car, blending into the landscape like a grizzly bear in the Arctic.

Passing the five-kilometre mark, I finally feel like I've left the mainland behind; the island beginning to feel like an entity onto its own.

Manor

The name is embedded in my brain.

Bras d'Or Manor.

There's only one place on the island that could be. A mansion, a huge structure built by a Glace Bay fisherman who hit the Lotto years back. Rene and I slowed and gawked whenever we passed, like your average awestruck tourist. The immense property sat atop a hillside in the village of Aberdeen, set off the highway, overlooking Bras d'Or Lake. One-hundred acres of surrounding wilderness backed onto Hunters Mountain, a winding tree-lined driveway traversing the hillside; the entire estate gated and under surveillance. The place resembled a highbrow hotel, adorned with an elaborate entranceway flanked by cascading fountains and Roman pillars. It was rumoured the home had twelve bedrooms, an indoor Olympic-sized pool and a wedding gazebo out back that could hold two-hundred guests. Soon after it was built the locals started referring to it by the name of a certain ominous hotel in a 1980's horror movie—not that the place was ever home to an evil presence, or housed a hedge-maze; more so because it stood out, towering and foreboding. I always played Berlioz whenever we passed, seemed appropriate.

There's no other Manor I know of.

I brake.

Up ahead, cars are parked on either side of the roadway, dozens, lined up like some post-apocalyptic Park & Ride.

I turn off the car and kill the lights. There's no movement, no sounds, not even crickets. The night is still, no indication anyone's been around, but something isn't right.

After a minute, I start the Flex and ease forward.

The cars are parked nose to nose, back to front, bumpers almost touching. The occasional car has a white towel or shirt in the window. I've seen this before on drives to Florida, abandoned cars on the side of the road with shirts in the windows. I assumed it was a sign that everything was okay, that the vehicle was broken down and not abandoned. In Ontario, the Provincial Police left orange tags on abandoned cars to alert other officers that the car had been checked. But this was different. This was done after the fact, and it made no sense.

What was the purpose of parking them out here, in middle of nowhere?

I continue on past until River Denys Road comes into view, a side route running east and west from the highway. An old Winnebago blocks the passage on the left, the right leg clear.

As I continue, I pull out my phone and access the GPS, figuring it's worth a shot. I set the phone down and light a cigarette while I wait to see if the satellite will connect.

Kilometre marker twelve is dead ahead, and past it, something is blocking the roadway. I slow down, shifting into neutral and turning off the engine and headlights, letting the car glide forward in silence.

A giant mining trunk, Tonka Toy yellow, with a bucket large enough to hold a Dodge Ram, blocks the highway. I brake to a stop and turn on the headlights. Beyond the truck the roadway is impassable, jammed with abandoned cars, vans and buses, a junkyard, as far as the light touches.

Who the fuck had time to do this?

Likely it was the same contingent responsible for barricading the Causeway. Failsafe number two. I take a drag on my smoke and scan the area, considering my options. River Denys Road is two kilometres back. I've taken that route once before, back when the police had shut down the 105 for a serious accident, forcing everyone to detour right or left. It took a bit, but the road looped north and connected back with the highway. I just don't remember how long the detour was.

But that would mean doing as someone intended, taking the eastern leg; springing the trap.

I grab my phone, adjusting the map on the screen. According to the GPS, both legs of River Denys Road loop north, parallel to the 105, connecting back to the highway six or seven kilometres up.

I take a final drag and flick the smoke into the darkness. My options are dwindling. Heading back to the mainland and trying my luck on the eastern side of the island was risky. I'd have to go through Port Hawkesbury, and I've been there, done that.

I look to the distance, past the graveyard of abandoned vehicles. It's another forty kilometres before I reach the Cabot Trail. By foot, I could make it in a day if I had to, but I'd be exposed, exhausted, nowhere to run, no backup plan if shit went sideways.

I put the car into drive and make a U-turn. A minute later I'm at River Denys Road grabbing my rifle and stepping out. The roadway is clear, at least until the bend. But that's intentional. You don't set a trap by leaving clues.

I wonder if they took Allie this way?

I step to the front of the car, angle the butt of the rifle, and smash out the headlamp.

CHAPTER 18

Halifax is the largest metropolis on the east coast, four hundred thousand people, four times that of the entire island of Cape Breton. Once upon a time that is.

After I'd crossed into Nova Scotia, I stopped to look for gas in Truro. Halifax was forty-five minutes south, but I had no intention of a detour, certainly not for curiosity's sake. On past visits, Halifax was always the first stop, especially when we flew in. The drive from Stanfield Airport to downtown Halifax was short, less than thirty minutes and we were at the hotel. We always stayed on the waterfront, close access to the boardwalk; a world of restaurants, shops and attractions, all the way to Pier 21.

Pier 21.

The entry point for generations of immigrants, Canada's version of Ellis Island. Tudyk came through Pier 21. He always wanted to return to Halifax to visit the museum, look up his name in the book of signatures, the infamous ledger capturing each immigrant's arrival to the new word. I didn't have the heart to tell him the book didn't exist, that it was a common misunderstanding, so much so they had to explain on their website that no such registry existed. Families would arrive, hoping to track their ancestry, peruse the great book of names, looking for the date their grandparent became a citizen, only to be disappointed. I knew the facts because we'd toured the museum, not that Rene or I had kin who immigrated, but because Pier 21 represented a piece of Canadian history, our roots, the tapestry of our nation. Rene always suspected my interest in naval history had more to do with the fact the Alexander Keith's Brewery was across the street. But I argued there was nothing wrong in celebrating our country's stoic legacy with a cold pint on a warm day.

I can't imagine the state of the waterfront now. Halifax was a major port city on the Atlantic, a war zone. Ships waiting to dock, requesting assistance, medics, supplies, were likely quarantined, turned away, or worse. I imagine like the Causeway, survivors weren't fucking around. I doubt there were any open-armed welcomes for foreign ships carrying strange diseases.

Come to Canada and start a new life.

How many thousands of immigrants, all dreaming of new lives and new beginnings, embracing freedom in a country of peace, had it all cease in an unceremonious final curtain call? Like a giant Monty Python foot, ending humanity with a single stomp.

Halifax was ravaged, I'm sure of it, down to the last soul. A conglomeration of Mad Max Escaping New York, only in a confined arena, just as violent, just as devastating.

Part of me wanted to see for myself, to witness the carnage. I wondered if like the Causeway, the Macdonald and MacKay bridges crossing from Dartmouth were tampered with, decommissioned or demolished. I wouldn't put it past any of the crazy fuckers.

Halifax was off the list. No boardwalk, no museum, no Keith's, not this trip.

Not ever again.

CHAPTER 19

I scoped out a small industrial park south of Truro and pulled in. I figured the main drag would be too risky. My only option for fuel was syphoning, gas stations relegated to taunting reminders of the spoils of a dead era.

I pulled in behind a row of nondescript storefronts, businesses with limited signage, not a place frequented by the pillaging hordes. Three beige panel vans sat parked at the rear of one of the loading bays. They looked clean, not picked over. As I got out and grabbed my syphoning supplies, I noticed a billboard across the highway, one I'd missed coming in. The original backdrop was faded and peeled, but some talented hack re-purposed the billboard with their personal, post-world artwork. The word 'Terminus' was spray-painted in blood-red three-dimensional letters, an arrow pointing south, towards Halifax. I smiled as I pried open the fuel door on the first van. It was rumoured they filmed a season of the *Walking Dead* right here in Truro, the hub of Nova Scotia, back in the day. I got a kick out of the fact I was retracing their steps, Rick, Daryl, Michonne's, only my post-apocalyptic nightmare wasn't catered.

I got the gas flowing without swallowing a mouthful. The van's tank had plenty, although it was always a hit and miss. Anything less than half full was more trouble than it was worth, and by the time I figured that out, I smelled like a mechanic's rag. I always kept a change of clothes handy; I couldn't have the RV soiled. Some things needed to remain tidy, clean, pre-world condition. It was my attempt at maintaining a sense of decorum, sanity, in a society gone apeshit.

Halifax.

I dreamt I was standing on the boardwalk, gazing out across the water towards Dartmouth. The scene was surreal, no Rene, no one familiar, but there were people. A shit-load of them, and they were looking at me as if I was someone important, someone they were expecting. There was a ship in the harbour; an ocean liner docked at the old Pier 21, one that looked remarkably similar to the Love Boat.

I'd forgotten that dream.

My container near full, I removed the hose, careful not to splash myself, and reached for a second can.

The Love Boat.

Humanity dead and I'm dreaming about the fucking Love Boat.

CHAPTER 20

The quiet of the surrounding wood is intense. River Denys Road is a mere pathway, an alternate avenue, a manmade escape into the depths of the island abyss. In the darkness, I can make out only more darkness, pine trees as thick and dense as cement walls, beyond them, a forest of arms continues for kilometres until land touches the sea.

I keep the car to the centre of the road, potholes the size of craters feeding off the car's suspension, daring me to pick up the pace. Three kilometres in and nothing of interest has surfaced, no cars, no traps, no signs of an ambush. But I'm at the halfway point now, an ideal place where anyone with an inkling of ruining my night, may be waiting. My foot off the gas, the Flex cruises at a slow speed, finding each pothole while my senses remain on watch, absorbing the smells, the sounds, the direction of the breeze, like an animal alert to predators, ever vigilant.

But there is nothing.

I begin to think there may be nothing. It's possible the blockade was yesterday's news. Back when things were hotter, when townsfolk were struggling to survive, infecting one another, that's when the need to restrict movement, to impede intruders, was at its pinnacle. That would make sense. But how many survived? Surely not enough healthy, motivated locals to create that logjam of cars back on the 105? That would have taken a crew of twenty, perhaps more, working under a leader. Why the fuck else would they do it? Who emerged as a leader in a land of followers?

In the land of the blind, the one-eyed man is King.

The guy in the uniform.

Him and the bald-headed prick, the one with the pending anal insertion. Bull.

They had that quality about them.

A clunking emanates from the back tires and I stop the car. I climb out to find a six-inch wooden board stuck to the rear driver's side tire. I kneel down, inspecting it. Several nails protrude from the board, one impaled in the tread.

I stand and peruse the area. I can't see past fifty feet, the darkness of the surrounding pines swallowing the moonlight, reminding me of how night vision is a younger man's domain. I wonder if I'm being watched, if unseen eyes had tracked me all this time. Images of snipers lying prone, watching my movements through green-imaged night vision goggles, are difficult to shake. But I'd already be dead, or at least leaking. I walk forward, scanning the ground, counting at least a half dozen more boards spread along the roadway.

Phase one of the trap.

While it's possible the boards were placed here months ago, long since forgotten, it makes no difference, I've sprung the trap. The tire is holding air for now, but not for long. I grab my rifle from the back seat and head further up the road, watching where I step, knowing a rusty impalement would not bode well.

I remember a run-down mechanic's garage in my hometown, owned by an old curmudgeon, the only shop in the area. It was well known the old bastard served time in jail back in the 70's for killing his wife, convicted of manslaughter. He specialized in tire repair, carried all the brands, sizes, makes. The location was perfect, a parallel artery that led to the highway, lots of tourists and visitors heading north to Toronto or east to Niagara Falls. He did a lot of business, unusually high; it seemed a lot of people got flats within a kilometre or two of his place. And he'd charge a hefty price for roadside service, especially after hours. I guess he pissed off the wrong people. The police did a sting and found the cocksucker was dropping weighted nails and screws on the highway near his garage. He'd been doing it forever. A year before the authorities got involved, a girl from Brantford, seven months pregnant, blew a tire, rolled the car and burned to death. Twenty-four years old and a baby on the way. She died two hundred metres from his garage. Unfortunately, by the time karma caught up with the old fucker, he'd dropped dead from a heart attack, two days before his trial. Never saw the inside of a cell.

They say karma is a bitch, but I saw way too many assholes who did just fine.

Until now.

I could chance changing the tire, clearing the rest of the deflation devices, but as I gaze further ahead, something tells me that would be futile. Fifty feet from where I stand a school bus blocks the roadway. I head towards the ditch and creep forward, my boots oozing with mud as I slosh through the stagnant water. The bus looks operational, tires intact, moved recently. It's a gate, a barrier, another page from my playbook, only they took a more practical approach. The back of the bus sits in a laneway that leads uphill, a farmer's road, no doubt a property up there, house and barn, homestead. There are few abodes on this stretch of roadway; I wouldn't be surprised if this was the original Denys family home, the road's namesake.

I approach, crouching down, peering underneath the bus. The other side is clear, no logjam, the road continues on, unobstructed. It makes sense; they controlled who passes. With the other leg of River Denys Road barricaded, this was the only passage back to the 105, a choke point, a rat trap.

I take a few steps up the laneway and I can just make out a corner of a two-story farmhouse at the top, typical Cape Breton residence, old and decaying. A light glows from within and I can hear voices, music playing. Two vehicles sit parked out front, a third, a white pickup, sits halfway up the laneway. One of the vehicles looks to be an Escalade.

I weigh my options.

I can return to the car, try driving another route. But which one? Even if I swap out the tire, without headlights, I won't make any decent time until the sun's up.

Option two is grabbing my bag and heading out on foot. It's three kilometres to the highway and from there, another thirty-five to the Cabot Trail. Depending on how many unwelcomed pop-ins I get, I could make it in eight hours, maybe ten, not quicker, it's not as if I can hang out a thumb. Hitchhiking isn't an option, not even in days gone by, not on this stretch of road. You won't hear banjo music, but fiddle music from the backwoods might make you think twice.

From the Cabot Trail I've got another thirty klicks to my destination. That's a lot of walking, but an option—one I'd better get used to. Most people have no fucking idea that gas supplies are already going bad, in a year's time, unless properly stored, gas will be useless. The shit will clog up every engine from here to Meat Cove, cars, motorcycles, generators, lawnmowers. All gone for a shit. Give me a Tesla or a Pontiac Volt, and we might be in business, but this is Cape Breton, eco-friendly never made it past the Causeway, and no one here has that kind of money. With any luck, a surviving egghead somewhere might figure this shit out, but I won't hold my breath. Forget Fitbits and fitness trackers, those of us left will be at ten thousand steps before our first morning piss. Walking is back in vogue.

I never like abandoning my car, but survival dictates.

I squeeze myself between the bus and the culvert, examining the open roadway ahead. A portable toilet sits off to my left. Even in the apocalypse, you have to take a shit.

I hear voices, shouting, from the farmhouse. It sounds like the party is picking up, it's time to decide.

I reach into my shirt pocket and remove Allie's pendant, running it through my fingers like it's a rosary.

Is she up there?

I hear a car door shut.

Time to bug out.

CHAPTER *Twenty-one*

I haven't thought of anything except reaching my destination, spreading Rene's ashes, and living until I die. Maintaining a steadfast trajectory, staying immune to external stimuli and outside interference was my focus. My instinctual side took care of a lot, and considering the blackouts were becoming more frequent, more intense, a part of me felt like I was being guided. I was the protagonist of my own story, only the plot line was linear, mundane, no subplots, no secondary characters, no dialogue. Unless you count the conversations in my head, the internal debate, the lively and all-consuming endless banter. Even in sleep, the conversation between sane me and insane me raged on, unraveling the hidden layers of my damaged psyche.

I wasn't a believer in the supernatural; ghosts, spirits, angels and demons, all that shit. Not really. But Rene was. She believed in it—to a fault. She was into Tarot Cards, chakras, premonitions. I found it amusing. I mean I enjoyed watching scary movies, horror, anything to do with a séance, Ouija Board or a possessed kid was entertainment, but those were films. I read *The Exorcist* years back, a great book, based on true events, except that the child was a boy, and every other detail was embellished. But I didn't buy the premise. Sure the concept was compelling, frightening, but the reality of mental illness, abuse, psychotic drugs, all much more reasonable explanations. There are more things in heaven and earth, I agree, but an unflinching belief in God and the Bible was a tough sell. I wouldn't call myself an atheist, an agnostic maybe, a doubter, but whatever the end result, I kept my beliefs to myself. I wasn't an asshole about it like the pricks with the Darwin Jesus fish on their cars, mocking the Christian faith, broadcasting to the world that they're so intelligent, ridiculing the naïve. I never owned a Jesus fish, but whenever I spotted a

Darwin hybrid on some asshole's Volvo, I had the urge to kick in a tail light. I never did though, that would have been a sin.

Goddamn Darwin elitists.

Rene and I were opposites, that's why we clicked. She was the Yin to my Wang, as I liked to say, a phrase she despised. But that's what I loved about her. Her devotion to her beliefs, her passion, gave me hope, kept my mind open. When a person of her intelligence, an IQ that dwarfed mine, believes in this stuff, you question whether there's something you've overlooked. Rene was beyond smart, academically, intellectually, emotionally, a rare gift to this planet.

But my dreams of her stopped. The first month I dreamt of her every night, but as time passed, the dreams became less frequent, and when she did appear, her glow diminished, like she was moving away, drifting into another realm, a realm where I wasn't welcome. Whether or not I believed she was speaking to me from beyond, I can't say. A part of me wanted to believe, had to believe. A part of me still does.

But that all dissipated when my dreams changed. The memory lapses intensified, the recurring fever, the little blue pills. Dreams mutated into vague images of people I didn't know, a ship, strange music, a gathering of survivors.

It wasn't until I saw the third sniper I contemplated the what-ifs. *What was the connection?* How had the world changed? Things were different, and not just because everyone was dead; there was something in the air, a shift, an unidentified energy that affected the mind, an invisible spectrum of thought, transcending the cosmos at warp speed. It was as if it had always been there, undetected until the great purge, like the herd's thinning brought it to light. One only had to tune into the signal, tweak the receptor to capture the flow of energy. I sensed it in waking hours, but the signal magnified when I slept. During a night of sobriety, the dreams were vivid, real. Self-medicating dulled the connection, inhibited recall, kept me sane.

The snipers tuned into the signal, that was a given. What it told them, how they interpreted it, I don't understand. The messages I received were like pieces of a puzzle—a five thousand piece 'polar bear in a snowstorm' puzzle, difficulty level—expert. I made no headway deciphering the message, the intent, nor did I want to. One thing was evident though, one thing I was sure of; picking up a high-powered rifle and shooting people, was not in my repertoire.

The dream of Halifax, of the survivors and the ocean liner, that recall was different; crystallizing from nothing to a clear recollection. It was as if something within me kept it hidden, buried deep within my subconscious, allowing my survival instincts to take the helm, keep me as far from Halifax as possible before the memory came to light. I wondered what it meant, why that dream was clear when others were dim, why my mind would archive that memory, and not others. It made no sense.

But it was the dream of Allie that broke me. That dream confirmed I wasn't losing my mind, at least not entirely. It signified something more was taking place, something other-worldly. A person might refer to it as an episode of ESP, the mind's ability to read thought across time, distance and space. The moment our eyes met, a part of my brain engaged with hers and I read her thoughts, extracted her name. It's one theory, but any respectable scientist, if any remain, would call bullshit on it.

The more I thought about that dream, the more I wondered if I'd heard her name. That was a logical explanation. I overheard the name, filed it away, retrieved it from the archives to enhance a macabre dream, inventing a reality where there was none. But how it related to her appearance in the motel room, I can't theorize; was it an apparition or a cerebral meltdown?

My scientific side says meltdown. Blame it on psychological trauma, all due to a little thing like surviving an apocalypse with a dollop of alcoholism, pills and fever on the side. The more I considered it, the more I became James Randi, the famous Canadian paranormal debunker, dismantling my theory, one fantastical claim at a time.

I felt comfort with science, comfortable in the knowledge my behaviour came down to stress, fatigue, illness. No one chooses to abandon their faculties. They say truly crazy people don't know they're crazy, but I'm not sure I believe that. As frightening as losing one's sanity may be, the fear of the unknown is a greater threat. Not just the unknown of day-to-day survival, the unknown of what lies on the other side of existence. Is it an end, consciousness terminated, or is it Rene and a beam of light, or an innocent child, abandoned? Or is it Lucifer, playing Blackjack with Adolph, Bin Laden and Sinatra? It's the not knowing that eats away at the mind, the soul, the sanity.

I can't shake the feeling that the closer I get to my destination, the further I drift from reality.

Rational explanation or not, the world has changed. This much I know.

CHAPTER 22

I sling the backpack and pull my enormous bug-out bag from the rear hatch. I can't afford to travel light, hence the need for a roomier option. Rene rides with me on my back with a few essentials, the bulk of my gear needed a bigger home, and you can't get much roomier than a CCM hockey bag. My expedition is not a *Survival Man* episode. Sure, Les Stroud may be shaking his head, but I'm not out on a weeklong excursion, testing my survival skills against the brutality of the Temagami wilderness. I'm in this for the eternal haul, and with humanity's existence emptying like an hourglass, a million viral grains per minute, I need everything I can carry, not just a knife or a roll of duct tape—*handy* is the new handsome, in the apocalypse.

I grab the rifle and listen to the voices echoing from the farmhouse; I can't tell if it's a heated discussion or a Cape Breton kitchen party in full swing. And I can't wait to find out. Trying to back out on a flat would be futile, I'd not get far, not on this ill-fated potholed *Road to Avonlea*. I'd be on the rim in a minute, making a hell of a lot of noise and creating enough sparks to set the island alight.

Heading out on foot is my only option. And I have no time for debate.

I bid the Flex adieu and head for the bus. It's a tight fit around the front end, considering I'm hauling a bag large enough to hold a corpse, but I squeeze past. The voices have quieted, but that could mean anything. I can't be here any longer.

Moving quickly, I keep to the left side of the road, staying to the shadows. The trees lining the roadway are less dense on this side, if need be, I'd have a better chance of escaping into the bush. According to my watch, it's going on three, which means in four hours the sun will be up. The sky is cloud covered, but the clouds are thin and high up, it likely won't rain, and that's a bonus. I'll be on foot a couple of days. And that's if everything goes according to plan.

The quick pace and the weight of my equipment forces me to break ten minutes in. The dizziness is back, my energy level tanking, and something in the backpack is digging into my shoulder blade. I drop the hockey bag, remove the backpack and reposition my gun. The dizziness concerns me. I think back to the last time I ate or drank, but despite my better judgement, it's a cigarette I want, not food or water. Damn you, Hans. I decide against it and pull out a bottle of water, downing half of it. I pat the outside of the backpack out of habit, reassuring myself Rene is still along for the ride, safe, and secure.

My ears pick up on a noise. I stiffen, pivoting my body, scanning the darkness. I'm on a slight bend, surrounded by trees, but I have open roadway both in front and behind, a hundred feet either way. A vehicle I'd hear within a hundred metres and it's doubtful anyone could have tracked me. I wait a few moments longer, then sling the backpack, grab the bag and head off, my pace quickening and my ears alert. I have to be vigilant, especially now that I'm on their side of the playground.

I freeze.

Fifty feet ahead, I see her.

She stands at the shoulder of the roadway, completely still. Where she came from, I don't know. I close my eyes and open them again.

She's still there, only how is it I can see her in the darkness? My heart races, my mind searches for an explanation, then it hits me.

She's glowing. Allie is fucking glowing, radiating light.

She's as I've seen her in my dreams, long auburn hair draped in front, summer dress. I stare, transfixed, wondering if my dizziness has given way to full-blown hallucination, as she turns and looks in my direction.

She raises a finger to her lips as if shushing me.

Someone or something is coming.

Without conscious thought I am moving, hockey bag in tow, walking towards her. I can't feel my legs, my mind is paused, like I'm in a trance, my survival instincts awakened, overriding my paralysis. Whatever the explanation, I keep walking until I'm within ten feet of her. She turns and heads into the bush, her glow illuminating the branches and leaves around her. I tell myself it's a hallucination, not to follow, to wait out this psychotic episode, but my feet are moving. Holding the hockey bag in front of me, I plow through, my mammoth riot shield fending off the attacking saplings and branches. I reach a small clearing forty feet in and stop. Just beyond the clearing, the glow continues moving, heading deeper into the forest.

I hear a noise behind me and I drop the bag, falling prone.

Headlights flood the forest. I lie still, shielding myself behind the great bag, peering back towards the road, towards the source of the light.

It's a Jeep, decked out with four high-powered floodlights on the roof rack, reminiscent of the kangaroo poacher's vehicle in *Crocodile Dundee*. They're looking for someone.

I reach for my rifle, hoping to God I'm far enough in they

won't see the mound of black that shields my body. I look back, but Allie is gone.

The jeep reverses and a second vehicle approaches. It's a pickup truck, someone within shining a handheld spotlight up and down the tree line. The two vehicles meet in the middle of the roadway, across from one another, like two police cruisers meeting up for coffee.

Voices resonate through the trees.

"Same car as the motel, what did I tell you?"

"You didn't tell me shit."

"He's around here, gimme the light."

The light's a fucking beacon of doom, and as luck would have it, they've picked the right side of the road to search. I'm forty feet in, praying the undergrowth is thick enough to conceal me.

The beam flashes above my head, illuminating the trees behind me. I keep still, my hand clasping my rifle, my other hand securing my backpack. If things go sideways, and they just might, I dump the big bag and leave light.

A car door opens and closes. Voices are on top of one another; I can't make out how many.

"Where you goin'?"

"Tracks here, toss me that flashlight."

"He could be anywhere man—this is a waste of time. He ain't gettin' far."

"Go tell the boss that."

"I fucking will!"

"Have another drink."

"Fuck you."

"Shut the fuck up, both of ya. Tracks here, recent, he came this way."

Another car door opens and closes.

"Right there, see."

"That ain't a footprint you shit."

"Damn straight, it's fresh, like an hour old."

"Oh, you're a tracker now? That ain't a human footprint shit fer-brains."

"Mikey, come and take a look at this!"

"He ain't getting out of the truck, he's gotta take a crap."

"He's always gotta take a crap. I say it's a footprint."

"It ain't no fucking footprint. I'm goin' back. We'll find him daybreak heading north, they always head north."

"It's a goddamn footprint. Nike, size ten."

"Oh, Nike, size ten. You keep tellin' yourself that. I'm havin' a smoke."

The flashlight beam dances around the trees, touching everything around me. I hear a car door open and close again.

A horn blasts and a muffled voice calls out.

"Let's go, I don't trust that bitch."

"Boss said to be sure."

"I'm crowning."

"Boss said to be sure."

"My sphincter's sure. Fuck the boss, let's go."

"I'll tell him you said that."

"Fuck you!"

The flashlight beam stops—right on the bag. Fuck me. Did it have reflective tags? Shit, rooky mistake.

"Hold on, I think I see something."

Footsteps approach, twigs snap.

The horn blasts again.

The footsteps stop.

"What goddamn sissy-ass shit can't take a dump outside? Ever dawn on you we're in a fucking apocalypse?"

The light is gone.

"Pansie-ass wimp."

The footsteps retreat. I let go of the rifle and breathe.

I enjoy toilet humour, but I'm not smiling, not just yet. I raise my head and peer over the bag, watching as the jeep peels away, heading south, back towards the farmhouse. The pickup heads north, out of site, but I don't move yet, opting to lie still and wait. Sure enough, a minute later, the truck passes by, heading south.

An eerie stillness hangs over the woods.

I stand, looking back to where I last saw her. The dizziness has returned, and I let the backpack fall to the ground and sit, straddling the hockey bag. I want to vomit, beads of sweat form on my forehead and my hands shake.

I can't travel, not like this; the risk is too great. And who's to say the three stooges won't be back after Moe wipes his ass? I have to stay off the road, at least for the next few hours.

I turn on my flashlight, the beam miniscule, but sufficient, surveying the area, looking for something, anything.

And I see it.

Where Allie was last standing—a clearing, a pathway in the bush. I stand, testing my balance, gauging my nausea, then sling my backpack, grab my supplies and move towards the path. Sweat streams down my face, the salt stinging my eyes, but it is a path, and considering I'm in the middle of nowhere, it means something's nearby. Another fifty feet in, the path opens to a clearing, and something unexpected. The flashlight beam exposes a structure; one surrounded by pine trees, balsams or firs, perfect eight-foot tall Christmas trees. It's a shed, in the middle of nowhere. I shine my light in all directions, looking for the house that goes with it, but there's only forest.

Who the fuck would build this out here?

I drop the hockey bag and move closer, rifle in my hands, examining the structure. It's a recent build, newer lumber, new shingles, solid. No windows, just a single door, overgrown weeds lining the base, suggesting no one's been here in a while. I think of Allie, or whatever it was that led me here.

A sharp pain radiates behind my left eye, a new addition to my medical chart. I feel weak, lethargic, like a diabetic crashing hard, and I reach for the knob. The door opens, flattening the weeds that grace the entranceway.

The flashlight beam illuminates the interior.

I blink, struggling to comprehend what it is I'm seeing, the image not registering. I step in, lowering the rifle and unslinging my backpack.

Holy shit.

Is this a hallucination, or am I dreaming?

The sharp pain returns and I buckle.

CHAPTER 23

I'm not awake, and I'm not asleep. It's the feeling in between, when you're entranced in a fading dream, yet able to distinguish the world around you. My head pounds, a pain I'm familiar with. It's likely I'm dehydrated, malnourished, among a host of other issues. There is no discernable light I can sense through my closed eyelids, yet I don't want to chance opening them. Not to preserve a dream I can't remember, but to preserve the feeling of serenity, of safety, comforts of a lost world.

I think of Allie, how her appearance averted my capture, how her eyes looked at mine with recognition, like we knew one another, in another time or parallel existence. We connected, but why, and on what level, I can't discern. Was it her, or was it something else, something other-worldly?

I recall Rene telling me about ghost stories and hauntings in the Maritimes, Nova Scotia especially, she'd read up on it before our first trip. Cape Breton had some of the more cryptic stories, tales of forerunners; spirits of recently deceased relatives who pay impromptu visits after death. Story after story recounted how after a mysterious knock at the door, an unexpected visitor would show up—then vanish, never saying a word. Minutes later the phone would ring with the bad news; Aunt Gertrude kicked the KFC bucket an hour earlier, three hundred kilometres away in hospital. The stories were engaging, unnerving, great fodder for the campfire, but difficult to accept, given man's tendency to fabricate, exaggerate and lie. I never held much belief in folk tales.

Until now.

She wasn't dead. At least I hope not. I hope what I saw wasn't a forerunner, not in the traditional sense.

My eyes sense the light overtaking dark. I know my quiet time is ending, reality waiting, but I delay the inevitable, imagining myself submerged in warm water, encased in a lightproof vestibule, a cocoon, safe and familiar, quiet and peaceful. I lay still and pretend, but as the light intensifies, so does the pain in my head.

I open my eyes.

I'm on the floor of the shed, my head resting against the hockey bag, sunlight peeking through the frame around the doorway. Sitting up, I rub the back of my neck, ignoring my pounding head, trying to establish my bearings. I passed out clothed, and just as well, the night air chilled the interior of the shed. As I pull myself up, I glance to my rifle, guarding the doorway like a silent sentry. On cue, my survival mode kicked into autopilot; I'd secured the door with a plastic zip-tie, the kind police use as temporary handcuffs. Not the sturdiest of locks, but enough to buy some time in case of intruders. I rub the sleep out of my eyes, looking around the interior, reacquainting myself with my surroundings.

This is not your typical backwoods Cape Breton shed. Far from it. Someone took great effort in transforming the interior into a pub—British style, complete with a solid oak bar, matching panelled walls with black accents, and four leather-backed stools. They were called man caves back in the day, or pub sheds as some referred to them. I've seen them before, and this one was no slouch. An assortment of bottles, glasses, and mugs adorn the shelves behind the bar, along with a rack of wine glasses hanging from the ceiling. A beer fridge sits tucked into the corner, stocked with cans of Coors Lite, Moosehead, an assortment of Coolers. Two beer taps and a six-bottle liquor dispenser, the kind that holds bottles upside down, adorn the centre of the bar.

I climb into a stool. A forty-inch flat screen is mounted to the wall across from me, connected to a Marantz receiver and pair of Paradigm speakers. Sports memorabilia, hockey and Canadian Football mostly, line the walls, and flags; one Canadian, one Cape Breton, and one American, cover the ceiling. I reach across and pick up an overturned can of Coors Lite. There's no surprise my head is throbbing. I count seven empties and a twenty-six-ounce bottle of Canadian Club, missing half its load. I'd had myself a party last night.

Looking around, I wonder how the shed was powered; a generator likely, one that would have been confiscated, assigned new duties when things got bad. A place like this, a man cave, became a level zero priority when death came calling.

It's obvious no one's been here in months, if someone had, I'd be bright-eyed this morning. Shame, there's more than enough alcohol to wipe a dozen memory banks clean, at least temporarily. I pull out a cigarette and light it, looking around, appreciating the effort and craftsmanship that went into this barfly bunker. This was someone's little slice, a hideaway, a place to regenerate, recharge, and get pissed.

I could hold up here a while, maybe settle in for a longer haul, follow Bubble's example. Living in a shed might not be the worst idea I had.

I smile, despite the pulsing in my temples. That's the hangover talking. Reaching into my pocket, I remove my pill bottle, wondering how many I popped last night, but not caring. I need one now. Once the alcohol kicks out of my system, my mood will sour, worse than it already is, my problem-solving ability will go for a shit, and my decision-making will resemble a squirrel trying to cross the 401 in Toronto at rush hour. I pop out a pill and wash it down with a half empty can of beer, hoping to hell I didn't just swallow a cigarette butt. The beer's flat, but it hits the spot, better than OJ in the morning.

I stand and remove the zip-tie on the door handle, allowing sunlight to flood the interior, the morning air crisp and welcoming. Above my head the sky is clear blue, a hawk soars above the canopy, keeping watch on the newest intruder. The birds are onto me, that's a given. I step out and look to the pathway. It's not much; I'm surprised I was able to find it in the dark. Beside the door I notice an electrical outlet, a double external plug affixed to the outside of the shed, a foot up from the ground. There's no cord, but I look straight out, to where an extension cord may have once been, and I see a second pathway, one I'd overlooked. This path was more prominent, and I knew where it led. This shed didn't have a generator, it used hydro.

Fucking hell.

There was a house beyond the trees, not a hundred feet away. I step back into the shed and begin gathering my things, then pause. I grab my rifle, pull the door shut, and head for the path.

CHAPTER 24

The house is an old relic, rotting white clapboard exterior, sagging front porch in dire need of a paint job. It sits on an acre of cleared land at the base of a hillside. Not a farm, no barn that I can see, but likely a home to generations of islanders, each one growing up in the modest abode, dreaming the dream of every Easterner; to head west to Toronto like Pete and Joey in *Goin' Down the Road.* I wonder how many of them made it off the island, how many stayed, how many perished during the great cleansing.

I approach cautiously, scanning the length of the gravelled driveway, knowing that River Denys Road lies just below. My estimation that I'd spent the night less than one hundred feet from a house was correct, another careless move, a snap decision that jeopardized survival, as if a part of me wanted to sabotage my quest. Part of me probably does, but I'll blame it on fatigue.

I catch a strong whiff of the unpleasant, and stop. The stench is familiar. I bypass the front steps and head towards the rear of the home; the smell is stronger, thicker. I cover my nose and step wide around the corner of the house.

Propped up against the white clapboard are what I can only imagine are the homeowners, what's left of them. They are both dead, months now, blackened skin that's fallen from their faces, exposing their skulls, pieces of flesh torn away by animals. It looks like a husband and wife. They sit unnaturally, their backs against the wall, feet extended out in front of them as if they were having a picnic. This wasn't random. They didn't crawl out here and die, not like this. Some asshole staged this for his morbid amusement. How do I know? Scrawled into the siding above them in black marker, the words 'Walking

Dead – Zombie Casting Call', an arrow pointing down. Someone had a macabre sense of humour in the apocalypse. I think to the billboard back in Truro and wonder if there's a connection, a common thread of insanity, rampant in the new world.

I back away, clutching my rifle a little tighter. I don't sense anyone's been here, if they had, Bubble's Pub would have been dry, but I can't take chances. The porch steps bend under my weight, the pillars leaning, barely supporting the sunken roof. The front door is ajar, and I pause to listen.

The door opens into a hallway, just beyond that the kitchen. Drawers and cupboards are opened, overturned, items scattered throughout. I step inside, the rifle barrel leading the way. Cape Bretoners were renowned for their uber-stocked pantries, always prepared for an apocalypse, but I know this one is bare, anything edible long since taken. Past the kitchen is the living room, a rotting pile of filth and debris, rainwater leaking in from the damaged ceiling. The mouldy stench is strong, but nothing compared to the bonanza of aromas outside. Just beyond the living room is a hallway with three doors, two likely bedrooms, one the washroom. I pause, my senses suddenly tingling. Two of the doors are ajar, but the last one, the one at the end of the hallway is closed.

My eye catches sight of something. On the living room table, amidst the clutter of ashtrays and newspapers, sits a shiny revolver and a pair of handcuffs, items placed there recently.

I've seen that gun before.

I hear a grunt. I raise my rifle, turning towards the closed door.

The washroom.

The door opens.

Grimes steps out, adjusting his Molson Canadian belt buckle. Our eyes meet. Neither of us says a word.

"You don't eat pop tarts do you?" I can't help myself, but my poorly timed humour is lost on him.

"Ah, no."

"If you move, I will shoot. Understand? I want to shoot. Understand?"

He nods. I back up a step. "Turn around and get on your knees."

"I got no beef with you man, just takin' a shit. I didn't know this was your place."

"You didn't notice Ma and Pa Kettle outside? Do it now, or I shoot you in the face."

"Okay, okay, fuck me."

Numb-nuts turns and drops to his knees. I reach over and pick up the revolver, checking to see if it's loaded. It is, with one in the chamber. I set the rifle down and pick up the handcuffs.

"I'm just passin' through man. Don't want any trouble. We should be helping each other out, no?"

"You got a key for these?"

"What, the cuffs, yeah, yeah I think I got one somewhere. Got them off a dead cop, figured they might come in handy, you know—if someone ever pulls a fucking gun on me!"

The sarcasm is lost on me.

"Hands behind your back, palms facing outwards. Do it now."

"What are you Dirty Fucking Harry? We don't need to do this, just give me my shit, I'll be on my way."

I consider putting a bullet just over his head, it's not my ammo so why should I care, but I quell the urge. A shot, even inside a house, will carry, and I don't need to alert his pals, at least not yet.

"You're right, where are my manners. Go ahead, get up."

Grimes rises and turns to face me. He smiles, revealing a set of choppers that haven't seen a toothbrush since Joanie met Chachi. He reminds me of a cross between a pedophile and a guy who steals scrap metal for a living.

"Cool man. We cool?"

"Kitchen," I motion with the revolver.

"No problem, no problem. What's your name bro? I'm Sketch."

Sketch, what kind of a name is Sketch? I step back allowing him a wide berth. He stops at the stove. I toss him the handcuffs.

"One wrist. Not loose."

"Aww fuck really man, we doing this?"

I nod. He clicks the cuff on his left wrist. "Put your other hand in your pocket and face the stove."

He giggles to himself. "You believe this guy, I stop to take a piss."

He turns and digs his hand into his pocket, and I'm on him, threading the open cuff through the oven door handle, then snapping it closed on his right wrist. In a flash, he's hogtied to an Amana.

"What the fuck man?"

"Anything in your pockets?"

"I got shit man, smokes, that's it."

"Don't move."

I do a quick pat down for weapons. He's clean other than a half-pack of Marlboros and a fancy two-hundred dollar lighter, the kind rich cigar smokers carry. I confiscate both.

"Hey, that's my last pack."

"You can thank me later," I reply, placing the items in my shirt pocket.

I step into the living room and retrieve my rifle, tucking the revolver into my waistband before searching the other rooms. I can hear the oven door rattling open and closed.

"Don't do that," I call out.

"What the fuck did I ever do to you? This ain't even your place!"

I rejoin him. A part of me wants to knock the crap out of him, for no other reason than he's a piece of shit, a kidnapper, a rapist, your typical clichéd post-apocalyptic dirt-bag. I'm surprised he didn't have a Mohawk, leather pants and fucked up face make-up. That would complete the picture.

I pull out one of his Marlboros.

"Tell me about the girl."

"That one of mine?" He cranes his neck, watching as I light his cigarette.

"The girl. At the motel," I say.

"No fucking idea what you're talkin' about. No skirts left, not on the island. Where you been hibernating? Give me a fucking smoke."

I pace the kitchen floor, dummy glancing back at me, more concerned about his cigarettes than this dwindling time on earth.

"A couple of days ago, Highland Motel."

"Drawing a blank here boss. Gimme a goddamn smoke!"

I step into the living room re-emerging with a pile of magazines.

"What are you doin'?"

He jerks and twists as I stack the magazines in the doorway leading to the living room. Living rooms tend to light up like matchsticks I find, not sure why, but it always seems that way. But that could just be the pyro in me talking.

"What the fuck are you doin'? I told you I don't know shit." He begins struggling.

"Don't do that," I say, propping a couch cushion against the magazines.

He stops struggling, a bead of sweat forms on his pimply forehead.

"You can't tell me anything about the girl?"

"Are you thick as fuck, I told you, I don't know what you're talking about."

I take a pull off the Marlboro and lay it atop the magazines. His eyes widen, fixating on my fire-building skills.

"You can't fucking torch this place, you piece of shit." His arms flail, but all he's accomplishing is punishing his puny wrists. The cuffs will hold, a three-hundred pound steroid abuser on PCP might snap them, but scrawny-wrists doesn't stand a chance.

I step closer to him, eye to eye.

"Go ahead and try. Even if you manage to drag that heavy bastard across the floor, it won't fit out that door. That's a special order oven, oversized, probably for that once a year thirty-pound turkey, a bit much for this place, I agree."

His eyes look to the door as if assessing my claim.

"She won't fit, not without removing the hinges, and that's assuming you can turn the knob with your teeth."

The smell of burning paper drifts upwards, reminding me of my youth, of magnifying glasses and fried ants.

"Fuck you."

"Last chance."

I watch with mild fascination as he tries yanking off the handle with his noodle arms.

"You can scream if you want to, there is no shame."

"Fuck you and the cock-sucking horse you rode in on," he cries. His arms are flailing now, the oven door opening and closing in a fury of slams.

I look over but the cigarette's gone out, my James Bond moment ruined. I remove dipshit's two-hundred dollar lighter, tear out a page from a magazine, crumple it, and light it. I toss it atop the pile, greenish blue flames flickering with delight.

"Your funeral."

I grab my rifle and head for the door.

"Fucker! Fuck you, you piece of shit!" His arms are rocking back and forth like mad now, the entire oven nudging forward a centimetre at a time.

I'm out the door. I pause, glancing inside. Flames lick the sides of the cushion, seconds from spreading across the floor and up the walls.

"Okay, okay! The girl, the fucking girl Allie. That's the one right? I'll fucking tell you." His voice is calm, sincere.

I step back in, kick the cushion aside, and stamp out the flames. Sketch sits quietly, the oven door hanging open, one hinge askew, droplets of blood covering the floor. He looks comatose. I light a cigarette and place it between his lips.

"Tell me."

He looks up and smiles, a ghastly grin that exudes insanity. He inhales, maneuvering the cigarette with his lips like someone who's been smoking since they were six.

"First, you tell me," he says.

I light my own cigarette.

"What you dream of bro? Fiddles?"

CHAPTER 25

I did dream last night. It came to me, like a brilliant wash of colour overtaking a monochrome memory, like a flashbulb in the blackness.

I dreamt of the ship, the ocean liner in the harbour. And of people, a hundred at least, huddled together on deck, as if bidding adieu to family and friends as they begin a journey, one from which they will not return. I think of photographs, black and white news clips of the doomed passengers leaving port on the Titanic, half of them destined to perish. It was like that. Only something was different. Something was familiar; not the boat or the people, but the setting, the feeling in the air.

And there was a violin. A giant one with a bow. It stood sixty feet high, a monument, a grandiose fixture guarding the port, and the ocean beyond.

It was then I realized I'd been dreaming of Sydney, Cape Breton's port town, largest municipality on the island. A place we visited only once, but the impact and memories stayed with us. I snapped a shot of Rene standing beneath the giant violin, as does every tourist who visits, Celtic music softly playing, each note reverberating across the wharf.

I remember being corrected as I pontificated, drawing from my vast well of knowledge on Celtic culture, Rene doing her best to hide her eye rolls. To her credit, she was always patient, always let me finish my disjointed conjecture before correcting me. And I always needed correcting.

But it was a nosey bystander who chose to interrupt my history lesson, pointing out that it was not a giant violin at all.

It was a fiddle. And there was a difference.

I dreamt of a giant fiddle.

CHAPTER 26

ALLIE

I drop the revolver into my bag and tuck a spare clip for the Glock into my back pocket. I remove the hockey bag and backpack, ditching them in the middle of a cluster of smaller trees and bushes. Regardless of what happens, I need my equipment; I can't afford to travel light, not with a long trek ahead of me. Sketch's friends will be back, and if I can believe anything he says, they'd be here soon. Once that happens, I'm back on the FBI's Top Ten Most Wanted list, sitting at number one, not that I'm not already, but if things go as planned, they won't like me much.

I sling my rifle, grab the bolt cutters, and head back to the house.

All is calm within; Sketch whistles the Barenaked Ladies tune, given up trying to free himself, satisfied to fight another day. He's content to wait it out and face the consequences of his actions. As I head down the driveway, I wonder just how much he told me is the truth and how much is bullshit. He confirmed Allie was at the house, captive in a bedroom, chained up for trying to run—*chained up like a bitch in heat*, as he put it.

If there's only one guarding her, if he was telling the truth, I'll have an advantage. But I have to move fast, get there, deal with the threat, and go. Hopefully, they'll be adequate hosts and provide me with a getaway vehicle. Otherwise, I'll be winging it, not that I haven't been all along.

Deviating from my mission is a difficult decision, but I can't abandon the girl, not again. It's the right thing to do, and a part of me suspects that wherever she is, Rene is annoyed. Despite everything, we're civilized people. Rene was that type, one who would stop to help anyone, anytime. Borderline careless I often thought, leaving herself vulnerable, but then again, who was I to judge? I've never been first in line to help those in need, or stray from my comfort zone to do the right thing. Maybe that's the cause of the recurring dreams, the hallucinations; we all know guilt manifests itself in sinister ways. But when I think of Allie, alone in this world, caged, betrothed to the self-appointed leader of a group of fucked-up misfits, I can't ignore the gnawing truth. Not anymore. If I can believe anything dipshit told me, this guy in the uniform, this Victor; a killer, rapist, all around piece of shit, is not a nice person.

I glance up and down the roadway. Clouds have moved in, rain on its way, but that doesn't matter. The wind scatters leaves across the road as I break into a trot, the weight of the rifle and bolt cutters throwing off my gait, but I don't have far to go. After a couple of minutes, I slow to a walk, my heart pounding.

I see the truck before I hear it, it's moving that fast. I don't have time to reach the tree line, and I don't bother trying. I drop the bolt cutters and raise the rifle.

The truck skids to a stop.

The driver's door opens and Allie steps out. Her blouse is torn, stained with blood. Around her neck is a leather-studded collar, the kind you see in sex shops, S & M bondage gear. A length of chain attached to the collar drags behind her, as she looks but says nothing. Her face is expressionless, pale and worn, like she hasn't slept in days, aged a decade overnight. Stress, panic, tend to fuck with you, in every way imaginable.

I lower my gun.

"Allie."

She says nothing and climbs into the passenger side, pulling the length of chain inside with her. I grab the cutters and get into the driver's seat.

"I'm Jack."

"We should go." Her voice is flat, monotone. I put the truck in gear and pull away.

"You okay?"

A long pause.

"Pretty far from it."

I look at her, she stares straight ahead, clenching her hands together, wringing them like a mental ward patient. She's been through hell, but like Winston Churchill said, 'when you're going through hell, keep going'.

She picks up the bolt cutters and snips the leather choker, severing her chains.

"I have to make a quick stop," I say.

She lowers the window and tosses the chain and choker out. I glace to the rear-view, watching the items tumble across the blacktop.

CHAPTER 27

"I have to grab my gear," I say, pulling to a stop in front of the house. "Two minutes." I look to Allie, but she doesn't acknowledge me. Sketch is hollering from inside the house, the arrival of a vehicle prompting his cries.

"Don't mind him. He's not going anywhere."

Allie nods, her attention drawn to the front door of the home. I climb out and hit the path running. A branch catches my forehead, causing a flash of searing pain, but I continue, time evaporating by the millisecond. At the rear of the shed I uncover my booty, sorting through the backpack, ensuring I left nothing of importance inside. I sling the pack and grab the hockey bag when I hear the shot.

I drop the bag, running flat out, pulling out my Glock and envisioning the worst. As I burst through the trees, I see Allie stepping out the front door, the rifle in her hands. She glances in my direction, then climbs into the truck.

I approach her, my adrenaline on overdrive, my mind running through the possibilities, none of which make any sense. She sits, placid, rifle across her lap, staring out the window like she's medicated.

"What happened? Why did you go in there?"

She doesn't respond, checked out.

"Allie? What did you do?"

"We have to go. They're coming." Her voice is calm.

My mind is reeling, time slipping away, but this new development is disturbing. I head for the porch and open the door.

Sketch is dead. Shot at close range, the blood spray painting a horrific portrait of his final moments.

Reality consumes me, I feel ill, like vomiting. I've never fainted, but the blood and bits of organs and tissue covering the walls override my circuitry, and I feel like dropping. An hour ago I was talking with this piece of shit, and now he's as dead as Ma and Pa Kettle out back. Not that he was a saint, not that I didn't threaten to unleash my own particular brand of poetic violence, but this was final justice. I'm not a killer. Not unless my life's on the line, and if that's the case, sorry for your luck, but my survival trumps yours. This was not like that. This guy didn't have to die.

And yet she shot him, point blank, in the back. Maybe she killed the others. What horrors did she endure to want to exact revenge like this?

The horn beeps.

Not a wise decision, but she's right, it's time to go. What's done is done. Now is not the time for a debate on the subtleties between homicide and self-defence. I step away from the bloodbath and pull the door shut behind me. Allie watches as I pass by, heading towards the pathway to retrieve my gear. When I reappear, I drop the hockey bag into the back and climb into the truck. Allie looks different, the child, the abandoned innocent, back.

"Thanks for coming for me."

"Don't mention it."

Of all the accusations and questions swirling in my brain, that's the only response I can manage.

A long moment passes, neither of us saying a word, as if we're each waiting on the other, each awaiting the floodgate to trigger. But we don't. We sit, like disconnected souls, drawn together on a desperate journey, strangers in a strange world, oblivious to social convention.

Across from me sits the girl who appeared to me as an apparition, spoke to me in my dreams, owner of the locket I carry in my pocket. And all I can say is 'don't mention it'.

I turn on the ignition.

Allie leans over and kisses me on the cheek. A shudder runs down my spine.

I look over, and she's smiling. Smiling like the promise of a new dawn is upon us. Smiling like death wasn't just beyond the front door, handcuffed and warm.

"Where will we go?"

I hit the gas.

"I know a place."

CHAPTER 28

It was to be a spiritual retreat, hidden in the vast Cape Breton wilderness, far removed from roads, neighbours, and civilization. The owners bought the sixty acre farm intending to create an oasis, a sanctuary, a place for visitors to escape the world, to rejuvenate, to recharge. Situated in the highlands at Middle River, Gillis Farm was four kilometres from the nearest road, the only access a lonely dirt laneway through the surrounding forest to the base of the mountain. Ten acres of land was cleared, once farmed, now overgrown, a new post and beam cottage sat at the base of the mountain, the only other structure, an old barn, surrounded by apple trees. The plan to build three individual cottages fell through, the owners ran into financial problems, or so the realtor explained, and only built the one. The place wasn't large, only one bedroom, one bathroom and a loft, but it had a wrap-around porch and a magnificent view of the valley and westerly sunsets. The owners never completed the interior, the only partitioning walls around the bathroom, but the open concept had a certain charm, one Rene and I fell in love with the moment we saw it. It was our third visit to Cape Breton, and we'd decided over the winter we wanted a place of our own. There was a well and septic, but no electricity, no hydro lines within six kilometres, and no chance they were coming anytime soon.

Gillis Farm was completely off grid, the house and barn not visible from the road. Without power or phone lines, no one except the realtor and a few farmers knew the place existed. It was what we were looking for. Surrounded on three sides by a spectacular valley that stretched out forever, and shielded by the highest mountain in Middle River, this was privacy at its most invasive. The surrounding land was government owned, a protected wilderness reserve, so there would be no neighbours, ever. Middle River was renowned for its natural beauty and abundance of wildlife; bald eagles, salmon, foxes, deer, even bears. A stream split the property in two, winding its way from the base of the mountain out towards Margaree River and beyond.

We were impulsive and put in an offer the same day. There was something extraordinary about the place, the natural beauty, the solitude; it fed our passion, made us excited, like kids on Christmas. I'd always been the type who researched ad nauseam, before a major purchase, spending weeks comparing prices, trends, pros and cons. Whether it was a new car or a laptop, I did my homework. It drove Rene crazy.

But Gillis Farm was different. We both sensed it. I didn't care that it was on the market forever. I didn't care about mortgage rates or realtor's fees. It was the excitement of the moment, the fascination and wonder of the island, staring us in the face, daring us to walk away. Our future lay here, at Gillis Farm, we were sure of it.

I guess in retrospect we went in too high, our offer was accepted the same day. But it didn't matter. We were ecstatic.

In celebration, I drove out to the NSLC store in Baddeck, demanding their finest bottle of champagne, confident I'd be spending no more than sixty bucks on a bottle of Moet or maybe Veuve Clicquot. Little did I know they kept a bottle of Dom Perignon on hand for the occasional high roller who sauntered in—me and my big mouth. The bottle set me back two hundred and twenty, but it was worth it, even after enduring Rene's ribs at my faux pas. We drove back to the farm, spread out a blanket, and toasted to our future, drinking sixty-dollar-a-glass champagne in paper cups.

Three months later when we returned, the property was ours. It was early October and the weather was turning, the valley already sparkling with swatches of fiery red and brilliant yellows. I took more pictures that short trip with my Canon 5D than I'd taken the previous two years total. We brought in a few pieces of furniture, bed, kitchen table, chairs, but we weren't intending on furnishing the place, not just yet. Without partitioning walls, there was no need to. I picked up a small generator as a backup, but the wood stove kept the place comfortable and cozy. The Canadian Tire in Port Hawkesbury had an end-of-season sell-off on solar panels, I bought out the store's stock, figured I'd start our off-grid adventure in the spring.

We wanted to stay the week, but Rene had a Specialist's appointment, one she'd made after our last trip, the kind of appointment you don't re-schedule. They assured her it was precautionary, not to worry, told her not to let it spoil her summer.

But it did. She played it down, but I saw the change in her. I struggled as well. At times it felt like we were both living a lie, ignoring reality, deflecting depression, I hated feeling like that. Watching her going about her day as if nothing was wrong, staying positive, making plans, took its toll on us both. But I hoped for the best, I even prayed, something I'd not done since childhood, but, like foxholes and atheists, desperate times called for extreme measures. And we forged ahead, counting the days until we were back on the island.

I carved our initials into a birch tree at the stream's edge the evening before we left for home. We sat together, hand in hand, sipping Shiraz out of Dollar Store wine glasses, listening to the trickle of the water, watching the sun descend beneath the hills, the vibrant colours dissolving into grey. It was a moment unlike any other, the two of us, our souls merged, amidst nature's glory, watching daylight fade to darkness, our journey drawing to a close.

That was the last time Rene saw the island.

After her diagnosis, things fell apart quickly. I struggled to deal with her affairs; Wills, insurance, palliative care. Cape Breton was the furthest thing from my mind, memories I wanted to bury, to delete, to purge for all eternity.

A month before she passed, I did a selfish thing. Rene lay dying, a little each day, but she worried about me, about my weight loss, my lack of sleep, my drinking. She asked me to take a trip, just for a few days, told me to visit the cottage and send her pictures. Bring her back a rock from the stream, and a branch from the birch tree, the one with our initials.

And I went.

Shameful as it was, I went. I was weak, selfish. I couldn't watch her slip away, not another minute. I needed time, and I went. Her sister was mortified, disgusted, never spoke to me again. I stayed three days, calling so often her sister stopped answering, but I felt no relief. Deep inside I knew I deserved punishment, penance for being spineless, gutless. I barely ate, didn't sleep, I walked the land for hours, zombie-drunk, until I passed out.

By the time I returned Rene's condition had worsened and she was back in hospital. I stayed by her side for four days and nights, until she'd regained some strength, started eating again. We spoke of the cottage, of our trip together. But we didn't speak of the future.

She was better, her spirits lifted, she was ready to go back home.

But it wasn't to last.

When she died, Cape Breton died with her. The island represented only pain, sorrow, an end. I never planned on returning. But fate has a funny way of fucking with you, especially when you think you can't possibly be fucked with, any more.

CHAPTER 29

"I could go for a hot bath. Is that too much to ask? A little 'me' time now and again?"

Allie ignores me, tearing into the jerky, ravenous, savouring the cardboard texture with each bite. She stares out the window. Unlike the southern extension of the highway, void of cars, void of any evidence of the apocalypse, this section shows the extent of the great purge. Dozens upon dozens of cars lie abandoned, pushed off the roadway into the ditches, someone's attempt at keeping the highway clear. This was accomplished afterward, and it must have taken great effort. We pass vehicle after vehicle, damaged, dented, overturned, like a welcome wagon from a bygone era, a parade route, lined shoulder to shoulder with the relics of a lost civilization.

But there are no bodies, no evidence of drivers, passengers, pedestrians. Allie senses it too, her eyes scanning back and forth, absorbing everything but saying nothing, focusing on nourishment, her mind adrift in a purgatory I could not imagine. *What was she thinking about?* Cold-blooded murder had to take a toll on one's mind, even in the new world order. Civilization is not out of our systems, not yet, we were born wired to acquiesce, to fit in, to live and let live; it's later we acquired the taste for violence, the win at any cost mindset.

I break the silence.

"Why did you kill him?"

I glance at her. She stops pulling at the jerky, then resumes.

"Why didn't you?"

I slow down. There's a shack up ahead, an old structure held together by particle board and scrap tin, remnants of a 1950's Coca-Cola sign hanging above the door.

I know this place. We're entering First Nation's land, a community running along this stretch of the 105. The shack was a tobacco hut, one of a couple on this route, sold cheap cigarettes and cigars to locals and passing tourists. Not that I was a smoker back then, but a pack of Players ran you sixteen bucks at the local convenience store, and that kind of coin was rare, especially with locals. The tobacco huts gave you a cheaper option, an alternative, a clever way to flip the government the bird. Between cigarettes, liquor and beer, Nova Scotians were hosed on anything deemed 'unhealthy' by the government, another excuse to ram more taxes up their puckered assholes.

"There."

Allie points to a second shack up ahead, this one larger, more elaborate, animal carvings and deer antlers adorning the front.

"Shit."

I slow down.

It's the first sign of life, or death rather. A body lies atop the roof, what remains of the arms and legs tethered to the corners with rope, as if being drawn and quartered. Dressed in traditional Aboriginal garb, the corpse is soiled and damp, a cesspool of deadly microbes, rotting under the crisp blue sky. Tied around the neck is a violin.

Allie whispers under her breath. "Fiddle."

I look over to her. She's looking at something else.

I hit the brakes, skidding to a halt in the middle of the highway. A body lies on the road ahead, unmoving.

Another corpse, this one wearing a hockey jersey. I can't make out the team, or the number, but it's a jersey.

"Drive," says Allie.

I take my foot off the brake and ease the truck forward.

"You know about them?"

She nods. "Drive, don't stop."

I look at her, then back to the body. It looks dead to me, but then what the hell did I know? I speed up and take the left shoulder, giving the body a wide berth, my eyes peeled, looking for the trap.

Just as we're passing, Allie grabs the steering wheel and yanks it right. The truck rears towards the centre line—towards the body.

"Christ!" I yell, yanking the wheel just in time to see the body leap to its feet and dart towards the shoulder. It was an L.A. Kings jersey, long greasy hair obscuring the number on the back, but I know what it was. No rifle that I could see.

A shot rings out, and I hammer the gas pedal. Two more shots, but we're soon out of range, clear sailing ahead. I keep one eye on the rear-view as we hit one-forty, but no chase cars come, no one follows. After a minute, I disengage warp drive.

I check my breathing and loosen my grip on the steering wheel.

"Can we hold off on the Death Race 2000 shit next time?" I

say.

Allie opens her bottle of water and drinks, like it's all in a day's work. She offers me some, but I decline.

"They'll be a next time," she replies.

I glance at her, then focus on the approaching village. Aged dwellings line the highway, some dilapidated some newer builds, little changed from a year prior. Side streets branch off to the left, leading to an array of smaller houses on large, unkempt lots. The Volunteer Fire Department building is on our right, a sad looking structure that's seen better days.

Four kilometres ahead is the village of Whycocomagh, an urban centre with a gas station and Tim Hortons, hardware store and pharmacy, the last metropolis before Baddeck. If a trap were to be sprung, it would be there.

We can't risk passing through. Reservation Road is up ahead to our left, a side-road that runs west through the reserve, connecting with the 395, a less travelled highway that intersects with the Cabot Trail. It's the long way around, but a safer bet. Staying on the 105 is what they'd expect, and seeing possum-boy back there confirmed any doubt I had. He had an accomplice, and if they have access to two-way communication, our arrival has already been announced. Even if we were to make it through Whycocomagh, there were more choke points ahead, plenty of opportunity for an ambush.

And then there was the Manor.

It was straight ahead, less than fifteen kilometres from here. Passing through would be suicide, especially if they know I have one-half of Thelma and Louise riding shotgun.

The 105 was not an option. The 385 would add an extra

twenty-five kilometres to the trip, but it would be an easier go, there wasn't much up that way as far as I remembered, a few farms, trailer park, nothing more.

"It's pretty here."

Allie gazes out over Bras d'Or Lake to our right, the water a crisp, shimmering blue, oblivious to humankind's dilemma.

"That it is."

She reaches her arms back, pulling her shirt up over her head revealing a white tank top beneath; a Marlon Brando wife-beater, classic undershirt of the old Italian gentleman who hoses down his cement driveway in socks and sandals. She lowers the window and discards her garment.

"I have clothes, in the back," I say.

Allie glances over, rubbing her neck, wincing as her fingers disturb the raw skin inflicted by her chains. I notice a tattoo just below her clavicle, over her heart, the number 'twenty-one' written in fancy script. Allie catches me looking, and it's just as well—I'm on the shoulder—another second and we'd have had a bigger problem than my wandering eyes.

"Sorry about that." I feel my face go red.

I slow as we approach a bend in the road, the town of Whycocomagh dead ahead. My eyes scan a row of shanties to my left, boarded up windows, sunken porches, peeling paint.

"I need to pee," Allie says, shifting in her seat, adjusting her undershirt, one that is clinging tightly to her skin.

"We need gas," I say.

"There."

She points to a restaurant, new to the island by the looks of it; at least I don't recall it the last time I was here. Several school buses are parked out back, a good chance their tanks might be ripe. I turn left, checking the front for signs of movement. The windows are smashed, a garbage can sits wedged inside the doors. I bypass the entrance and pull around back, parking between the buses.

Allie is out of the car in a flash.

"Wait!"

I jump out after her.

"Where are you going?"

She turns and holds up the revolver. *When the fuck did she get that?*

"I'm good. Get gas, I'll be right out."

She tucks the revolver down the front of her pants and re-adjusts her clinging tank top.

"I've got clothes in the back," I repeat.

She ignores me and heads for the rear entrance. I should go with her, but I don't. She can handle herself. And I wish she'd put a shirt on.

"Try not to kill anyone," I mutter under my breath.

I scan the area. We're on Reservation land, winding streets that branch out into cul-de-sacs, sprinkled with modular homes on large overgrown lots. First Nations people were often shortchanged on housing, and Cape Breton was no different. Even during better days, a few of the homes were run-down— aging boxes held together by duct tape and coat hangers.

I grab my syphoning gear and start on the first bus. The tanks are deep, but I have the long hose, and an extension if needed. We're close to fumes in the pickup, and with dusk closing in, running out of fuel on the 395 means walking. We need twenty litres at least, more if I can manage it.

The first tank is empty, or close to it. I move on to the second one then pause, stepping out from between the buses, eyeballing the rear of the restaurant.

Did I hear something?

No noise, all is quiet. I resume my task, and with luck, the fuel begins to flow.

I hear a crash. From inside the restaurant.

I drop the hose and run for the rear doorway, fumbling to get my Glock out, preparing for God knows what. I step through, the gun trained in my grip. The interior is unevenly lit, the back section dark, the front bathed in light.

"Allie?"

No response. I step further into the restaurant.

"Allie!"

The place is a Boston Pizza clone, decorative jars of pasta and peppers lining the booths and windowsills, blue and red coloured paint, sports memorabilia on the walls. The restaurant's been looted, but not in bad shape overall. The bar area is barren, pillaged, not a bottle in sight, at least not any full ones.

"Allie?"

I navigate a collection of discarded chairs and stools, moving towards the front, shards of glass littering the entranceway. To my left is a hallway, a 'Gents' and 'Ladies' sign displayed above the doorway.

"What do you think, better?"

I spin.

Allie appears, hands on her hips, wearing a Pittsburgh Penguins hockey jersey. The shirt is huge on her, down to her knees. She does a half turn and I see it's the Captain's jersey, number eighty-seven.

"Authentic, signed," she says, pointing out the signature in black marker across the Penguin's logo.

"W-where did you…"

She points to what's left of an ornate boxed frame behind the bar; the glass smashed out. It was a piece of sports memorabilia, likely the restaurant's showpiece, considering he was from Peggy's Cove, a hero to the Maritimes and all of Canada. I'm surprised it wasn't taken, but then again, number ninety-nine seemed to be the preferred collector's item 'round these parts.

"You know who you look like?"

"Only I don't miss."

Allie picks the revolver up off the floor and tucks in under the jersey.

I look around, but unless sports memorabilia has any value in the new world, it's unlikely anything salvageable remains.

"We should go. I gotta use the can first."

Allie nods. I watch as she steps behind the bar, her eyes alight, inspecting everything like a barfly on an all-inclusive pub-crawl. The jersey looks like a dress on her, but it works. At least she's covered up.

I push aside an overturned table and head towards the washroom. Bypassing the lady's room out of habit, I enter the Gent's. Bad choice. The stench is horrid, urinals stained yellow, glistening with black mould. I light a cigarette to lessen the nasal intrusion and push open a stall door. The toilet's worse, but it'll do. I can't recall the last time I took a dump, but nothing's currently pressing in the intestinal zone, and I'm not eager to coax one out, not here, not now. I always wondered why it is you never see anyone taking a shit in the apocalypse. Men take the occasional piss, but not the women. All those third act scenes, the cannibals converging, the zombie herd's final push; no one ever stops to take a shit. Considering few stragglers were eating a balanced diet in the after-world, it's highly likely your average survivor had the runs—all the time. I never understood that.

I unzip, freeing my bladder, dragging on the cigarette, the first smoke I've had since we became the dynamic duo. Thelma and Jack. My lungs fill, my bladder empties, a moment of bliss, one of life's simple pleasures in a complex world. I finish my business, reach down to flush, realize there's no point. Glancing at my cigarette, I think back to my university days, when hanging out in a pub was an everyday occurrence. I remember urinals filled with chipped ice, people smoking joints in the stalls, it all comes back in a rush. I used to play *sink the battleship*, at least that's what I called it, back in the days you could still smoke in restaurants and bars. Errant smokers would drop their butts in the toilet bowl and neglect to flush. When you went to take a leak and saw one, you focused your stream, maintained precision, and bombarded that cigarette like a water cannon until the paper disintegrated, releasing the tobacco like a tiny oil spill. *Sink the battleship.* I hadn't thought of that in years.

I bypass washing my hands, that's old world etiquette, nothing a few pub germs will do to me that Mother Nature hasn't already tried. I step out.

Allie is gone. But why wouldn't I expect that? I peer out the door and see her at the pickup, syphoning gas. I take a final look around the bar then head out.

"Careful, you don't want to ruin your shirt."

Allie smiles and closes the fuel door. I take the can from her and start filling the pickup's tank.

"I'm guessing you're a Leaf's fan. You have that unflinching-faith-in-miracles look about you," she says, smiling. I smile back, contemplating my retort when I hear the explosion.

Allie freezes.

I can't tell where it came from, or how far away, but it dawns on me just how exposed we are. Stupid move.

"W-hat was..."

"Shh." I cut her off.

There's a second explosion, closer this time, somewhere on the 105. A thick plume of smoke rises into view north of us, less than a kilometre away. A car fire maybe, or something worse. Whatever it is, we can't hang around to find out.

"Let's go."

"Wait."

Allie takes a few steps out into the open and cocks her ear.

"What?"

Car engines, I hear them now. It's hard to tell where they're coming from or which direction they're headed. We shield ourselves behind the buses and peer out towards the highway.

Two cars race past, southbound. Something's happened. Or someone's ratted us out. We jump into the truck and I jam her into drive. Thirty seconds later we're racing up Reservation Road. Clusters of abandoned homes streak by, makeshift play parks, rusted bicycles and broken trampolines, all remnants of island life. Soon we're on the 395, surrounded by bush on both sides, heading north, away from trouble.

"I'm guessing they discovered your handy work," I say, looking up to the sky, now scarlet red, the sun slipping behind the mountaintop.

"Yup," Allie replies.

I look over to her. The 'C' on her jersey signifies 'Captain'—the team leader, but beneath her Adidas armour lies another number. One that must also have meaning.

"You're on the wrong team," I say.

Allie looks down, examining the logo.

"No, we're on the right team. I'm pretty sure of that."

CHAPTER 30

The struggle to understand recent events, what was happening and why, incapacitated my ability to rationalize. It's said that in solving complex problems, conundrums, it's best to avoid thinking about the issue directly, instead, set it aside, focus on the here and now, let the larger problem simmer. Use this tactic and a solution will present itself. The theory made sense, not that I ever tried it.

But in the new world, amidst this blank canvass of societal abandonment, the back-burner analogy has promise. I've come up with a theory, as far-fetched as it may be, on how these supernatural, other-worldly events are occurring—on how it is I dream of people I've never met, and know things I couldn't possibly know.

Quantum physics.

The concept that life is composed of energy, vibrations. Solid objects are not solid, not on a quantum scale, everything is fluid, vibrating atoms, moving, changing, evolving. Our thoughts, our emotions, emit this energy, knowingly or otherwise, sending out vibrations to the cosmos, attracting similar energies. What you put out to the universe, you get back. Positive thoughts of compassion and peace attract more of the same—and the reverse is true; send out bad vibes, and the universe responds in kind. I'm no scientist, I'm not even particularly bright, but it's the way our world has always been, only few realized it, and even fewer embraced it. I remember a scene from a favourite movie of mine, *Joe Versus the Volcano*, Meg Ryan's character explaining how her rich father said that most of the world was asleep, except for a few people who lived in a state of constant wonder and amazement. That line, that analogy, impacted me, I didn't understand why at the time, but I'd filed it away, only to be retrieved from the archives at world's end.

And why?

Because I was among the masses, asleep, existing, and nothing more.

Until now.

Our thoughts project, they transcend distance and time, they always have. The polar shift occurred when six billion energies were eradicated, the airwaves now clear, air traffic control on autopilot, vibrations and messages, unencumbered. That's why humanity was always on the verge of catastrophe, no matter the century or technological sophistication, man warred. Murder, starvation, exploitation, all fed off an infinite supply of negative energies, a continuous loop of jealousy, barbarism, and hate.

But the great cleansing cleared the way, purifying the environment, re-establishing the channels of cosmic communication. Thoughts, feelings, emotions became free once again, free to transcend the universe, unfettered. Awake or asleep it didn't matter, there was no off switch.

Humanity was never in control.

I dreamt of Allie, a girl I'd never known. I saw her forerunner, her spirit, her essence, whatever the terminology, and I learned her name. There was no logical explanation. Call it a sixth sense, or a seventh, the theory holds merit, and it comforts me, reassures me I'm not insane. Adapting to this paradigm shift is a radical leap, but I've tuned in to the signal; the ethereal radio station of the apocalypse, one that broadcasts from the highest peaks of existence.

The snipers caught the signal also, which stream, I can't say. I'd wager they've connected to the lunatic channel, one that broadcasts self-indulgence, aggression, murder. They have their signal to decipher, I have mine. Part of me wonders if Allie is the key, the antenna, drawing survivors towards her like metal shavings to a magnet. She is the conduit, the core, not the frightened child I thought, but a formidable spirit with a warrior's mindset, mitigated by a gentle soul. She is maturing, evolving, having been a target, a prize, in a world without justice. I don't blame her, in fact, I thank her. Since our meeting my mind has cleared, the memory lapses, the dizzy spells, gone. She did that.

I don't have the answers, but I know where they lie. They lie with her.

But then again, maybe I am just fucked.

CHAPTER 31

She stands on the shoreline, gazing out over Lake Ainslie, her jersey catching the breeze like the tiny sail of a ship. Moonlight dances on the crests of crashing waves, the sound of the surf serenading the desolate campground.

I wedge my crowbar into the lock and heave, forcing the door open. The trailer is enormous, a park model, larger than my ride on the mainland, a virtual homestead on wheels. She's not been abandoned long, unlike the other trailers in the park, their doors hanging open, pillaged, havens to mice, squirrels and scavengers. These rigs belonged to seasonal visitors, islanders who lived an hour or two away by car. A home away from home, a place to swim and fish, relax and enjoy the peace and tranquility of lake life.

I pull the door open and shine my light inside.

"This one has potential," I say in a whispered shout.

I look over my shoulder. Allie is inspecting a burned-out trailer two lots over, an old Airstream, the kind shaped like an aluminum Twinkie. The unit is gutted, recently I'd guess, the smell of charred plastic and metal still lingering in the air.

Allie steps up. "Why's this one intact?"

"No idea. I'll take the front, you start at the back. Anything, cans, food, water, medicine, we'll take it all."

Allie moves off to the rear, her flashlight beam dancing about the cramped quarters. I move to the front, inspecting the kitchen area. The cluttered interior smells damp and stale, but it's in fair shape, inhabitable. I open the fridge out of curiosity, the smell horrid; inside is an expired container of coffee creamer and the remnants of a package of wieners, the contents a science exhibit. I close the fridge and open the overhead compartments.

Jackpot.

I pull open the adjacent compartments on the other side, also full.

"Allie."

She steps up. "Just blankets and fishing gear." She looks. "Holy shit."

The cupboards are stocked; bottled water, canned food, candles, boxes of Macaroni and Cheese. I'd been craving pasta since day one, and Mac & Cheese with its mildly toxic powdered cheddar was always my favourite. That shit will never go bad, not even in an apocalypse, like Twinkies and hard candy. Millionaires crave it, that and Dijon ketchup.

"This will do. We should bring the truck closer."

"This belongs to someone," Allie says, inspecting an unlabelled can.

"Yeah, to us." I begin pulling items out. Allie shines her light in my eyes.

"You don't think this is unusual, a locked trailer? Maybe it's a trap."

"Not likely." I continue unpacking. "I trust my instincts. You want to get the truck?"

Allie furrows her brow, pauses as if to reply, then steps out. I peruse the bounty; cans of corn, beans, soup, instant coffee, tins of tuna and salmon, sardines. This was a lucky find. I start stacking the items atop the kitchen table, then stop. I hear a noise.

Music.

Violin music. I drop the cans and head outside.

Allie stands frozen, her gaze fixed on something or someone I don't see. I move past her, straining to focus in the dim light.

The music continues, an eerily haunting ballad, familiar, the notes rising above the sound of the surf, reverberating off the trailers.

It's a person. An old man. He stands in the shadows, dressed in orange overalls, a yellow slicker and baseball cap, a fiddle tucked under his chin, the bow moving with slow precision across the strings.

I take Allie by the arm, pulling her back, but she resists. The music stops, the sudden silence, deafening.

"I taught you was one of them arseholes." He lowers his instrument. "Dat shirt you got on."

We both look to the jersey, the Penguin's logo translucent under the moonlight.

"No sir, we're just passing through," I say. "Sorry if this is your place, we were looking for food."

"If you were dem other fellas, I'd a been holdin' a shotgun. I'd a told ya to get your Jesus arse on outa here."

He steps up, favoring one leg, smiling.

"Don't get many visitors. Come this way, don't mind the limp, I'm an old man."

Allie and I glance at each other. There's a glint of concern in her eyes, distrust, the survival mode emerging, but I nod to her, indicating it's okay. We follow behind as the old man leads us to a small trailer, an eighteen footer at the water's edge. He opens the door and ushers us inside.

"Welcome to Lake Ainslie," he says.

He lights a butane lantern and invites us to take a seat. The cramped interior is jammed with supplies, every inch of counter space piled high with boxes, clothes, bottles. I count three First Aid Kits, a pair of fire extinguishers, a shotgun, crossbow, flashlights. Allie and I find a seat on a pull-out couch, squeezing our arses into the tight quarters.

The old man rummages through an overhead compartment and removes two cans of Moosehead. He hands us one each, grabs one for himself, and wedges himself behind the kitchen table. He pops open his can.

"To new friends."

We toast. The beer reminds me of home, of my apartment, of old man Tudyk.

"Thank you." Allie's eyes have softened.

"I'm Allie, this is Jack."

"Cecil. Pleased to know ya."

He takes a long drink.

"I won't ask ya where yer father's from, you're both

mainlanders."

I nod. "That obvious? You live here alone Cecil?"

"Yup." He reaches over and lights a candle, setting it down precariously close to a container of butane. The flame flickers and grows, illuminating the grey stubble on his chin, the crease lines on his weathered face. He's lived an islander's life, no doubt there.

"I'd been waiting for my son. I taught maybe you were him."

He plucks a book from atop the table and hands it to Allie. She opens it, angling the pages towards the candlelight. It's a scrapbook, photos of happier times. Allie flips through it.

"The family moved to New Glasgow. I figured after the power and phone went out, he'd be down to check on me."

I take a drink.

"How long have you been here?"

"Cape Breton—all my life. From New Waterford, moved to the lake years back, looked after the trailers for the seasonal folk."

"You've been here all this time?" I ask.

"Went into town once, that was enough."

"These pictures are lovely." Allie glances up. "You mentioned you thought we were someone else."

His eyes dim, his demeanour stern.

"Those boys came by a few weeks after the power went out. I

was the only one left, everyone else gone or dead." He sets his can down and looks up. "No one came for them. Not the cops, fire department, nobody. I dug their graves, up on the plateau, away from the trees."

He takes off his hat. A swatch of grey hair falls across his furrowed brow.

"Marked their restin' places as best I could, figured the families might wanna know one day. When those boys showed up, they took what they wanted. I couldn't stop them."

He swallows hard.

"Then these two important fellas pull up. A bald-headed giant and an arsehole in a cop uniform. He wasn't no cop, I knew that right off. They had a chat with the others, then left."

Allie flips through the book. I glance over; she's paused on a series of photos of a family standing around a Christmas tree, one with so much tinsel it looks like an aluminum silo. She looks up and smiles.

"I waited them out, figurin' they'd leave once they took all they could carry."

He stares into the flame.

"Next thing I know my trailer's on fire—and I can't get out, the door's buggered. I hear 'em laughing outside, cars starting."

"They set your trailer on fire?" Allie closes the album. "How'd you get out?"

Cecil reaches over and takes the book from her, his bony fingers caressing the binding.

"Underestimation. There wasn't a brain between the lot of them. Stunned they were. Like they were doped up or drunk, maybe both. I used the axe, chopped a hole through the floor. Guess they figured I'd just curl up and die."

"They figured wrong," I say, smiling.

"That they did."

I finish my beer, too quickly, and the old man takes my empty.

"Another?" he asks.

I could go for a dozen, but politely decline.

"She's gettin' warm in here. Not used to the company, not that I'm complaining." He removes his slicker letting it fall to the floor. Tattoos cover his forearms, blue inked patterns, faded with age.

"Have they been back?" I ask.

"A couple times, but they figure the place is cleaned out and move on. That's why I'm spread all over now, never in the same place."

"Smart," I reply. "You get many others up this way?"

"Nope. Not in weeks."

"What is the significance of that?" Allie leans forward.

"Tattoos?" Cecil asks. "Which one?"

"That one," Allie points, "the number."

Cecil angles his left forearm towards the light. The tattoo

depicts the number 'twenty-one', an elaborate crucifix separating the number 'two' and 'one'.

"Oh, that one."

Cecil pauses, as if searching his thoughts.

"Twenty-one miners died in the explosion at Glace Bay, back in '78. One of the worst in Maritime history."

"You worked in the mines?" Allie asks.

"I did, and I worked in that mine, right alongside those boys. I knew them all." His eyes lower.

"What happened?" Allie leans forward, intrigued, her hip digging into my kidney.

"Fate's what happened my dear. The wife went into labour, three weeks early. I was in hospital in North Sydney, holdin' my baby boy when I heard the news."

He rubs his fingers over the faded tattoo.

"The fella they got to fill in was new, first day in the mines. He was eighteen."

Cecil looks up and smiles.

"So I remembers them, twenty-one souls, twenty-one men who never got to see their family again. And I should have been one of them."

"I'm sorry," Allie says. "Things happen for a reason sometimes."

"Well, after all this time I can't think of the reason. The Lord and me, we didn't always see eye to eye, but my wife said it was a miracle. Me, I ain't so sure."

I shift in my seat, but Allie is oblivious, content to sardine me. I catch her eye, urging her to drink up. It's time we got moving.

"She was a long time ago, but even now, when I hear the music, I remember their faces."

"You play beautifully." Allie smiles, downing the rest of her can.

"You're kind, but I'm not that good. Been practising though. What else does a lonely old man have to do? That's a tune I only just heard on the radio."

"Radio?" I take Allie's empty and hand it to Cecil.

"Beside you there. Started workin' one day, all on her own."

I pick it up. It's an old AM/FM portable, circa 1975, missing the volume button, and void of batteries. I set it back down.

"You use a generator at all?" I ask.

"There's a few in the park, but I haven't bothered, at least not yet. Need gasoline for that."

I look to Allie then stand.

"Cecil, we appreciate your hospitality, the beer was great, but we should be going, it's late, and we have a ways to go."

Cecil stands.

"Where are my manners, keeping you like this. Before you

head off, help yourself to whatever you want, I got more than an old man needs. Stuff's stashed all over the park, in case the arseholes come back."

Allie and I glance at one another.

"Maybe just a few cans of food, water, one of your First Aid Kits, if that's okay."

Cecil grabs a milk crate and promptly dumps the contents on the floor at his feet. "I'll clean that up later. Let's go shoppin'."

Fifteen minutes later, Allie and I are loading supplies into the back of the pickup. Cecil appears, holding an eight-pack box of Mac & Cheese. He hands it to me.

"I hear you're partial to it. Don't care for it myself. Not the same without butter and milk."

I take the box.

"Thanks Cecil. For everything. And I'm sorry for the door."

"Don't mention it. I'll fix her tomorrow." He turns to Allie.

"And for you my dear," he holds out an ornate oval brooch, gold, encrusted with emeralds. "I want you to have this. The stones match your eyes."

Allie shakes her head. "That's not necessary, I couldn't take that Cecil."

"Go on now, it'll bring you luck. I was supposed to hand her down, but I don't expect I'll be seeing my granddaughter before I die. I'd like you to have it. Make an old man happy."

Allie takes the brooch.

"It's beautiful. Thank you."

Cecil nods and turns, looking out over the lake. He's silent for a moment.

"We're all that's left, ain't we?"

I nod, realizing it's a rhetorical question.

"We'll come visit once we're settled, see how you're doing," says Allie. "We aren't going that far."

"I'd like that," Cecil replies. "I'd like that."

The winds have died down, the water calmer.

I look to the burned-out trailer, Cecil's home, meant to be his casket. He's a survivor, like us.

Cecil and I shake hands, his grip firm, the miner in him very much alive. He smiles, his eyes filled with warmth and sadness.

"Thank you," I say, climbing into the driver's seat. Allie hugs him, kisses him on the cheek. She opens the passenger door and gets in.

Headlights illuminate the ghostly remnants of the abandoned trailers, massive tombstones in a graveyard of lost moments.

Cecil steps over as I lower the window.

"I know there ain't no batteries in that radio. But I heard the music, just the same." He waves.

"We'll check on you," Allie yells.

"I'm countin' on it."

Allie buckles up, and I put the truck into gear.

"Did you recognize that song he played?" she asks.

I shake my head as we pull away.

"I do."

CHAPTER 32

Are there shades of grey in the apocalypse, or only black and white—good and evil? Books and movies all point to the latter. When a mass exodus of humanity occurs, those left, the lucky, or unlucky depending on where you lie on the glass half-full, half-empty spectrum, choose sides. Or perhaps the sides choose them. Whatever the case, people emerge as one of two things; inherently human, caring, compassionate, civilized, eager to carve out the remainder of their pitiful lives in a positive light, or, conversely, they embrace humanity's darker side, a path that knows only self-preservation, violence, greed, a breach of Commandments, one through ten.

The consensus of twenty-first-century authors suggests the predator-prey scenario wins out in an apocalypse, the strong exploiting the weak, evil eviscerating good.

Is there a middle ground? Is there a sub-category of post-apocalyptic misfits who side on their own, fulfill their needs, avoid interaction, but also live and let live?

There doesn't seem to be.

Not in this apocalypse.

There's good and there's bad, and then there's me, a lone soul adrift in the non-existent middle ground, traversing the abyss with a solitary goal. My priorities are conflicted; at my core I'm good, yet I lack integrity, one who won't jeopardize safety for another. I will make it to Sanctuary and live until I die. End of story.

Then along comes Allie, a leader, team captain, rallying the troupes while I sit on the bench as a third-string sub, hoping never to be called upon. It's not that I don't play well with others, it's my selfish streak, my tragic flaw, an obstacle I cannot—or choose not, to overcome. Doomed to internal conflict and questionable motives, I exist in a periphery, hidden in shadow, segregated by choice, hounded by guilt.

Allie champions hope. The others, the pillagers, murderers, rapists, pledge their allegiance to those without souls, men without remorse or conscience, men with a taste for blood. The vicious never acquiesce; never ease up, never stop coming. There is always more to covet, higher ground to conquer, opponents to annihilate. If the history of humankind has one constant, it's that man's inhumanity to man is resolute, a single truth proven century after century.

But the new morning has dawned, and with it, humankind's prowess over the earth has been silenced. Global warming, deforestation, species extinction, has been halted. Nature found a way to extinguish the threat called humanity, humbling the few who remain, reminding us of just who the fuck was in charge the whole time. It wasn't us. With all of our technological advancements, all our best intentions, our greed and lack of respect resulted in twelve billion lungs suddenly silenced, oblivion, brought on by our own actions.

Rapture or brimstone?

Who chooses?

There can be no middle ground. No shades of grey.

Not in this lifetime.

CHAPTER 33

SANCTUARY

We arrived under cover of darkness. Allie continued to doze, having fallen asleep shortly after we bid adieu to Cecil, the elderly escape artist. The drive up the 395 was uneventful, the roadway clear, less travelled, no signs of life, no evidence of inhabitants.

Allie continued to sleep soundly, undeterred, as I fished out my handsaw and set about cutting a pair of trees that had fallen across the laneway. This was a usual occurrence; I'd found out the hard way last year when a half-dozen trees had come down over the winter. I kept a chainsaw stashed in the barn, but that would have meant leaving Allie alone and hiking twenty minutes in, then twenty minutes back—and hoping the damn thing started. I kept certain essential items in plastic totes hidden in the barn, camouflaged. Off-season break-ins, even in the most rural areas of Cape Breton were commonplace. Most things we can afford to lose, but a chainsaw wasn't one of them.

I'd planned ahead, months earlier, and picked up a small folding handsaw, for just such a development. The trees fell fifty metres apart, each one blocking the road entirely, too large to move without Lou Ferrigno sized arms; not that I'm supporting a pair of noodles, but well beyond my weight class. It took me a while, working up a sweat in the process, but gave me the opportunity to enjoy a couple of smokes in the cool night air while Allie slept, my first cigarettes in a while. I don't think she knows I smoke, not that it should matter. Thankfully each tree only needed a single cut before I could drag the section far enough to the side to drive past. I made a mental note to a drop a few after we'd settled, to prevent any surprise vehicular visits. It was a good idea, the kind of thing I needed

147

to think more about.

Allie didn't flinch as I climbed back into the truck.

THE CABIN

I pull around back, the long grass scraping against the undercarriage, the tires carving a pathway through the undergrowth. Allie shifts in her seat as I turn off the engine and jump out to inspect the perimeter. All looks good, doors locked, windows intact. With no electrical hook up, I keep the place stocked with candles and a pair of Coleman camping lanterns; the lanterns stashed in the barn with the generator. That stuff I can get in the morning, at first light, no sense in trying to navigate the dark quarters at this hour. I'll be lucky if I remember where I stashed everything in daylight, never mind in the dark.

Unlocking the rear door, I step inside, the air damp and musty. I light three candles and space them out across the cabin. The place is reminiscent of a house under construction, open concept, no separating walls, no drywall, just the shell, the distinct smell of fresh cut timber thick in the air. Above, the loft runs half the length of the cabin, unfinished also, accessed by a ladder attached to the wall near the front window. The gables and beams cast ominous shadows spurred on by the flickering candlelight. I think of Rene, of our final hours together, our ghosts still lingering within the walls.

Exhaustion and fatigue overtake my adrenaline, and I remove the urn and place it on a coffee table beside the wood stove. The damp in the air confirms summer has passed, the evenings longer and cooler. I open the back door and peer out, inspecting the firewood stacked neatly against the exterior wall, untouched since last year, home to families of spiders, moths and ants. I'll get a fire going once we're settled.

I grab my flashlight and head to the truck.

Allie opens her eyes, acknowledging me with a smile, a glint of serenity in her eyes until reality overrides comfort, and she's up and out of the truck. She stands in the shadow of the mountain, rubbing her eyes, gazing at the cabin, the faint amber glow flickering from within.

"Welcome to Sanctuary," I say, as I grab the hockey bag from the truck.

"Let's get inside. I'll get a fire going. I'll give you the grand tour in the morning."

Allie nods and heads into the cabin. Inside, I drop the bag by the ladder leading to the loft, then bolt the rear door. Allie circles the cabin, as if inspecting it for weaknesses. She stops and peers out the front window, scanning the landscape, gathering her bearings.

"The futon's yours, there's a blanket and pillows in the bag underneath."

Allie turns and glances around the room. She sits down on the edge of the futon, her energy drained.

"Where will you sleep?"

"There's a double mattress up there." I point to the loft, Allie looks. "Washroom's there, the only private space. I won't have the water working 'til morning, but you can use it."

She shakes her head. "I can pee outside, I'm a big girl."

I step out back, returning moments later with a handful of firewood. Within a few minutes, the wood stove is alight, flames poking through the air vents, warmth on its way. I always loved a fire, indoors or out, it didn't matter, the sense of warmth and safety, Mother Nature's security blanket, transcending technology, luxury, the banality of modern existence. Fire, water, air and earth, that's all humankind ever needed.

Allie is asleep. I step over and open the vacuum-sealed bag, removing a blanket and a SpongeBob SquarePants pillow, lifting her head, sliding the pillow beneath. I cover her with the blanket and pause to look. She can't be more than twenty. Despite everything she's been through, despite captivity, starvation and abuse, she is beautiful, innocent and desirable, a unique mix, unaffected by the horrors of the new world. She mumbles something, turning onto her side, and I take that as my cue to dial back the stalker mode, and let her sleep.

I gaze about the cabin, wondering if I'd made the right choice. I was here. At great effort, at even greater risk, but the journey was complete. *So what now?* I step towards the kitchen and pause. The candles flicker in unison, as if some unseen spirit just entered the room. As I listen to the soft roar of flames growing within the stove, the emptiness of the Sanctuary is suddenly very real. I look to the urn, the flames reflecting off its copper casing, casting amber hues that look like tiny moving pictures on a cylindrical screen.

We're here. And we have a friend.

My heart knows Rene would have done the same, only sooner, without hesitation.

"We made it," I say aloud.

Allie shifts in the futon and I slink to the floor, my back sliding down the main column like a drunk passing out after last call. I sit where I land, feet laid out in front of me, facing the stove, watching the urn, the amber hues, the tiny moving images dancing in delight.

Around me, candlelight flickers, heat from the woodstove warms my face. I hear Allie, murmuring in her sleep.

My eyes close and I realize I'm smiling.

As sleep overtakes me, one word escapes my breath.

"Sanctuary."

CHAPTER 34

Allie is gone.

I've been asleep a while, the candles burned down. Cold creeps across my skin, the wood stove reduced to embers. I struggle to stand, my neck aching, the cobwebs slow to clear. What time was it? It must be almost dawn. I look to the washroom.

"Allie?"

My voice cracks the silence, the frigid stillness of the enclosed void. I hear only the sound of my raspy breath, harsh and quick. The blanket lies on the floor next to the futon; the front door ajar.

I grab the flashlight and head outside. Dawn is on the horizon but the night is still dark, the pale glow of morning distant over the tree line. I shine the flashlight beam back and forth, tall grass and weeds catching the light, glistening with dew. Ahead I see something. As I move closer, I recognize what it is. Allie's jersey. I pick it up, slinging it over my shoulder.

"Allie?"

No response.

Further ahead, more clothing; Allie's pants, socks, underwear—a trail of garments, like a desperate housewife's last-ditch effort at reigniting a dying love-life. Eventually, the path of pending nudity leads towards a cluster of trees in the distance, beyond that, the barn. I walk faster, my eyes scanning the night.

Allie is there.

She stands facing the closed barn doors, naked, silent, entranced in something I cannot see or hear. I move closer, the flashlight beam exposing a tattoo at the base of her spine; elaborate script in Chinese lettering. I step up beside her. Her eyes are open, glazed over, unseeing. She's sleepwalking, likely due to exhaustion, an over-active mind, the horrors she'd experienced, stuff that fucks with you, never lets you go, not even in dreamland.

"Allie."

I place my hand on her shoulder. She trembles, her skin cold, alive with goosebumps. It's then I notice she's wearing her pendant. The one from the motel room. I reach into my pocket confirming it's the same one. *How could it not be?* And when the fuck did she get it? I shake her gently, but she continues to stare, trance-like at the door, like something of tremendous importance stands beyond the withered boards and rusted hinges. I slip the jersey over her head, noticing her 'twenty-one' tattoo has tiny script beneath, words too small to decipher. As I pull the jersey over her arms, I see she has something clenched in her hand.

My phone. It's off, the battery dead, I hadn't thought of charging it on the drive here. But why did she have it? I pry the phone from her hand and pocket it.

Mental note, charge it, and hide it.

"Allie, you awake?"

No response. I look to the doors, wondering what she sees, what she senses. Somewhere in the distance an animal scurries through the bush. Allie trembles and I put my arm around her and begin leading her down the embankment, towards the cabin.

We walk in silence, the light in the east brighter now, dawn on the horizon. Once inside, I lead her to the futon and lie her back down. She's asleep immediately as I pull the blanket over her, watching her eyes moving beneath closed lids, wondering what it is she's dreaming of, who it is she's dreaming of. She mumbles something, words I can't make out, then turns on her side, and is quiet.

I head to the stove, opening it and examining the smoldering contents. Moving quickly, I fill the hearth with wood, watching as the birch bark ignites, flames reintroducing themselves to familiar surroundings. I close the cover and go about extinguishing two of the three candles, taking the third with me. Pausing to check on her, I lock the front door then glance at my watch. It's 6:40, daybreak upon us. I need sleep. We both do. I grab the Glock and climb up to the loft. From up here I have a clear view of the floor area below, and both doors. I make a mental note to fortify the entrances in upcoming days, not that any visitors are expected, but we've made enemies, the kind that might just show up uninvited, a pop-in of the worst kind.

There is much to do in the morning, but for now, sleep.

I lie down on the mattress, the material cold, smelling of stale neglect, but despite my exhaustion, my mind races. Reaching into my pocket I pull out my vial of pills, popping out two and crushing them between my molars, allowing the powder to absorb into my bloodstream. I blow out the candle and set the gun down beside me. My mind drifts to Allie, naked, distant, away in another dimension, another realm. What did she see, or feel, what was in the barn? And when did she snatch her chain from my pocket?

Tomorrow all will be clear. There is no urgency, no rush, not anymore. No need to keep moving or staying one step ahead. I am home. We are home. I try to picture Rene's face, her beauty, her radiance, but the image is unclear, distorted, gone.

CHAPTER 35

The generator starts on the first pull. Eight months stored in a cold, damp barn, and it starts without so much as a sputter. I knew investing in the Honda was the way to go. Sure, the thing costs triple your typical entry-level ear-shattering model, but Hondas were quiet and reliable. And considering I'm in the middle of nowhere, I don't need sound travelling when it shouldn't be. I reach down and adjust the choke, the engine responds, the decibel level lowering. I let the generator run while I examine my gasoline supply. Two five-gallon containers, full, the gas is on the stale side, but shouldn't do any harm. Down the road, months, years from now, it will be a different story altogether. But I've got time now, plenty of it, to figure things out. And there's nothing saying I'll outlast the gas, not with enemies, a plague, and whatever else Mother Nature cares to throw my way.

Sunlight peaks through the cracked boards, throwing diagonal rays of light throughout the interior. The barn is original, came with the land, eighty years old at least, aging by the minute. The steel roof kept the place standing, weathering the storms, but sections are missing, bent, askew, the results of unpredictable weather and the wrath of the island. Part of the original Gillis family homestead, the barn survived, unlike the farmhouse that was demolished years ago. Two hundred acres were parcelled off after the remaining family members died, the back sixty was our piece. I had grand plans for the barn when we first explored it. I imagined get-togethers, Ceilidhs, kitchen parties, fresh-caught lobster and salmon under the stars.

But it wasn't to be.

The stars.

I'd forgotten what it was like to look up and see the Milky Way in all its glory. Cape Breton never disappointed. A blanket of speckled light, shooting stars, asteroids, it was a feast for the senses on a clear night.

But that's all moot now. New York City, Toronto, L.A., London, whoever remains, wherever home is, nature's nightlight is back on.

The generator revs loudly for a moment, then settles back to a quiet hum. Satisfied, I reach down and turn it off. Beyond the generator and fuel lie four new solar panels, still in the boxes, along with a pair of deep cycle marine batteries and an assortment of hookup gear. I did my homework over the winter months, figuring out how to retrofit the cabin to run on solar and marine batteries, a generator as backup. We'd be off grid, completely.

It looks like I was onto something.

In the far corner of the barn, furthest from the doors is an area cluttered with rusted machinery and discarded furniture. A tarp that resembles an old red-checkered tablecloth, the kind you'd see in a Fifty's Diner, plastic, gaudy and ketchup-stained, covers something of considerable size. I don't recall putting that there. The totes containing my other equipment I found straight away, lodged beneath an old trailer, a storage area for the excess lumber and materials from the cabin build. I'd examined every inch of the barn when we first bought the place, just as I had the cabin and the sixty acres. I was that type of person. First day here I was out in a nor'easter, armed with a compass and a property map, trying to locate the six survey markers that defined our property. I found four of them before the lightning started, Rene hollering at me over the walkie-talkie to get my ass inside. I never found the last two, but it looks like that won't be an issue, not anymore. I liked to know what was mine, what belonged to me and what didn't. And that's why I couldn't for the life of me, remember what was beneath the tablecloth.

"Why didn't you wake me?"

I spin. Allie stands in the doorway, backlit by the sun, a silhouette, my eyes squinting, compensating for the blinding contrast.

"I always heard you don't wake a sleepwalker," I reply.

She steps into the barn, her eyes canvassing the interior. She wears Rene's clothes, a pair of grey sweatpants with the Roots logo in big letters on the rear. I always loved them on Rene, reminded me of university girls during exam week, dressed for comfort, but sexy as hell. Allie wore a Madonna t-shirt, also one of Rene's, a throwback from her retro days. I remembered that was one of the bonuses of buying a vacation property. All the stuff you no longer used but refused to part with; clothes, furniture, dishware, gadgets, all that shit found a new home. The cabin, and especially the barn, were a hoarder's paradise.

Allie looked nothing like Rene, not in face or physique, but there was something about her, something unique. She was younger, and she was entrancing. This much I knew. This much I wish I didn't.

Allie paces the interior, inspecting, taking stock of everything within, old and new, tracing her finger over random objects as she passes.

"You remember last night?" I ask.

I watch her, avoiding the logo.

"Which part?"

I replay the events in my head. "Surprise me."

She pauses and opens a large cardboard box marked 'Kitchen Shit' in black magic-marker, removing a cleaver the size of a cricket bat. Why we brought that to the cabin I'll never understand, unless we envisioned feasting on mutant lobsters.

"I remember the drive was bumpy." She runs her finger across the blade, her eyes focused like a serial killer reliving a moment.

I pull out my cigarettes, but decide against it.

"And the striptease?"

She places the cleaver back into the box and turns.

"I'm working on it."

I watch as she pauses in front of the tarped mystery object, her fingers touching the checkered cloth, tracing trails in the soot.

"What's your connection to this place?" she asks.

"You mean the island or here?" I want that smoke, but hold off.

"Both." She places her hand on the tarp as if sensing what's beneath.

"We fell in love with Cape Breton, most people do. We wanted a place to call our own. The listing had been on the market a while, we thought what the hell."

"And you bought it."

"Sort of your classic impulse buy. Mind if I smoke?"

Allie glances up at me, her eyes narrowing, but says nothing. I take that as a no, but light up anyhow. I inhale, the smoke trail swirling up to the rooftop, catching rays of sunlight as it dissipates into the rafters.

"You were staring at the doors, like something was in here."

Allie turns and approaches.

"There is an energy here. The land, this barn."

She snatches the cigarette from my hand, inhaling like a two-pack a day trucker, exhaling through her nostrils. Her eyes continue taking stock of the interior, looking for clues, answers.

"You want one of your own?"

She hands the smoke back, shaking her head.

"Your decision to buy wasn't by chance. There's more than this. Something infinitely more."

Okay, I was expecting this. Other-worldly shit.

"You had my phone with you," I say.

She ignores me, her thoughts engaged elsewhere, like she's channelling information from another source, transcribing it.

"You were drawn here. Before, and now. There are no coincidences."

She stops in the centre of the barn, holding out her arms as if embracing an invisible aura. She cranes her neck back, slowly spinning, gazing upwards at the rotting beams and abandoned spider webs.

"And that you're back now is no accident. You've felt it?"

I exhale and contemplate my response. Allie stops her slow spin and looks at me, her gaze intense, almost unsettling, like she's sizing me up, like she knows my secrets.

"You've dreamed this. I know you have," she says.

I offer her the cigarette but she waves me off.

"Can I ask you something?"

"That depends," she replies.

"On what?"

"On what you ask me."

I smile.

"Fair enough. What's the significance of the number? You didn't work in the mines did you?"

She absently rubs the tattoo over her shirt.

"And my other one, are you curious about that one too?"

She stares, her eyes like lasers penetrating my core. I'm suddenly aware that I'm blushing. A grown man, survivor of the apocalypse, blushing.

"I wasn't, looking-looking, I put your shirt back on you—it was cold."

Her expression softens.

"Ignore me, I say stupid things sometimes." She marches past me, out into the sunlight.

"You already know the answers," she says. "You just don't realize it. That will change. A part of me was very much awake last night."

I can feel the colour of shame dissipating, but far too slowly.

"We can talk. You have questions, I get that. But first, is there any way I can take a shower?"

I nod. "If you don't mind cold water. It'll take the generator a while to warm the tank."

"This isn't a Marriott, cold is fine."

She turns, then pauses.

"Thank you, for last night. You were sweet." She heads off.

"No problem," I say, watching the Roots logo saunter away.

Mind games—was she awake or wasn't she? I sigh and lean over the generator. I struggle with it, although small, it's heavier than a bucket of cement.

"I wasn't staring," I mutter under my breath.

I look up to the rafters, blue sky peeking through the slats.

"And I wasn't talking to you."

I exit the barn, lugging the Honda cement bucket, cursing myself for not bringing the truck around.

CHAPTER 36

The outlets work, only small loads, but we have electricity, so long as the Honda's running. Out back, the orange extension cord runs eighty feet to the tree line, the generator hidden behind a makeshift enclosure for added soundproofing. I close the door and listen. Perfect. I plug the standing lamp into the power bar and flick the switch. *And we have light.* I switch out the lamp for the battery charger and connect the cables to a deep cycle marine battery. I thought the generator was a pain to carry; the batteries were worse, heavy and awkward, my lower back paying the price. I considered using the truck on the second trip, but decided against it. We needed to conserve fuel, and more importantly, we needed to keep movement to a minimum. Despite seclusion, we weren't invisible. Sacrificing my body was the safest option, at least for now.

I hear a door open and turn to see Allie exiting the washroom. She's wrapped in a towel, working a toothbrush back and forth, acknowledging my electrical prowess. Had she stepped out a second sooner, I'd have graced her with a clear shot of my plumber's butt. Good timing.

"I can promise you lukewarm next time," I say.

The towel slips from her shoulder, but she catches it.

"I hope you don't mind," she says, holding out the toothbrush.

"Not at all."

"I also helped myself to the tampons in the cabinet."

Okay, a little too much information, but I nod as I plug my phone into the power bar.

"Funny how you never hear people talking hygiene in the apocalypse," she continues, still brushing. "Why is that?"

I shrug, watching as the phone's screen lights up.

Allie leans over the kitchen sink, glancing at me for approval. I nod. She spits.

"Expecting a call?"

I look to confirm the charging icon is on and set the phone down beside the battery.

"Checking Facebook."

"You don't mind me wearing your wife's clothes? If it's weird, I won't."

"I don't mind."

"She had nice taste, your wife."

"Rene."

"Rene. That's a pretty name."

I glance to the urn atop the table. I've been avoiding my obligation, telling myself I had to secure the cabin, prepare for the long haul before I could carve out time to remember, to acknowledge the real reason I'm here.

I bend over to examine the battery charger and my lower back spasms, a sharp searing pain, like a hot poker in the kidney.

"What's wrong?" Allie steps up.

"My back, I'm okay."

"You should put heat on it."

"I'm good." I smile, despite the lingering spasm. Lack of nutrition over the past couple of months is taking its toll, my body falling apart one arbitrary piece at a time. I walk it off.

"I'll have this place rigged with solar panels eventually. With the marine batteries and the generator for backup, we can hold up through winter."

Allie glances to the batteries, to my phone.

"They'll come looking. They've been looking since I left. They'll find this place."

I look over. Allie's leaning over a storage bin, wearing only a bra and panties, sorting through clothes. Her skin is pale, translucent in the morning light. I do an abrupt heel spin, like a Nazi Headmaster on point. I focus my attention on the gauges, careful not to bend beyond my breaking point.

"All the more reason to be prepared," I continue. "We need supplies, fuel, food. There's a neighbour up the road, I'll scope that out tomorrow. There's a good chance it'll be intact, I doubt anyone ventured up this far."

"I'm dressed, you can face me now," Allie says.

I turn. She wears a pink Polo golf shirt, one of mine, and a pair of black Adidas gym shorts.

"What did you mean 'no coincidences'?" I ask. "Is that like an M. Night Shyamalan thing?"

Allie sits down on the edge of the futon, towel drying her hair. My movie reference doesn't register.

"There are none. Not then, not now. Everything that's happened, everything that's happening now, is happening for a reason."

"Signs?" I ask, smiling.

She looks up, ignoring my comment.

"Do you think it was dumb luck you not only survived the illness, you survived the journey here—without getting wounded or killed? You think all the snipers are such bad shots. All of them?"

Truthfully, I had. I figured they were dolts. By my estimation, nowhere in the rules of an apocalypse did it stipulate only intelligent and adaptable humans were spared. Dolts, morons, skids, all had the same odds. Like the Powerball, it only takes one ticket to win. Plus, it was early days; the snipers were likely honing their skills. I just got lucky.

"You're saying there's something else, something bigger than this?" I ask.

She sets the towel down and runs a brush through her wet hair.

"You asked me about the number." She tugs at her shirt, revealing the top of the tattoo. I glance over, then turn away.

"You want to know the significance, what it represents, why a young woman would deface her body in such a ghastly and permanent way?"

I shrug. "A running tally of how many walkers you killed?"

She doesn't acknowledge my reference—again. What show was I thinking of anyway? Even I'm not sure anymore.

"Have you heard of Angel numbers?"

I shake my head.

"Numerology?"

I ease myself down into a kitchen chair like an old geezer climbing into a sitz bath.

"You need heat on that. Lie down, I'll give you a Mr. Miyagi massage, my specialty, it really works."

"I'm good. I'll take some aspirin in a bit." My words say aspirin, but my mind is thinking little blue pills—the magic cure-all.

"Numerology, kind of like horoscopes, certain numbers hold meaning?"

Allie puts her brush down and sits on the floor, crossing her legs in front of her in a yoga pose. We sit facing one other, fifteen feet apart, her on the floor, me shifting my ass from side to side with each unique twinge of pain. From outside the cabin a bird of prey squawks, a high-pitched shriek that reminds me of where we are.

"Sort of. I didn't believe in horoscopes or fortune telling, but things happen that challenge your belief system. Sometimes your whole world changes, and you adapt."

Allie's gaze falls to the floor.

"My dad was a Paramedic. He was killed on the job, stabbed in the throat by a patient high on meth. I got the call just before midnight. I was out with friends celebrating my birthday."

"He died on your birthday?"

"February 21st, three years ago. My twenty-first birthday."

Mental note, she's twenty-four.

Allie pulls her legs in tight.

"Hundreds came to the funeral, maybe thousands, paramedics, firefighters, police. I didn't know any of them. I remember standing in church, listening to a Minister I didn't know, drone on and on about a man he'd never met. All I could think about was how he died on my birthday."

Allie closes her eyes.

"Sad coincidence right? My special day. Twenty-one on the twenty-first."

I shift in my chair.

"It wasn't long after I started seeing the number everywhere. On licence plates I'd look at for no particular reason, addresses. On my watch or phone, every time I'd look at the time. After a while I figured I was subconsciously looking for it, fixating, picking out random configurations that meant nothing. I thought it was my way of dealing with grief."

"Your mom wasn't in the picture?"

Allie ignores me.

"I did some reading, more for sanity than anything else, to confirm I wasn't bonkers, like Alice down the rabbit hole. The number meant different things depending on what you read, what century or culture. But a common thread kept popping up—it was a number that symbolized sin, rebellion, depravity."

She opens her eyes.

"Wilful wickedness."

I picture her tattoo in my mind, the tiny lettering beneath the number, that's what it said.

"I was mad at God. Mad at my dad. Mad at the world."

"I think you had right to be upset," I say, shifting again.

"The number followed me, in my waking hours, my dreams, day and night. It was an obsession. Then one day I was passing a Tattoo Parlour and thought, fuck it. I went in and had myself branded."

"It's not your standard butterfly on the ankle. I like it."

Allie straightens her legs out in front of her, stretching forward.

"You know what I found out later?"

I shake my head.

"Pagans believed the number meant rebirth, a new beginning. Twenty-one signified strength, the ability to lead. I somehow missed that one in my research."

"I prefer that," I say.

"I'm not so sure."

Allie stands and walks to the kitchen, grabbing a bottle of water.

"You branded yourself to commemorate the worst day of your life."

169

Allie jumps up onto the kitchen counter, taking a seat. "What about you, does that number mean anything to you?"

"Not much use for numbers," I say. "I don't know what day of the week it is, I barely know the month."

"It's Thursday, the 19th, and you know the month."

My brain accesses my internal weather network, trying to remember when it was the winter weather would be upon us. I needed to start planning.

Allie continues.

"This is all connected. The dreams, this place, the music."

I look at her.

"The music?"

Allie offers me the bottle, I decline.

"You've heard it."

I shrug, non-committal.

She looks to my phone on the floor.

"Is that why you had my phone?" I ask.

"Maybe. I know something is coming, something's upon us, I just don't know what."

"The end maybe?" I stand up, my back aching. "You ever consider we're just puppets, playing out our last days for some higher power's amusement?"

Allie watches as I feign walking normally.

"Or maybe there isn't more than this. Maybe when you're dead, you're dead. Asses to ashes as a friend used to say. Maybe atheists nailed it. Our time is up. We have to accept it."

Allie shakes her head.

"You don't believe that. You've seen proof, heard it. Why aren't we dead then? You've had the dreams. You dreamt of me, returned my pendant. Tell me Jack, what else have you dreamed of?"

Returned, that's an interesting choice of words. The pain in my back kicks up a notch, and my thoughts fall to alcohol and pain medication.

"I stopped dreaming. What happened at the motel, out on the road, I can't explain it, I had a theory, but it seems foolish in broad daylight. Thing is, I'm here now, I made it, I achieved my goal, that's more than a billion other poor bastards can say. I have no desire to understand any more than what's in front of me right now. I'm in my zone, no desire to stray, no need to."

"Your sanctuary," Allie interjects.

"Right. Maybe this is as good as it gets. We're better off than most, I could be the guy having the eternal siesta atop of the Tobacco Hut. How'd things work out for him? And his buddies?"

I grab my cigarettes and step gingerly for the door.

"I'm prepared to defend what I have here, but that's it. My destiny is this place. There's nothing for me out there, nothing I care to know about. Selfish, yeah, but that's me."

"You came back for me."

I smile. "We all leave our comfort zones occasionally, and then we fall right back again. People don't change. I'm not fighting a battle I didn't start, I'm not killing people I don't need to kill."

I take out my lighter and open the back door. "I'm going for a smoke."

"I'll come with."

I step out, Allie following. The sun's rays are Florida hot, unusual for this late in the season considering how cold the evenings have become. I've had Margaritas poolside in weather cooler than this. I offer Allie a cigarette but she shakes her head. I light mine and walk out towards the tree line, Allie following.

"It's in our dreams where reality lies," Allie continues. "Now especially. I think I've always known it, it just took the world dying before things started to piece together."

Allie looks up and I follow her gaze. A pair of hawks circle the cabin. Those damn sentries never let up.

"Do you know how they control their own people, the ones in their gang?"

"Who, Victor?"

Allie nods.

"Pharmaceutical drugs. Fentanyl mostly. They snort it, inject it, ingest it. He dispenses it, and they take it willingly. It's like heroin, only stronger, more concentrated. They're addicted, all of them, dosed every night. Do you know why?"

"It's fun to be high."

"So they can't dream."

Allie pulls a clutch of blue wildflowers from the grass, bringing them to her nose.

"They pass out, remember nothing."

"At least they have a drug plan," I say, flicking my ash towards my boot, taking care to stomp it out. A brush fire would not be ideal.

"He's created a gang of post-apocalyptic drug addicts, complete control."

"How do you know all of this?" I ask.

Allie takes the cigarette from me—I don't mind sharing, but it's like having your date decline dessert, then eat half of yours.

"I can be quite charming when I'm not shackled."

She inhales and blows three perfect smoke rings into the still morning air. I watch as the rings grow and spread, one after the other, dissolving into nothing.

"He told me over a romantic dinner, one where he spiked the wine that I pretended to drink. He worked with the Mounties, not as a cop, in a civilian capacity, but when the crisis hit, he got his hands on the drugs, enough to last years, apparently."

"Clever. Looting an evidence room. I'd never thought of that. Why does he wear a uniform if he wasn't a cop?"

"Why do the snipers wear jerseys, I have no idea. All I know is he's a deranged narcissist with a pile of dope."

"Why's he killing people?" I ask.

Allie hands me the cigarette back.

"Some by accident, most on purpose. My dad told me about opioid overdoses, people going VSA left and right a few years back. Fentanyl was the drug of choice for a while, it's fifty times more potent than heroin, a hit the size of a grain of salt was enough for an extended high, any more than that, you pass out, your heart stops beating."

"That must be some high. What about the guy we saw, Tobacco Tom?"

"Intentional. A warning to others. Anyone he didn't like, anyone who declined the drugs, didn't want to be part of his merry band, was eliminated. He hated Aboriginals especially. From what I'd heard, they tended to be the strongest dreamers. He took great joy in explaining how he neutralized three of them by slipping a few grains into their rum. He even sat and drank with them, watching them drop, one by one."

"Nice guy." I point towards the roadway, Allie nods and we both start walking in that direction, following the tire tracks in the tall grass.

"Addicts get worse," I say. "I can't see this as a long-term solution. Unless he's expecting newcomers to fill the ranks, it's a faulty strategy."

"That's exactly why we can't stay. There are no more people coming. The odd straggler, maybe. But the odds of finding another female, he knows how unlikely that is. He won't stop until they find me, and kill you."

I look out over the field toward the entrance to the property. How long before we get visitors I wonder?

"We need to move soon, find the others."

"Others? You mean the people you dream about?"

Allie stops.

"You've seen them, heard them, maybe not clearly, but you have. We're safe for the moment, but that window is closing— fast. We need to act."

"And do what?"

"Let ourselves dream. This is exactly where we need to be. We're here for that reason. It sounds crazy, far-fetched I know, but it's real, it's all happening, right now. And they're out there, looking for us, trying to stop it."

"Stop what?" I ask. "Stop us, because we killed a couple of theirs? That's not unreasonable when you think about it. The way I see it, it's about vengeance, an eye for an eye. I've thought about this, and the more I think, the more I'm convinced that there is no master plan, no higher power. This isn't a battle of good and evil, it's just assholes being assholes. King of the castle shit, nothing more."

Allie drops the flowers.

"What are you hiding?" she asks. "What am I missing?"

I turn and start heading back. The fresh air is exhilarating, but it's time to start getting shit done, and between my lower back and this topic, I'm not having a blast. And what's an apocalypse for, if you're not having a blast?

"That's it, our walk is over?"

"Tell me Allie, why did you feel it necessary to kill that guy back at the house?"

Allie pauses, considering the question.

"Because it means one less of them. You want to know the truth, it's simple math, the new reality. There's no compromise, not anymore. It's us against them and if you want to live beyond tomorrow, you need to accept it. You've only seen them from a distance, you don't know what they're planning, what they're capable of, what they're creating at the Manor."

"And what's that, exactly?"

"An army."

"Of drug addicts," I reply. "That sounds like a problem that will take care of itself in time. That threat will erode from within."

"It won't," Allie replies. "It's growing. No place will be safe."

I pick up my pace. Allie hangs back.

"I think we should get Cecil, bring him back. He's not safe," she yells.

I continue.

"I know what's in the barn. Under the tarp. I dreamt it."

I pause and turn. Allie stares back, defiant.

CHAPTER 37

The stream wound its way along the east side of the property, just beyond the tree line, hidden from view. We stumbled upon it by accident. Clear spring water traversed its way down from the shadow of the mountain, the mountain that protected our cabin and watched over our land. I'd been here in the dry season, when the stream was barely a trickle, impeded by the smallest branch or clump of vegetation, and I'd seen it in the high season, a mini river, flowing with the onslaught of melted snow and heavy spring rain. Either way, it belonged to us, at least our portion of it. I'd followed it one day, off our property onto the next, and onto the next, until the woods became too thick, the land too soft to continue. I imagined at some point the stream connected with the great Bras d'Or, fresh spring water fusing with the brackish depths of the world's largest inland sea. And from there, onto the Atlantic Ocean, home to seals, whales, and lobsters, and those who fished for them.

It was our stream. Rene's and mine.

I used a weed-whacker, whipper-snipper as the locals call them, to cut a pathway through the tall grass towards the stream; a path I imagined would take hold and grow old with time, imprinted with the memory of our visits, our picnics, the sunsets and sunrises. Our tiny river of dreams.

But it wasn't to be.

I sit at the stream's edge, the water level low with the lack of rain and stifling late season heat. Above me the sky has clouded over, rain on its way, a respite for the waning current.

I put the bottle to my mouth and swallow. The rye tastes harsh but I fight the urge to choke it back up. It was only a month ago I was drinking it like Perrier. That shows you what a few weeks of sobriety—at least partial sobriety, can do. But then again, the little blue pills have kicked in also, my lower back silenced, my spirit rekindled. I recap the bottle and set it down beside my seat, a portable hunting chair, camouflage coloured, powder-coated steel, maximum capacity, two hundred and twenty pounds. I was well under that now, at least fifteen pounds below my fighting weight, lean, mean, serene.

A few of the trees are turning, it's still early days, but I can see occasional spots of colour in the white birch that lay hidden amidst the dense pine. Peak season was still weeks away, synchronized with the start of the Celtic Colours Festival, an event that drew thousands with the promise of glorious foliage and lively music. We'd only been down once to see the leaves, and it was spectacular. Middle River, the endless valley surrounded by mountains and hills, was the most beautiful of all. We made a promise to come every October, to take part in the festivities, and to visit our cabin, our stream, our slice of glory.

I reach over and pick up a piece of bark, tossing it into the middle of the stream. The current catches hold and it's soon floating along with errant leaves, off towards a new resting place. As kids, we used to play *float the stick*. A stream ran through our neighbourhood where I grew up, and when the water level was high enough, we'd race sticks, pieces of wood, whatever we could find, following them along the banks, prodding them with branches or unleashing a barrage of stones whenever they got stuck. Whoever's ship made it the farthest was the winner. I always lost, every time it seemed, but the competition was unimportant. It was about having fun, enjoying nature, allowing our imaginations to take us away, dissolve our problems, not that we had many back then.

Unlike now.

I watch as my ship bounces off a rock and becomes stranded in a snag of twigs and leaves. Now would be the time I come to the rescue. Instead, I take a gulp of rye.

The urn sits between my feet.

My mind will not focus. My thoughts are disjointed. I think of Rene, of her ashes, of my journey here, my goal and purpose. I have difficulty picturing her face, and it terrifies me. The dreams have ceased, I no longer feel her presence. The memories aren't gone, but they've been eclipsed, placed into storage, like a time capsule to be opened years from now.

But I don't want them to be.

I pick up the urn, my finger tracing the inscription; the name, the dates—the dash. I hated that reference, ever since I read the poem. The fucking dash.

I set the urn down and take another gulp, the amber liquid no different from the copper coloured water flowing at my feet.

No different at all.

"I miss you," I say aloud. Somewhere in the trees above my head a chipmunk chirps in response, no doubt angry I've infiltrated its domain. I remove my wallet. Why I continue to carry one, I never quite understood. It's as if a part of me still expects to turn a corner and run into a 7-Eleven, or a Hilton, or a bank machine. Like I may yet need to prove who I am, where I came from, who I was, back in the world of yesterday.

I remove a photo from the insert. It's the picture of Rene and I standing beneath the 'Welcome to Cape Breton' sign. I stare at it for a long time, my anxiety dissipating, sedated by the gradual numb of rye in my veins. I remove a second photo, this one of Rene smiling, a photo taken at her graduation. I lay them both down, side by side on a rock at my feet. In that moment, I allow the sudden rush of recollection to take hold; the beginning of the end, the onset of the illness, the progression, the pain and sadness, our late-night talks, her final wishes, it all hits me at once, like a Mike Tyson left to the jaw.

A tear trickles down my cheek. I'm alone, it's okay I tell myself. Just this once.

Minutes later I'm standing, the urn opened, clasped between my hands like I'm holding the World Cup of Soccer. I tilt the urn and release the ashes into the moving current. The greyish brown sand spills from the container in a puff of dust, each grain dispersing on impact, merging with the cool spring water, off on a journey. A final adventure.

I watch as my life, my dreams, all that I lived for, floats away into the abyss of the afterlife, into the unknown. As I look, my ship, as if given a push by an invisible hand, frees itself from the tangle of debris, and accompanies the ashes on their final quest.

I look to the urn, empty, void, a barren receptacle of what once was.

Maybe there isn't more than this. Maybe when you're dead, you're dead.

My own words haunt me.

I set the urn down and drink. The warmth of the liquid is soothing, no longer harsh, my senses dulled, that familiar feeling creeping back, like an old friend.

I look over my shoulder, towards the barn in the distance, stoically poignant, a reminder of business unfinished. And I think of Allie.

How did she know?

CHAPTER 38

An hour earlier I stood frozen, my mind trying to comprehend what was happening, why it was happening, and why to me. The checkered tarp drops from my hand, I don't even notice. I stand transfixed, as if consumed by an alternate reality.

Before me are items I have never seen before. I did not leave them here. And Rene sure as hell didn't. Someone had been here, and recently by the looks of things. All the items were carefully stacked and arranged, protected from the elements in case the roof overhead should fail. I break my trance and step up, removing a small plastic container and examining it.

Ammunition. Brand new, an unopened box of rifle shells. I set the container back, counting at least half a dozen more. Standing upright is a beige canvas gun case, military grade. I begin rummaging through the bounty. A hard plastic case marked 'FLIR Thermal Vision'. A two-way radio. More ammunition. Clothing, a bulletproof vest, lettering on the back that says 'Tactical Unit'.

Combat gear. Someone stored it here, likely when things started to go bad. Maybe a cop, but probably just some schmuck who was smart enough to pillage the local police detachment.

But why here?

And how the fuck did Allie know?

I replace the tarp, my mind reeling, my thoughts in disarray.

CHAPTER 39

I place the urn at my feet and drink.

Reaching for my cigarettes, my wallet falls out. I pick it up and consider the contents. Nothing that I need, not anymore. I remove my driver's licence; the photo depicting a younger, heavier me, not overweight, but not the post-apocalyptic buffed cheesecake I've evolved into. I stare at the address, my descriptors, and finally, my date of birth.

1978/12/21

I was born on the twenty-first. What were the odds? One in thirty I guess.

I tuck the licence into my back pocket then stand and hurl my wallet into the stream, watching it bounce like a skipped stone, disappearing below the surface. I sit back down, reaching for my bottle but it's empty. Fuck me. I fling the dead soldier against a large rock, the bottle shattering like expensive crystal on cement. Birds squawk overhead, alerted to the sudden commotion.

I turn.

Allie stands atop the hill in the distance, watching me.

I snatch up the urn and the photographs. Moments later, I'm heading back up the pathway, the chair and urn under my arm, cigarette in my mouth, emptiness in my soul.

CHAPTER 40

Solitaire. Pastime for the lonely soul. I played my share way back when dial-up modems were the norm, and PlayStation 1 was state-of-the-art gaming. But despite technological advances, there was something about playing with an actual physical deck that personified the feeling of being alone, of having no one.

Allie sits cross-legged on the floor, flipping cards, candles on either side of her. The cabin's grown dark, despite the hour, the first drops of rain pelting the windows, a storm looming. She hasn't spoken a word or taken the slightest interest in my meal preparation in the past hour. The cold shower cleared my cobwebs, sobered me up, and now it was time to put away childish things, memories vanquished.

A flash of lightning illuminates the cabin. I peer out the kitchen window, watching the trees swaying in the wind, like seaweed in a strong current. This storm has the potential to become a true nor'easter, the last of the summer heat colliding with the approaching cold, a late-season atmospheric death match.

I stir the Mac & Cheese atop the wood stove. Beside it, a frying pan sizzles and pops, the creamed corn steaming, slightly burnt, ready for serving. I remove the pan and empty the contents into a dish on the counter. The table is set; candles, matching plates and silverware, wine glasses, napkins, and my last bottle of Australian Shiraz.

Another flash of lightning, followed by a tremendous crack of thunder. I glance to Allie, but she doesn't flinch, doesn't acknowledge the weather, just continues laying down cards, as if entranced with the falling rain, absorbed by the storm.

"Dinner's ready," I announce, plopping a ladle full of gourmet Mac & Cheese onto each plate. I take a seat, reaching for the corkscrew, realizing it's a screw top.

Allie sits down, placing the deck of cards on the table beside her.

"Looks wonderful. How's your back?"

"Better." I unscrew the wine and reach for Allie's glass. She puts her hand over it.

"No, thank you. You go ahead."

I fill my glass then reach over and fill Allie's with bottled water.

"Thank you."

Rain begins to hammer the windows and roof.

"It's picking up," I say.

"Is the generator okay?" Allie asks.

"It's off, and covered. I think we're okay without it tonight."

The pasta tastes authentic, without milk or butter, the old world flavour still coming through. Or maybe I'm just starving. Allie picks at her pasta, one tiny tubule at a time.

"I used to play Solitaire until computers killed the thrill," I say, trying out the corn. It's burnt, but edible.

"It's calming, like yoga," Allie replies. "I see patterns in the cards sometimes."

I nod, taking a sip of wine, the vintage a perfect accent to the wonderful feast. Allie twirls her fork in the burnt corn, not actually eating it, but going through the motions, like a kid avoiding broccoli, not that I can blame her. The candlelight twinkles in her eyes, the glow accentuating her lips and dimples when she smiles. The ambience is amazing, better than a Paris Bistro in springtime; I'm pleased with myself.

"Sorry for spying on you earlier. I didn't know where you went," Allie says.

I wave it off, shoving a forkful into my mouth.

"Forget it."

Outside there's a loud crack of thunder. We both jump. Our eyes lock and we smile.

"I love storms," I say.

"It must be difficult being here now. The memories, me wearing her clothes."

"No more difficult than the last few months." I raise my glass in a toast. Allie raises hers.

"What are we drinking to?" she asks.

"Sanctuary."

"Sanctuary," Allie repeats. We clink glasses and drink.

"So I know your first name, I know you're twenty-four, I know you have tattoos, tell me more about Allie."

"Like what?"

"Where are you from? How'd you end up here? Cat person or

dog person? Coke or Pepsi? What'd you do before all this?"

Allie smiles. She salts her corn, then ignores it.

"Cat person, definitely. Dogs make me nervous. Coke. The person I was six months ago—is gone. I wouldn't recognize her if she walked through the door. I was in Dartmouth when it started—the dying that is. I knew I had to get out of the city, I had two choices, west towards New Brunswick or east. I went east."

I take a sip of wine.

"So you're from here, the coast?" I ask.

"No, not originally."

"What were you doing in Dartmouth? School?"

"It's complicated."

"Why east?"

Allie continues picking at her pasta, staring into her plate.

"I don't know."

"No family, boyfriend?"

She shakes her head.

"You were alone the whole time?"

"I kept my head down, headed east, avoiding the towns. I saw no other women, no girls, I knew that couldn't be a good thing. Eventually I made it to the big drink and ran out of running room."

"How'd you get across?"

"Canoe."

"Really?"

Allie nods. "What about you? Who were you in your past life?"

The rain intensifies, the storm gaining momentum.

"Nobody. Recent widower as you know, not that that garners any sympathy considering everyone's lost everyone. Allergic to cats. Pepsi. The rest is yesterday's news."

We both pause, listening to the storm, watching the candle flames flicker about the cabin.

"You still think there's a greater purpose, an underlying path for humanity, for those of us left?" I ask.

"Yup."

"Dreams and visions?"

"That's part of it," Allie replies.

"Explain," I say, reaching for my glass. "What's causing it? What's the common denominator? Similar dreams, bizarre behaviour. Is it a mass psychosis, like PTSD, only on a macro scale?"

"The behaviour is bizarre, but it's patterned," Allie replies.

She sets her fork down.

"The dreams are a signal, a beacon. The first few weeks after the sickness there were no dreams. Little sleep, no dreams. I was convinced it was only a matter time before my turn came to die. In every apocalyptic story I've ever come across, at some point, the living envy the dead. That's how I felt. Then the dreams started, things started making sense. I believed there were others out there, like me—people whose first inclination wasn't to kill me or fuck me."

I glance up from my plate. "What'd you dream?"

"Survivors, like me. A group. Good people, frightened."

"How does the music fit in?"

"I was asleep the first time I heard it. I'd pulled over to the side of the road, exhausted. I woke up to music playing from the car stereo, the engine wasn't even on. Violin music. It scared the shit out of me, and I jumped out of the car and just stood outside shivering, wondering if I was dreaming or if I had gone insane. A minute later I hear engines approaching, motorcycles. I hid and watched three bikers stop and inspect the car, then head off. If not for the music..."

Thunder rumbles, as if mimicking the sound of a dozen Harleys.

"That's when I knew it was connected. That the music was a sign, a signal, I was being guided. Things started to click. Thoughts I'd had before all of this started, images I couldn't understand, suddenly made sense."

"The onset of the sickness?"

Allie nods.

"People would have thought you were nuts, a crazy Mayan predicting the end of the world."

"Yup," Allie replies.

"You predicted the end of days?"

Allie shrugs. I offer her more pasta but she declines. I load more onto my plate. Neither of us seems to be putting a dent in the corn.

"Whether you choose to believe or not, we're a part of this. It's not supernatural, it's more of a psychokinetic phenomenon, like ESP, a type of energy, an electricity in the air. It's new, it wasn't here three months ago. A new reality, I know I keep saying that, but I can't describe it any other way. Like our minds are suddenly capable of receiving radio waves or television signals, only these are coming from a collective conscience. I liken it to a survival mechanism that kicked in when humanity faced extinction. Our brains evolved overnight. It's real. It's the new real."

I smile, analyzing the passion in her eyes. "You remind me of someone," I say, topping off my glass. "So everyone has these dreams—everyone who doesn't try to block them out?"

Allie shakes her head. "Not everyone. Very few in fact. I sensed that Victor didn't. Bull either. They abstain from drugs and yet they don't dream. I'd know it if they had."

"Don't get high on your own supply."

"It's more than that. They're threatened by this. You can see it in their actions, in their eyes."

"I guess I'm not off their most wanted list."

I pause.

"You told me your name in a dream," I say. "Then you

appeared in my motel room. I convinced myself it was a hallucination, but I found the pendant, and the writing."

Allie sips her water, watching me.

"How does that fit in with your collective conscience theory?"

"I don't know. I honestly don't," Allie replies. "Astral projection maybe, some type of spiritual connection, I can't explain it."

"Out on the road I saw you again. You led me to safety."

I put my glass down and lean back in my chair.

"Have you ever heard of forerunners?"

Allie looks up, a glint of surprise in her eyes. "I have. You think that has something to do with this?"

I shake my head, sliding my dish to the side, clinking the wine glass, almost knocking it over. The grapes are flowing nicely, no sense in over-lining my stomach and diminishing the effects. Plus, I've got a backup bottle of rye in my bag for a nightcap.

Allie glances to the wine bottle, half-empty now. Her eyes peer into mine.

"Can I ask you a question?"

"Depends," I say, smiling.

"I found these on the floor, they fell out of your pocket when you were taking a shower." She places my pill container on the table.

"This is anti-anxiety medication."

Found them on the floor.

I pick up the container.

"You know your meds."

"My mother had her demons," Allie replies. "It's not my business, it's just that I think I know why your dreams stopped."

I take a drink, no longer concerned about keeping up appearances.

"Anxiety during an apocalypse—now there's a shocker. It's more complicated than that. I'm not on your friend Victor's drug plan. Not yet anyhow."

Allie, unamused by my sarcasm, continues.

"Stimulants or depressants, meds, alcohol, pot, affect your mind, distort how you filter information, especially when you sleep. Why do you think he keeps them sedated? He can't tell who dreams and who doesn't, and no one will admit it if they do. That's a death sentence. They take the drugs willingly, they line up for it, like Pavlovian circus poodles, never questioning reality. It's a win-win. Even if they do dream, they think it's drug-induced, they don't know any different."

Allie's sold on her own story. As the wine numbs my senses, I look beyond the lecture to the girl, the woman, sitting across from me.

"He kills anyone he thinks may be holding out, anyone who may have a connection to the other side."

The candles flicker in unison, the air in the cabin shifted. We both glance to the door as if an invisible intruder just entered.

"I don't dream," I say. "And I'm fine with that. I think humanity, what's left of it, is fucked—pardon my French. God didn't give a shit three months ago, what's different today? Everyone we know died, horribly, family, friends, neighbours, newborns. This new reality, whatever you think it is, it's just desperation. Desperate individuals trying to make sense of horrific experiences. The mind trying to adapt to dire circumstances, knowing that survival is not in the cards. We don't even know that we're not sick right now, the virus hibernating, mutating, waiting to re-emerge and re-fuck the world."

Lightning flashes, illuminating Allie's face, her expression dark. I continue.

"There are a dozen nuclear power plants across North America that are failing as we speak. With no technicians, no grid, it's only a matter of time before they go up like Chernobyl. And depending on which way the wind's blowing, today or next week, we're all fucked. All of us, everything expired except cockroaches and Ramen noodles."

The wind whistles through the rafters, we both glance upward.

"The dreams of ships and giant fiddles, ballads from beyond, numerology, won't save us. Can't. Whoever stored those supplies in my barn is dead. Never came back for them. Things didn't work out for them. Why is that? They dreamt too, no?"

Allie peers at me, her eyes wide, like I let one slip.

"You dreamt of a giant fiddle? And people, on a ship?"
I lean back in my chair, placing my hands behind my head, nonchalant, refusing to be baited.

"You know it's different for us, you and I," Allie says. "We're different. We were meant to connect, here, and now, it's not random, it never was. Like pieces of a puzzle, only we won't know the picture until all the pieces come together."

"Polar bear in a snow storm, I know," I say. "Some puzzles are impossible, futile, the final piece always missing."

Allie leans forward, peering at me like an analyst on the verge of a breakthrough. "That's what I was missing."

"Sorry?"

"You've been self-medicating all along, intentionally drowning out the signal."

I down my glass and stare straight through her as if she was a ghost, a mirage, a figment of a wandering imagination.

"I'm not the person you think I am Allie. I came back because I felt like a piece of shit and I owed you that much. But we're square now. You're welcome to stay, I'd like you to stay, but I'm not leaving, I'm not chasing phantom fiddlers around a cursed island. This isn't fucking *Lost*."

"You're running from it," Allie responds. "The wine, pills, denial."

"A river in Egypt," I say, smiling at my own wit. "Speaking of Old Man River," I continue, "if you ask me, Cecil is fine where he is. The Sanctuary was never meant to be a commune, I'm not looking to host a survivalist love-in. We can check on him in a few days, but he's happier, probably safer, where he's at." Allie stands and clears her dish from the table.

"They'll torture him before they kill him, you know this right?"

"They think he's already dead, the crafty old bugger is one step ahead of them," I reply.

Allie cleans off her plate and places it into the sink.

"Don't forget your cards," I say, holding up the deck.

Allie looks. "They're yours. I found them in a drawer."

She steps by me and enters the washroom, pulling the door closed. Conversation over.

I sigh, filling my glass with the last of the summer wine. Glancing at the deck of cards, my thoughts fall to the stream, to Rene's final goodbye. I pull out my driver's licence, the one item Allie has yet to discover and pilfer, and study my photo, my surname, my date of birth.

I slip the licence back into my pocket and shuffle the cards, placing the deck face down, turning the top card up.

The Ace of Spades.

I flip the second card.

Jack of Hearts.

The one-eyed Jack.

Twenty-one.

Thunder rumbles overhead.

CHAPTER 41

The morning sun after a torrential rain has a unique quality, a brightness and warmth that restores man's faith in the dawning of a new day, in rebirth, in the knowledge that beyond every storm lies a pending calm.

And when you wake with a hangover, you can shove that brightness and warmth right up your shit-pipe.

I sit up, vaguely aware that I fell asleep clothed, socks, shoes, earbuds still in my ears. Even without an electrical grid, I still manage to keep my magical music box charged, generator or car battery, doesn't matter, all that does, is I have music to pass out by. I pull my feet off to the side of the mattress and sit up, acclimatizing myself to my surroundings, my tongue coated with a double thick layer of film, greasy hair flopping in my eyes. Outside it looks to be a marvelous September morning, the ground drenched and sopping, but the air full of promise.

Beside me on the floor lay an empty bottle of rye, one of two I pilfered from Bubble's pub. The pictures of Rene lay on the floor at my feet, placed on either side of the empty urn. I had myself a celebration of life last night, photographs, memories, sad tunes, libation to dull the senses. I shake my head, glancing to the living area below. The futon is empty, the covers neatly folded atop the pillow, untouched, or at least made very early this morning. Then again, what the hell time was it? I look at my watch, 8:30. She must have gotten up early, maybe in the shower.

I retrace the events. Solitaire, dinner by candlelight, Blackjack. I remember going out for a smoke, armed with an umbrella and glass of rye. Then it was up to the loft, more drinking, listening to my summer party mix until I passed out. I made a different playlist each year, encapsulating a mix of current hits, along with some Canadian content—bands like Wintersleep or the Great Lake Swimmers; it was my thing, music I'd listen to over and over. It drove Rene nuts, even though I always added some Hip, just for her.

I'm sure I fumbled my way down the ladder a couple more times for a cigarette, careful not to disturb her. I know I took my pills before I passed out, I remember saying the words out loud, 'perchance to dream', cackling at my own wit, oblivious that I was wearing earphones and projecting my voice like an auctioneer at a retirement home. But she never said a word.

And I didn't dream. Nothing. No ship, no fiddles, no people. I didn't dream at all.

"Allie, you up?"

All is quiet. I sense the chill in the air, the dampness of the night permeating the walls, the wood stove long since extinguished. I climb down, my head still lost in the cloud of last night's debacle.

The washroom is vacant. Allie is gone.

A note sits atop the kitchen table, the deck of cards standing upright like a placard, holding the page in place, lest an errant wind permeate the cabin walls.

The handwriting is tiny, exquisite. Allie has perfect penmanship, like calligraphy, difficult for my bloodshot eyes to decipher. I step closer to the window.

Jack,

I apologize for leaving. But the cover of darkness and the storm were necessary. Thank you for the clothes and supplies. I took only what I needed. I will keep your promise for you, I will check on Cecil before I head north.

And yes, I've taken the truck. Sorry, but it was mine in the first place. You are resourceful, you will find a replacement.

Stay safe. If you travel, avoid Baddeck. There is only death there.

Until we meet again, in this realm, or the next.

Yours,

Allie

P.S. I've taken your pills and disposed of your alcohol. No need to thank me.

I look to my bag. She's been through it. While I didn't have much, I had enough to last until my next liquor run. I drop to my knees, rummaging through the contents, confirming my fears. I stand and gaze about the empty cabin, sullen, crestfallen.

"Why is the rye always gone?"

I plop myself down on the edge of the futon, trying to ascertain what's happened, how big of a head start she had, where she was going. But what did it matter when my mode of transportation was downgraded to biped?

I open the rear door and peer outside. The truck is gone, my box of syphoning supplies left behind on the step. I close the door, rubbing my temples, my head pounding like a drum kit at an ADD pre-school.

"Fuck me."

I need a drink. I look around, as if expecting to find a bottle of Absinthe, dropped off by a passing green fairy while I slept.

No such luck.

Guess a smoke will have to do.

CHAPTER 42

I take a pull off my cigarette. My boots are soaked, the blades of grass retaining moisture from the overnight downpour, refusing to let the morning sun confiscate their bounty. The laneway is deluged with puddles, the clouds above reflecting in the standing water, merging heaven and earth into one. Walking the perimeter is something I'll get used to, a daily ritual; morning, midday, sunset. It's a necessary step in protecting what I have.

The rifle slung across my back, I remove my phone from my breast pocket, checking the timer's still running. Eleven minutes twenty-one seconds and counting. Timing my scouting mission will help me plan my days, prioritize my tasks. I replace the phone and step up the pace.

I considered keeping a video log of my adventure, capturing my day-to-day challenges and conquests, but decided against it. Who in the future will give a fuck? The apes? And with today being reality check day, with Allie gone, sobriety thrust upon me, there's no better time to focus on survival. Forced to face the bitter truth of my situation; stuck in the middle of nowhere, dwindling resources, no companionship, I felt like the chubby kid plucked from his bedroom and abandoned at Fat Camp—the camp that cures what ails you. Only calories weren't my crutch.

As I approach the gated entrance, I spot another bald eagle high up in a tree, perched there like a magnificent sentry, watching my every move, wondering what it was I was up to.

At least I'm not entirely alone.

Allie left in the night. She took the revolver and ammo;

unfortunately for her, she took the Glock ammo, so I'm hoping she doesn't need more than six shots. I wish her well, but despite her passion and tenacity, I don't like her chances. She's not a kid, not an innocent, but vulnerable just the same. I take a final drag and drop the cigarette into a puddle, watching the miniature ship fizzle out in the broad expanse of the tiny lake.

The front gate is closed. Muddy tire tracks lead out to the island proper. Allie stopped to close the gate behind her, not that it locked, not that the 'No Trespassing' sign would deter visitors. Signs held little respect on the island, often having the opposite effect on the criminals who preyed on vacation properties. Cottage owners often found their homes and trailers ransacked, anything and everything taken; electronics, air conditioners, liquor, beer, even toilet paper and bug spray. The culprits were island low-lives, scum who clawed their way through life, jobless, despised the wealthy, and thought nothing of leaving a steaming turd on the kitchen table as a parting gift.

But that was then. Anything goes in the new world. You loot I shoot; that's the new reality. Keeping what you have and protecting it, is job one.

Despite the sunshine, the rain has cooled the air, although the temperature is still above normal for late September. But that will change, and fast. I have to be ready.

I step around the gate and continue up the roadway, avoiding a puddle the size of a crater, impeding the entire width of the road. On either side, branches and leaves glisten with damp, the undergrowth bent and hanging from the overnight wrath. Venturing into the forest would be akin to taking a shower with your clothes on, you'd be soaked, ten feet in.

A breeze sweeps from east to west, and I catch the aroma of wildflowers, summer's last attempt at holding on, refusing to relinquish its seasonal grip. Nature never gives up.

I pause and look back up the roadway, to the path I'd just traversed. The cabin is barely visible in the distance, obscured by trees, but in a few weeks the leaves will be gone and the cabin exposed. Smoke from the chimney is already a concern. The barn is hidden from view but it's the cabin that would peak anyone's interest, anyone who happened upon this road.

My road.

I should double-back and finish walking the perimeter, time my first run properly, but my thoughts are fragmented, disjointed, pulling me in directions I'd rather not go. I pull out the phone and stop the counter. They'll be time for that tomorrow.

I remove a piece paper from my shirt pocket and examine it. My list of priorities, things I need to get done, and soon. I study my penmanship, sloppy handwriting reminiscent of a nine-year-old with cerebral palsy. Rene used to say I missed my calling, that I should have been a physician, I had the illegible cursive down pat.

I ranked the list in order of urgency, from critical to 'probably-a-good-idea':

1. *Vehicle*
2. *Fuel*
3. *Solar panels & batteries*
4. *Food*
5. *Firewood*
6. *Rye*

They say the first step to getting sober is admitting you have a problem. Writing out number six suggests I'm on the road to recovery, but the reality is, I'm stranded, no liquor stores, no cooking sherry in the cupboard, no pub shed. When I think back to the stockpile I left behind, I feel ill, like a diabetic driving past a Dairy Queen on two-for-one-Tuesday. Surviving I can manage—sobriety, I'm not ready for. Not yet. Too much has happened. Staples like food and water, firewood, fuel, I have enough to bide some time. But without my pills and booze, I'm in deep shit.

Why the fuck was the rye gone?

I gaze out over the terrain, hues of green melding beneath an aqua sky. The universe was speaking to me, and I might not get another warm, clear day like this. This was the day for a hike; it's the logical thing to do.

Our only neighbour is four kilometres up the road. We would have passed the laneway on our way in, but I was half-asleep; no way I'd have spotted it in the dark. McNeil was the name on the mailbox, Fred McNeil, typical Caper, our first meeting he handed me a bottle of home-brew and a twenty-box of Timbits, welcoming me, Cape Breton style. I'd had Newfie Screech before, but Fred's concoction put that to shame. He distilled it in his barn, called it gin, and had barrels of it, as I recall.

Barrels of it.

Some say *need* drives motivation, but I'll argue *want* is the better navigator. A vehicle is critical; food, water and fuel imperative, but there's a false idol I pursue. Even the eagle above knows it—it's that fucking obvious.

Fred drove an older GMC pickup, and his wife had a small Kia, with any luck, one will be roadworthy. I look at my watch; it's going on ten-thirty. Forty minutes at a fair trot should get me there. I consider going back for water, but decide against it; I won't be gone that long.

Picking up the pace, I keep to the shoulder to avoid the larger puddles. The storm took its toll on some of the older trees, several leaning, a few with trunks uprooted, glistening in the sunlight. Other than the potholes, the roadway is clear, and that was a good thing, especially if I get lucky and snag a ride.

Twenty minutes in, I hit the Cabot Trail, the road winding its way north and south from the intersection. Like most roads in Cape Breton, the travelled portion is in rough shape; even the infamous Cabot Trail wasn't immune to sunken patches and cavernous potholes. I head right at the crossroads, back towards Highway 105 and civilization. Swatches of darker coloured asphalt appear on this stretch of highway, the road crew's attempts at keeping the potholes from becoming lethal. The centre line was recently painted school bus yellow, the last work done before the world changed forever.

I glance at my watch again, taking a moment to adjust the rifle on my back. Another fifteen minutes at this pace and I should be close. I light a cigarette and scan the surrounding woods, scoping out the dense bush, knowing if I have visitors, the tree line is my best bet. Looking up to the blue sky speckled with powdery white clouds, I breathe in the glorious morning, focusing my thoughts on what I need to accomplish, what I'll do when I get to Fred's. With the cigarette between my lips, my hangover dissipating, I resume my pace, wishing I had an extra-large Double-Double waiting for me at end of my trek. After all, in Cape Breton, a coffee and a smoke were considered a balanced meal.

I stop dead.

Two hundred feet ahead, at the bend in the roadway, a vehicle sits stranded in the ditch. I reach for my rifle and step forward cautiously, my eyes and ears on alert, my heartbeat quickening.

It's the truck. Allie's truck. There's a dent in the left rear quarter panel, the taillight's smashed. It looks like the truck was forced off the road, the rear tire buried up to the rim in mud.

"Fuck me."

I spit out my cigarette and approach, my pace quickening as I close in.

The truck's empty, the driver's door ajar.

There's no sign of Allie, but blood droplets speckle the steering wheel and dash. The keys hang in the ignition; whatever happened, they weren't concerned with the truck—but then again, she wasn't going anywhere without a tow—or a winch.

I have a hand winch in the barn.

I lean my rifle against the door and slip behind the wheel. Cecil's emerald brooch dangles from the rear-view mirror, Allie's defective good luck charm. I try the ignition and she starts up. A quarter tank, not too shabby. I put the truck into drive, then reverse, then back again, but she's stuck, solid.

I run my finger over the blood spatter.

"The new reality," I say aloud. "Meet the new boss, same as the..."

A vehicle approaches.

Change of plans.

Time to go.

I snatch the keys, grab my rifle, and head for the tree line. I'm drenched within seconds, crawling my way up the steep hillside on my hands and knees, not stopping to look back. Rotting branches and wet undergrowth slow my ascent as I claw and grasp at the earth, pulling myself to the safety of the forest. My adrenaline on overdrive, I hear nothing but the sound of blood in my temples as I crest the top of the hill. I pull myself up and glance behind, the roadway beneath me now, but I see nothing. I turn to move, and my foot catches a root. Suddenly I'm airborne, landing with a thud and brilliant flash of bright light.

I lay still, soaked, trembling, blood seeping from my forehead, the warmth spreading across my cheek and down my neck. I reach up and realize my temple is split wide open. I try to sit up, but blackness consumes me.

CHAPTER 43

The right side of my face is cold and wet.

My eyes are open, but I register only darkness, a void. My head aches worse than a New Year's hangover, and considering I've experienced my share, that's saying something. I lay awkwardly, my left knee twisted beneath me, my bladder about to rupture. I prop myself up, ignoring the pain receptors that fire in disturbing sequence across my entire body. This condition is not self-inflicted, not self-induced misery caused by a night of lugubrious libation as I've grown accustomed. My body shivers as I struggle to comprehend my predicament.

I'm in the forest. It's night, and I've been here hours. As my eyes adjust, I can make out a faint glint of light from above, bluish-grey threads of luminescence emanating between the gaps in the tree canopy. Struggling to focus, I realize that something else is wrong. I reach to my right temple, the blood coagulated in thick clumps. Tracing my finger over my right eye I confirm the diagnosis—it's swollen shut. Not a raccoon-eyed pop-in-the-nose shiner, this was a haymaker, courtesy of fate.

In the land of the blind, the one-eyed man is King.

I reach into my pocket, fumbling for my lighter. Nausea grips me and I lean over to vomit, my stomach muscles contracting, the spasms rippling through me as I spew forth, unbridled. After a moment, I catch my breath, wondering if the end is upon me. At best, I have a severe concussion, and I've been unconscious for hours. That can't be good.

My eyesight halved and ineffectual, survival mode engages and my ears take over, scanning the area, gauging my predicament.

Somewhere off to my left, a small animal scurries in the brush, no doubt aware of my presence, either curious or drawn by the smell of blood, or a potential meal. Crickets and bullfrogs call out into the night, serenading my plight, oblivious to my peril.

I triage myself, my brain checking for injury, flexing muscles, contracting tendons and ligaments, wiggling fingers and toes. My left knee is sprained, twisted, but not incapacitated or broken. At least I hope not.

I ease myself up and flick on my lighter. I'm halfway down the embankment, surrounded by young pine trees and clumps of bushes and thickets. To my left is a solitary deciduous tree, an ash by the looks of it, a lone monster amongst a chorus of saplings. It was just my luck my head found the only immovable object within a twenty-foot perimeter.

I stand, unbuckling my pants, wondering if my urine will be bloody, but not wanting to know. I hobble over and mark my territory for what seems like five minutes, against the tree that nearly killed me. Seems fitting. I finish up and flick the lighter on again. Judging by where I went airborne, I have a short climb back up to the top of the hill, the roadway just below. Anyone who came looking for me is long gone.

My rifle.

It flew off mid-tumble. I scour the area on my hands and knees, feeling around, hoping to get lucky, but I realize the odds of finding it are nil. Flicking on the lighter only serves to illuminate the thousand potential hiding spots for a weapon that likes to blend in with its surroundings. I'll never find it, even in daylight I'll be lucky. I fumble around my pocket and remove my note. I approach the big ash, careful not to step in my own piss, and pierce the paper onto a small branch, affixing it to the tree. Despite having other guns, I can't afford to abandon the rifle, not without a proper search in daylight.

I turn and crawl up the embankment like a geriatric ape, wetness no longer a concern, better to be safe than dead. At the top I can see the roadway below, lit by stray shards of pale moonlight. My depth perception non-existent, I make my way down slowly, clutching each tree as I pass, stabilizing my footing and taking no chances. As I squeeze myself between the last two trees at the edge of the roadway, a branch whips back and smacks me in the temple. Blood flows once again, trickling down my cheek, dripping from my chin.

The truck is as it was, untouched. I pad the outside of my pocket confirming the keys are still there. In one swift motion, I remove my shirt and wrench the water out. The night is cold and soaked clothing is not helping my core temperature, hypothermia a reality. I wipe down my temple, careful not to open the wound further, and tie the shirt around my head.

The road is quiet, no movement, nothing unusual, just me and the truck. I look at my watch. It's eight.

I wait out a dizzy spell then start walking, my pace slow, deliberate. Despite a head injury, and the onset of hypothermia, I can't push myself beyond my breaking point; I need to make it back to the cabin, clean my wounds, and regroup. After a while, I quicken my pace, comforted that with each step I'm closer to safety, closer to home. If only Rene could see me now—Jack, with a self-inflicted lobotomy, bleeding and shivering, with nothing to show for my effort.

I stop.

Rene.

I dreamt of her—or hallucinated, I'm not sure how you classify a concussion-based experience. She was standing in the field, in front of the cabin. It was nighttime, and Allie was there. They stood fifty feet apart, facing one another.

I stood between them.

I resume walking, trying to recall what Rene had said, but the more I concentrate, the hazier the memory. Pausing to adjust my t-shirt, I wonder if the bleeding has stopped, but realize there was no way to tell. I was soaked through, my body numb, no longer able to sense cold or heat, hypothermia taking hold.

The road ahead curves left and I begin moving, keeping to the centre line; I can't risk drifting and tumbling into the abyss.

I remember Rene smiling. She spoke, words that resonated within my head.

"It's time."

I'd looked to Allie, but she had turned away, the Roots logo glowing neon green in the blackness. I was to make a choice, like a cherished pet, placed between feuding owners.

Then they were gone, and I was alone. I looked out towards the gate in the distance. Someone or something, was coming.

I stop.

I overshot the laneway, my mind preoccupied, swaddled in a hypothermic trance, running on overdrive. Backtracking, I stop to examine the roadway, dropping my lighter in the process, my hands trembling. I scoop it up and try lighting it again. Success. Nothing looks disturbed, no sign any vehicle has been here since Allie left. I pocket the lighter and start up the laneway.

Fifteen minutes later, I'm in the cabin, lighting candles, stripping naked. I wrap myself in a towel and examine my wound in the bathroom mirror. The bleeding has stopped, but my eye is swollen shut, a bloated purple mess, like a C-Horror

Movie make-up job. I need stitches, but unless the bald eagles have medical training, whatever I have in the Kit will have to suffice. If there's permanent damage, or if an infection takes hold, my Fat Camp days are numbered anyhow.

I consider firing up the woodstove as I sort through the Kit, but fatigue grips me, and I want nothing more than a dozen blankets and sleep. The generator is not an option—the million dollar question; to sleep or not to sleep. If I don't wake up, my problems are solved. If I do, they're just beginning.

Using an antiseptic wipe, I clean the wound then affix a gauze and pressure bandage. I admire my handiwork a moment, then grab a bottle of water and second blanket, and lie down. What I wouldn't give for a hot tub, cigar and snifter of brandy.

But I have more pressing matters to consider. Priorities. I have to be prepared, ready.

Ready for what?

Someone was coming. They ran Allie off the road, two kilometres from here. That was not a coincidence.

They were here looking for her. If they found her, they know I'm here, and they'll come. I force myself to stand and walk to the kitchen where I remove the truck's keys from my pants pocket. I lay the keys on the table and grab the flashlight; then it's back to the bathroom to re-examine my face.

Yes, I look like I have my shit together.

I shuffle to the futon and lie down, wanting to sleep. But sleeping with a concussion is bad. Pulling the double blanket over myself, I gaze to the flickering candle flame. Maybe a short nap? My body needs to recover, concussion or not, sleep is my motivator, I no longer have the strength to fight it. I lower my head onto the pillow and close my eye. I feel warmth, comfort.

Bang!

I sit up.

Looking to the kitchen, I stand, wondering where I left my Glock. I let the blankets drop and scoop up the candle, stepping towards the source of the noise.

The First Aid Kit lies on the floor, the contents spilled out.

I must have left it too close to the edge. I gaze about the cabin, wondering if I'm losing it, if my scrambled brain has rendered me unable to distinguish the rational from the imaginary.

I look down, holding the candle out in front of me, my eyeball struggling to focus in the flickering light. A roll of gauze lies unravelled on the floor, unwound ten feet, where its progress was impeded.

By my bug-out bag.

CHAPTER 44

The first of three vehicles, an Escalade, comes into view, a hundred and fifty metres up the laneway, no headlights or taillights, blending into the surroundings like a champagne flute at a keg party. A pickup is next, staying close to the Escalade's bumper, followed by what looks to be a police SUV, decked out with traditional markings and takedown lights.

I switch the binoculars for the thermal night vision goggles and the darkness opens into a surrealistic world of green pixilated imagery. Swelling around my right eye has gone down, but I'm still a one-eyed Jack. The aspirins have quieted my pain to a dull throb; I'm thankful for that.

The pickup truck hangs back, leaving the entourage. I grab the binoculars in time to see two shadows jump from the back of the truck. They're snipers, dark and light jerseys, one home team, one away. I watch as they separate, rifles slung on their backs, moving towards opposite tree lines.

The Escalade and cruiser continue to approach, barely above walking speed, until they both stop, side by side, a hundred feet from the cabin.

I examine my weapon, the unexpected gift from an anonymous donor. I've never shot a sniper rifle before, unless you count *Call of Duty* where I was a master. In the online gaming world, players referred to snipers as 'campers', a derogatory term for those who preferred to hide and wait for unsuspecting newbs to stumble into our midst. Campers were a despised bunch, no matter what platform you played, Xbox, PlayStation, computer; we were the hated few. But our death/kill ratios were outstanding.

Unfortunately, this was for real.

My rifle lost, my shotgun and Glock limited to close combat, the sniper rifle was my only long distance option, even though a shot would be heard all the way to the mainland. I managed to figure out how to load the gun and affix the tripod, but there was no time for a practise shoot. And being a one-eyed pirate, accuracy is a looming question mark. I can't afford to miss, not once.

I shift to my other elbow, peering at the vehicles positioned in front of the cabin. They're squaring off with whoever they expect is inside. And that would be me, by all accounts.

The passenger door of the Escalade opens and a figure climbs out. The silhouette carries a gas can and disappears into the night.

I scan for snipers, but I've lost them. They've likely taken up positions in the meadow, laid up on their bellies, waiting for the prey to be coerced out, and eliminated.

The quiet is intense. It's like nature has stopped, pausing, awaiting the showdown. No thunder, no fire, no rain. My heart beats double-time and my hands tremble; the dull throb in my head reminds me my odds of survival are remote.

I thought I had more time—time to plan, prepare an escape scenario when things went south, but it wasn't to be. Either Allie confessed, under coercion or worse, or they solved the riddle, deducting that their FBI Top Ten Most Wanted was down that remote laneway, in the middle of nowhere, hiding out in plain sight.

KABOOM!

I jerk, my eye squinting with a sudden flash of white light.

Fireworks.

Someone just lit a cannon, yet another page from my playbook.

Trails of white and blue light shoot skyward, cascading in circular spirals, illuminating the entire meadow from tree line to tree line. A nice attention grabber. I scan the area, trying to spot the snipers but the illumination is sporadic, movement impossible to determine. A second firework explodes, sending red and green shooting stars into the sky, one after another, repeating like a machine gun, smoke now gathering, hovering in the air; a malingering vapour of death.

The SUV lights up like the lead car in the Rose Bowl Parade, headlights, spotlights, take-down lights. Alternating strobes of blue and red ignite the entire clearing, reflecting off the surrounding trees, illuminating the cloud of smoke settling into the grass.

The Escalade's headlights come on, no strobe lights, but the powerful high beams add to the blinding display, lighting up the entire front of the cabin.

I reposition myself, reaching for the binoculars, then stop.

The distinct crackle of a loud hailer erupts, the distorted microphone click echoing off the mountain in behind. Then a voice.

"Pardon the theatrics, but you only get one chance to make a first impression, am I right?"

The distorted audio is raspy, the volume level too loud, the speaker blown.

"How'd you like me so far?"

I try to focus in on whoever's talking, but the cruiser's windshield refracts the light, I can't see who's inside.

"Here's the deal Jack."

They have her.

"I'm a fair man. But I sure as fuck ain't a patient man. But you probably figured that much out already. Thing is, we got to settle our differences—like men. Reasonable men. There's been too much killing, too much violence, there ain't enough of us left to keep this shit up, you get me?"

I shift my weight, switching to the night vision goggles. I see only one in the Cadillac, and it looks like one in the cruiser.

"You're a resourceful guy, an asset in a sea of liabilities, and that's fucking rare. That's why I'm willing to play nice, talk it out over a cold one. Shit, maybe we'll kick back, play some Chase the Ace, like the good ole days. This is still Cape Breton after all. I got the Community Centre up and running back in town. That's what I do. I bring back civilization where there was none. I restore order. And I need good people, leaders, on my side. What do you say? A cold beer and a chat. Just come on out the front, no weapons, and let's get this done."

The flashing lights play havoc with my vision, inducing a trance-like effect, an acid trip gone awry. I pan the tree line, looking for movement.

"Don't mind my boys, they won't hurt nobody, so long as we all place nice. Consider them my Secret Service, East Coast style, protection from those who would do me harm. They're no threat to you. What do you say?"

A long, uncomfortable pause. I pan the area.

"Remember when I said I wasn't a patient man Jack? Time is precious. Survival, growing older, is calculated in minutes now, not days or weeks, not years. We've been given a gift, you and me, the gift of life. Think about it man, millions dead, women and children, all wiped off the earth in a heartbeat, and yet here we are, Cape Breton of all places, alive and well, carrying on. We're special, we were chosen. But as the chosen, we got shit to do. Shit that can't be put off till tomorrow. Tomorrow's no guarantee. Patience is an old-world luxury, no one can afford that shit anymore, you get me?"

I switch to the binoculars and see his hand out the window, motioning to the Cadillac. Something is about to happen.

"What do you say, we do this like gentlemen? You come out, I meet you half way. No weapons, no one draws, no one dies. My word."

The cruiser door opens and he steps out. He wears a uniform similar to a military commander or police chief; the kind worn in parades and special events, more medals on his tunic than Edi Amin. Holding the microphone in his hand, he steps away from the cruiser, stretching the cord to its max.

"Tick Tock Jack. Tick Tock. You see, no weapons."

He pivots left and right, showing me he's unarmed. A long, silent minute goes by. He signals the Cadillac with a wave of his hand.

"You're trying my patience Jack. I offer you one over the plate, and you don't swing. Well okay then, let's try this a different way."

There's a loud whoosh, followed by a glimmer of light emanating from the right, in behind the trees. The light intensifies, flickering like an amber strobe.

"That's the barn Jack. Strike one. Tick Tock."

The light magnifies, merging with the pulsating cruiser lights, the meadow coming to life in a blanket of competing glows.

"I gave you my word Jack, and you're not being respectful. I appreciate that this is your land and you likely want to be left alone, live a hermit life, but things just ain't that simple. Not no more. You broke a couple of my Commandments—in my town, serious ones, but not anything we can't work out, *mano a mano*. But you gotta meet me halfway. This shit's gotta get dealt with. *Capiche?*"

He lowers the mike.

"Last chance Jackie-boy."

He likes to hear himself talk, that's obvious. But what colourful antagonist doesn't? He's the type who'll reveal his entire plan for world domination before succumbing to the down-and-out protagonist. I'm down-and-out, but I'm no fucking hero.

"We do it your way then."

The Escalade's door opens and Bull, the bald-headed prick emerges, still wearing sunglasses, no doubt a closet Corey Hart fan. Bull opens the rear door and pulls someone out, leading them towards the front of the Cadillac, positioning them between the headlights. The person wears a dark hoodie covering their head. I bring the binoculars up.

"You remember Harry fucking Houdini?"

Bull pushes the person down to their knees and pulls the hood off. It's Cecil. He looks battered, beaten.

"I call this the Apoca—litmus test. Get it?"

The mike clicks off, then back on again, as if for effect.

"Do-you-give-a-fuck-about-anyone-but-yourself?"

Another mike click.

"This is a pass or fail, Jack. True or false. Truth be told, gramps here ain't the best candidate for this particular test, considering he should have crawled into a coffin ten years ago, but he's all I got at the moment."

Victor and Bull exchange glances. The microphone clicks again.

"I'll sweeten the deal. You come out now, like a good boy, grampa here gets to see his hundredth."

Cecil remains motionless, oblivious.

"Nothin'? Well alrighty then."

Bull reaches into the car and pulls something out. I focus the binoculars. It's a long sword, a blade, like a scimitar, the metal gleaming blue and red in the flashing lights.

"I'm not normally one for grisly antics, but it is the goddamn apocalypse, you gotta keep things fresh. What's it gonna be Jack? Times like these a man's character is revealed—or not, your choice. I'll give you one minute to think about it."

The words echo throughout the valley. One minute.

I drop the binoculars and fix my eye on the scope. Judging by the cinders floating into view, the barn is engulfed. Smoke fills the valley adding to the chaos of light and shadow.

Bull positions himself behind Cecil. The old man's head remains lowered, he hasn't moved. My hands tremble as I struggle to aim the crosshairs. I look away a moment, blinking my eye, then refocus. Either he's a tactical genius or just lucky, but Bull's position behind Cecil gives me only one option, a headshot, otherwise I take out two for the price of one. The brightness of the headlamps distracts my focus, the tripod shifting under my weight as I re-aim. The distance isn't far for a scoped rifle, but with trembling hands and debilitating lighting, the odds of me hitting my mark are waning.

"Thirty seconds. You have anything to say, grandpa?" Victor looks over. Bull leans over Cecil, then straightens up, shaking his head.

"Nah, he's good. Ten seconds Jackson Browne."

I hold my breath, tensing my body, the wrong thing to do, but it works. The crosshairs steady on the Oakley's resting on Bull's gargantuan forehead. He towers above Cecil, clasping the sword in his grip, holding it like a batter waiting on the three and two pitch, his muscles tensed and ready.

I begin my trigger pull, conscious I need a slow, steady pull, otherwise I'll drop the shot and take out Cecil.

"Ten…nine…eight," the words are slow and deliberate.

Bull brings the sword back in a wide arc.

"Six…five…four."

Audible override, I hear nothing after the word 'five'. My finger pulls. Suddenly…

"Hold on!"

Victor breaks the stalemate. I release the trigger.

"Stand down."

I grab the binoculars, scrambling to see what's happening.

"Can't do it. Too fucking dramatic. This ain't how we do things, we're not animals. It's not what I'm about, not what we're about. Chopping off mother-fucking heads is too ISIS, I hate that shit. I don't want you coming away with the wrong impression of me Jack."

I steady the binoculars on Victor, wondering what he has planned. Smoke continues to fill the valley, accentuated by the artificial light.

"You called my bluff, well done. Or maybe I made a careless assumption, thinking you gave a shit about this old coot. Or maybe you're just a selfish bastard, there's that too."

Victor reaches into the car. He removes a shotgun. I watch as Bull walks over and grabs the gun, then returns to Cecil.

I line up the scope again, fumbling for the trigger. Within seconds I have Bull in my sites. Standing beside Cecil, not behind, I have a clear shot. Bull points the shotgun downward to Cecil's torso, the barrel two feet from his midsection. I check my breathing, focus, and start my trigger pull.

The mike clicks. I hear the word.

"Now."

BANG.

The muzzle flashes and Cecil falls forward.

My body convulses, I let go of the rifle, rolling onto my side, hyperventilating, conscious that I'm bleeding again. But I don't care. I just watched a man die.

"Strike two Jack."

I lay on my back, dazed, not believing what just happened. How I let it happen.

I try to control my breathing, but the smoke is beginning to overtake my lungs, sucking the oxygen from my system.

"Let me ask you something Jack, what kind of a God kills little kiddies, but spares a useless old fuck? You get where I'm going with this? You understand the complexity of what we're dealing with here? How I'm trying to make sense of this fucked up post-world shit storm? Do you have a fucking clue what it is I'm trying to accomplish?"

I force myself back to an upright position, choking back the urge to cough up a lung, picking up the thermal goggles. Bull stands across from Victor, opposite the cruiser, the shotgun in his hands. Cecil lies dead, basked in the glow of the headlights, surrounded in a haze of smoke, like the fucked up ethereal gates of purgatory.

"I bring calm to the storm. Unite the masses. Protect the weak. Under my vision, we cleared the roads, disposed of the dead, fed the hungry. Showed them hope."

Victor reaches into the cruiser, the siren wails for a second, then stops. He resumes.

"And you're trying to fuck with that. Over what? An old fart?"

He pauses, lowering the mike as if expecting a response. Then he smiles. He raises a finger, shaking it like he's chastising a naughty child.

"It's the girl. It's always been the girl. Am I right? I'm right aren't I?"

He taps his finger to his nose, the traditional sign for 'I knew it all the time'.

"What can I say, she's a hot commodity these days, a rare pearl in a post-world oyster infested shit parade. It is a shame, you and I could have worked things out, but some things aren't negotiable. Finders keepers Jack, no sharesies."

A silhouette approaches the cabin, carrying a gas can. The shadow disappears from the glow of the headlights. Moments later a window smashes, followed by an explosion.

The cabin's alight.

Sanctuary burning.

"Strike three."

I fight to control my panic, the smoke thickening with each passing second.

"No hard feelings Jack. And, just so you don't go away dejected and all heartbroken and shit, the girl, Allie, ain't who you think. This ain't a Disney storyline, no one's rescued a princess from the evil sorcerer, not even fucking close."

Glass shatters, followed by another whoosh of flames.

"Did she happen to mention her extended stay at the Forensic Facility in Dartmouth, psychiatric ward? No one gets sent to that place unless they're real nasty. By invitation only. Did you happen to chat about that over a bottle of Chianti and can of beans?"

Flames spread within the cabin, thick black smoke billows out the windows.

"I thought not. But I figured you might like to know. Don't worry though, I'll see she gets the help she needs. I've got her back on her meds, she'll be good as new."

Victor motions to the Cadillac, then turns and points towards the pickup.

"I'll tell her you said hi, shall I?" He chuckles into the mike. "Sayonara Jack."

He climbs into the cruiser and closes the door. Moments later, he's pulling away, the Escalade following. The snipers emerge from the shadows, like a pair of demented doppelgangers, taking up positions on either side of the cabin. A third silhouette appears, likely the pyromaniac of the group, moving towards the rear. They're setting up a visual on all exits, windows, doors, secret escape hatch, waiting to see if their target does a Richard Prior, and comes out in flames, begging to be shot.

And I watch. My mind reeling, my heart racing, consumed by loss and guilt.

Sanctuary is gone.

Cecil is gone.

I sit up, my muscles aching from lying prone. I reposition myself, the Glock in my lap, the rifle beside me. I have to wait them out. No one could survive the blaze, the cabin engulfed, a matchstick dipped in gasoline tossed into lava. And despite the reality of the situation, the assassins aren't leaving. Maybe they figured out I was never inside. Maybe they're waiting for the camper to slip up. Maybe they're dumb, but not stupid.

I grab the thermals and scan. Flames have breached the cabin's roof as a final window blows. From where I sit, hidden in my elevated position, I can see the entire valley, but only two of the assassins.

They don't know I'm here, and it's unlikely they'll climb the hillside to search. It's a waiting game. There's no reason to engage, there's nothing left to protect—except my cowardly soul.

I lay the thermals down and pick up the Glock, wondering how long this will play out, but not really caring.

Then I hear the music.

It begins softly, challenging my sanity; like hearing the ice cream truck two blocks over but doubting your senses.

With each refrain the melody grows louder, echoing through the valley. It's the familiar fiddle music, the haunting ballad, eerie and surreal. I can't tell where it's coming from, but it feels like it's in my head, music resounding from within.

Am I hearing this again?

The pickup truck's headlights turn on and it's suddenly motoring towards the cabin.

They hear this too.

The truck stops thirty feet from the inferno. Three silhouettes emerge from the shadows, running for the truck, climbing inside. A second later, the pickup is barreling up the laneway, heading for the gate, getting the fuck out of Dodge.

They abandoned their posts, relinquished their mission, fled like cowards.

All because of a little ditty.

I remain as I am, basking in the glow of Sanctuary lost, smoke and ash corrupting the sky; the ballad quieter now, fading, the sound of flames once again overtaking the night.

CHAPTER 45

I awaken with a jolt and roll out from under the tarp. Somehow I'd managed to fall asleep, likely a combination of exhaustion, head wound, guilt, defeat. The surrounding forest is wet, the rain that fell overnight still glistening in the morning sun. Trails of black smoke rise upwards to the sky.

The cabin is a charred cinder. Sanctuary lost. I climb out from my makeshift camp, my right eye able to see again, although only partially. I gather my things, dropping them into my bug-out bag, my last vestibule of survival gear. I grab the bag and rifle, and climb down the hillside.

I pause to look. Some of the larger beams are still standing, smoldering, the remainder of the cabin is a scorched remnant of yesterday.

I remove my First Aid Kit and mirror from my bag, examining my wound. The swelling is down, my eye partially open, but the gash is dirty, wet with fresh blood. I clean the wound, bandage and dress it. I do this robotically, without thought, trying to block out the reality that awaits me. Cecil is out there, not fifty metres from where I stand, but I don't have the guts, the spine, to look. Guilt, shame, cowardice, all telling me to just leave, just start walking, and not look back.

But I can't. I can't run. Not anymore. There is no place to go. My mind spins in circles, my thoughts rampant and confused. I need to regroup, think things out, prioritize. But my thoughts won't let me.

I walk towards the barn. The structure is leveled, still burning in places, thankfully the fire spread only to the surrounding grass and not the trees. I stand in silence, my gaze transfixed on the charcoal remains, the tiny trails of smoke rising and dissipating in the morning air.

Fuck this. Let's get on with it.

A few items in the centre of the barn survived the fire. Tools, casement windows, even the solar panels look to be intact. I search the area and find what I'm looking for. A shovel, the handle broken but it will do. I grab it and march off towards the creek, the opposite side of the valley. I don't look in Cecil's direction, but I know he's there, just the same.

I choose an area void of trees, less chance of stubborn roots to impede my progress. I break the soil with the first stomp, and start digging.

An hour later, I'm standing over Cecil's corpse. Curled fingers, clenched in death, draw my gaze. I think of him playing the fiddle with those fingers, smooth melodic strokes, a ballad recently learned. I roll him onto the tarp, securing the ends with nylon rope, then drag him across the field, towards his final resting place.

The grave is shallow, but I don't have the time or energy to contemplate frost lines or scavengers. It's the best I can do. Mechanically, without thought or feeling, I roll the corpse into the hole and start filling it. My mind blank, numb, I'm thankful for the menial task, part-time gravedigger, keeping me occupied, albeit temporarily. I always found it peculiar how the dirt you dig up is never enough to refill a hole, I never understood why, but it was a curious fact of life. I top off the grave with extra soil from a nearby pile, making sure it's packed down tightly.

Behind me the creek flows, heavy with overnight rain, encapsulating the moment with a promise of another lost soul's pending journey.

Satisfied the grave is sufficient, I kneel beside a large piece of shale, a stone I'd discovered at the water's edge a year back. The piece was triangle shaped, two inches thick and weighed fifteen pounds. I remove my knife and etch Cecil's name into the centre. I consider adding his last name, but I can't remember what it is. And what the fuck did it matter? I remove my phone from my pocket.

I should at least put the date.

It's September 21st.

My thoughts fall to that number, to Allie, her tattoo, her deluded ramblings—and Victor's comments about her past, her transgressions, her mental state.

But today was the 21st.

And there are no coincidences.

I carve the date beneath the name, careful not to sever a finger in the process. When I'm satisfied with my craftsmanship, I lay the stone atop the pile of dirt.

A bald eagle sores above me, the same one I'd seen a day earlier, at the start of my trek to seek out rye. Rye, not a vehicle, not gas, not food, but rye. I'm suddenly cognizant of the moment; the dawning of a new day, the eagle, the gurgling stream, death at my feet. I pick up a twig and toss it into the water, watching the current carry it away.

Rene left the same way.

Perhaps it's time to follow. There's nothing left here.

I look to the meadow, empty now, no longer a home, not a Sanctuary, just a stoic reminder of the evil that men do, the plague that humanity, what's left of it, has become.

I'm not like them.

But if I had been, Cecil wouldn't be dead, spending eternity four feet under, alone, in a strange place with no one to remember him. And Allie might be free—free to pursue her vision, free to help those who longed for a chance to live in peace, to exist.

Allie was right. I can't hide, I can't turn my back on humanity. Dying a selfish coward is not a legacy I want to leave.

You miss one hundred percent of the shots…

If I'd taken the shot, Cecil might be alive.

I look up to see my twig has reached an impasse, wedged between a rock and tree branch.

I pick up a stone and throw it; a direct hit, the twig freed, back on its journey.

"Rest easy Cecil."

I look off to the distance. "See you soon."

CHAPTER 46

I never understood the whole Chuck Norris thing. I mean he was a great martial artist, sparred with Bruce Lee in his early days, a respected tough guy, but he seemed laid back and reserved, as far as movie heroes go. I mean you take your Arnold, your Stallone, to a lesser extent Willis and Neeson, more of your traditional kick-ass hero types, those guys I understood.

But I'm no hero, I'm not a tough guy.

As I secure the cable around the tree trunk, my mind flips through random memories of days past; of a simple life predicated on television shows, films and books.

Lucky for me the winch's cable is just long enough to reach the closest large tree. I jump into the truck and shift her into neutral; then I'm back across the road. I work the winch with both hands, the cable tightening with each crank. Rated at two tons, I don't know if this contraption will extricate a full-sized pickup, but I figure it's worth a shot.

With each successive yank growing more difficult, the rear tires begin to move. Seeing progress, my forearms surge with energy, like Popeye after a can of spinach, and before long, the truck's free from the worst of the mud. My arms and shoulders burn with fatigue, and I pause to light a smoke, a well-earned reward for a job well done.

Detaching the cable was something I didn't anticipate, the instructions not particularly useful. Considering the tension on the aircraft-grade cable could decapitate me if done incorrectly, I take my time fumbling with the gadget, the cigarette hanging between my lips, smoke rising into my nostrils, choking me. I never understood how people could work with a smoke in their mouths for more than a few seconds, but after a minute, I'm able to disengage the latch without catapulting myself into oblivion.

Moments later, I'm in the truck, rocking her back and forth, alternating from drive to reverse, careful not to let her roll back into her original predicament. Mud flies, covering the wheel wells, but on the fourth attempt, the left wheel catches and the truck frees itself.

Let's see Chuck Norris do that.

I leave her running, disconnect the cable from the tow hitch, gather up my supplies, and dump everything into the rear seat. Then it's back to Sanctuary lost. Despite the grim scene awaiting me, having a vehicle gives me a sense of security, a jump-start, a well-needed kick in the arse.

The smoke lingers amongst the cinders, but the worst is over. I retrieve my hockey bag and sniper rifle, sorting through my supplies, removing a pair of black combat pants, the bulletproof vest and a police issue belt with holster. My Glock is a perfect fit. At least there's that.

I secure the rifle in its case and remove one final item from my inventory.

Allie's Penguins jersey.

Things are about to get frosty.

Game on.

CHAPTER 47

BEN

The Cabot Trail winds its way through Middle River, up into the surrounding hillside, a magnificent spectacle of nature's riches. A fortress of pines line the roadways, the mountains awash with cascading greens, save for the occasional glint of orange, a sign that autumn was hovering. The sun high overhead, the temperature remains warm for late September, a perfect day to bask in nature's unblemished beauty, and explore the island.

Only exploring is not on the agenda.

Approaching Highway 105, I near the intersection known as Buckwheat's Corners. I slow down, not knowing what to expect once I round the bend. A large two-story structure, an old farmer's barn converted into a restaurant and souvenir shop, stood at the corner, a familiar landmark for tourists and regulars alike. Rene and I stopped in often, almost every trip, usually for an early breakfast before heading north to Ingonish, then onto Meat Cove, sometimes looping down through Cheticamp on the trek back. The drive was surreal, each valley, each mountain, more picturesque than the last, a photographer's dream and nature lover's Eden.

I skid to a stop.

The barn is gone.

An acre of scorched earth remains, rubble piled a story high, surrounded by abandoned pickups and vans in the adjacent parking lot, a lot once home to curious travellers and island explorers. There is no movement, no signs of life. I take my foot off the brake and ease the truck forward.

The closer I get, the uglier reality becomes.

Dead bodies lie piled atop one another in the makeshift crematorium. Dozens, a hundred maybe, charred, rotting, decomposing in the afternoon sun. Vultures and seagulls circle the remains, a few feasting on the corpses, tearing putrid flesh from open wounds and empty eye sockets. As the stench reaches the truck, I close the windows, stopping to survey the devastation.

They chose this spot to gather and cremate the dead. That's what the abandoned vehicles were for, transport, Island Hearse Services. Why this place and not a secluded area off the beaten path, I don't know. While the risk of diseases like widespread cholera was a myth, this was intentional. This was a warning sign for anyone passing through, a calling card of death, a prelude to what lay further up north, in Baddeck.

The stench permeates the vents and I pull forward, turning at the crossroads, heading south on the 105. Ahead I see a pair of vehicles parked on the gravel shoulder, opposite sides of the roadway. A body lies atop each car, outstretched arms and legs bound, frozen in an eternal horizontal jumping jack—another message for the curious traveller. The corpse on the right has been dead for a while judging by the clothing, ravaged and soiled. Two ravens land on the trunk, a mating pair, ensuring the area is free of predators before settling in for lunch.

I pull over to the shoulder. I have six hours of daylight, and no plan, it's time I buckle down and formulate a strategy. Other than using the cover of darkness, my tactical expertise is limited and inadequate. I adjust the Glock that's been poking into my side for the past half hour, the gun belt uncomfortable and awkward. But I need to be armed, to be ready. I need a warrior attitude. It's them or me. There can be no compromises, no half measures, no retreat, no surrender.

I grab my cigarettes from atop the jersey strewn across the passenger seat. I light a smoke and search my mind for images of Bras d'Or Manor, trying to remember if there was a second driveway, a back entrance for servants and staff.

I see movement. I jerk forward in my seat, scanning, doubting my eyes.

The body moved. On the second car, across from the raven buffet, the head moved, I'm sure of it. The person was alive.

I grab a bottle of water from the cup holder and dart towards the vehicle, my eyes alert for an ambush.

Unlike the others, this person's wrists and ankles are bound with a thin gauge wire, crisscrossed through opposite car windows. This guy really pissed someone off.

"Hang on," I say.

He peers at me, his sunburned face and weathered skin suggesting he's been out here a while. He is Aboriginal, dark-skinned, pockmarked face with the nose of a hockey enforcer, broken at least twice, hair black as coal, wrapped in a ponytail.

I remove my multi-tool and snip the wires. He sits up and slides himself down onto the hood, his feet hanging over the edge of the car. I watch as he pulls each wire from the skin, the bloody welts ripe and festering with dirt and pending infection. He does this methodically, without flinching, until all his appendages are free from his wire snare. He lowers his feet to the ground and stands, a little unsteady at first. Hovering six inches above me, he's as wide as he is tall, a mountain in blue jeans. I offer him the bottle and he accepts it in silence, and drinks.

"I'm Jack."

He nods but says nothing. Finishing the water, he motions with his fingers, asking for a cigarette.

"In the truck."

He follows me to the pickup. I watch as he removes the elastics from his ponytail, freeing his mane, his hair down to his beltline. I'm reminded of Hans, back at the Causeway, long flowing hair like a Nordic warrior, and dead as a shit-sack.

I reach into the truck and grab the cigarettes, handing him one, taking one for myself. I light them.

"Dry throat, or you not a talker?"

He inhales deeply and just looks at me.

"I had a friend diagnosed with mouth cancer, had her tongue and part of her jaw removed. She didn't chat much after that."

The big man exhales a cloud into the heavens.

"Not my business, I get it. You must have done something to piss them off. Or they ran outa rope." I smile, looking for a reaction, anything that suggests he understands, or gives a shit.

He makes a walking motion with two fingers.

"You tried to leave?" I ask.

He nods.

"And that's a death sentence?"

He looks to the wounds on his wrists.

"I have a First Aid Kit in the back."

He shakes his head.

"They kill you for trying to leave?"

He looks at me for a long moment, inhales, then pulls up his left shirt sleeve, revealing a large tattoo covering his shoulder. The artwork is elaborate, colourful and intricate.

"Dream catcher," I say, recognizing the significance.

He nods and traces a single word into the mud on the pickup's fender.

Ben.

"Nice to meet you, Ben." He nods and accepts my hand, his massive paw dwarfing mine; it's like shaking hands with Andre the Giant. He points at my face, acknowledging my injury. I reach up and touch the bandage.

He makes the peace sign. I shrug, not understanding, then it hits me. It isn't a peace sign; it's the letter 'V'.

"Victor?"

He nods.

"Indirectly, yeah I guess so. Dream catchers make him nervous, huh?"

Ben cocks his ear as if sensing something, something I don't pick up on. My hand falls to my Glock.

"We should get off the road. Can I drop you somewhere?"

He points north, holding up three fingers.

"Three minutes?"

He nods. I toss my cigarette and open the door, climbing into the truck. Ben crushes his cigarette beneath his enormous boot and opens the passenger door. He pauses when he sees the jersey on the front seat.

"Toss it in the back," I say, putting the truck into drive. Ben squeezes himself in, a tight fit, his head almost touching the roof. The air becomes thick with the smell of sweat and piss, but I hesitate to roll down the window, not wanting to offend. Ben notices, glancing to his soiled clothes.

I pull a U-turn and head north. We pass a couple of driveways and within minutes, Ben's directing me to hang a right down a gravel laneway. The sign says Celtic Cottage Trailer Park, the roadway narrow and tree lined. A hundred metres in, Ben is tapping my shoulder and I stop the truck. A huge tree trunk blocks the road. No sooner do I stop then Ben is out walking towards the downed tree. In one swift motion, he crouches down, picks up one end and shuffles sideways, angling the massive trunk off the roadway. It's like watching a strongman competition, only without the grunting, or anyone shitting their pants.

Moments later he's back in the truck and we're moving. He's not even breathing hard. We round the bend and the roadway opens to a large field. Two log cabins are set off to the right, the shores of Bras d'Or Lake visible in behind. To the left is the RV Park, only a handful of rundown Cousin Eddy class motor homes parked in a cluster closer to the lake. This was no five-star resort. Ben points towards a large prefab building straight ahead, the Main Office and General Store by the looks of things. In behind the building is a Quonset hut, likely for storage for maintenance equipment and watercraft. I pull closer and see that the front doors and windows are boarded up, the place looted and since repaired. Ben directs me to pull around back.

I stop the truck beside a green Chevy pickup and we both climb out. Ben holds up a finger, telling me to wait. I watch as he heads towards the shoreline, shedding his clothes one garment at a time until he's buck. I follow, keeping my distance. A handful of picnic tables and fire pits line the sandy shores of the campground. In the distance, over the water, the island's east side rises into view, sunlight dancing off the ripples on the lake.

Ben walks straight in, impervious to the temperature, no hesitation, no flinching when the jewels hit the water. He disappears beneath the cresting waves, cleansing himself in the great Bras d'Or. I pull out a cigarette and look around. This was his Sanctuary, at least initially. I inspect the outside of the office building and the truck, noticing a large vehicle, covered in a tarp, parked beside the Quonset hut. There's something unique, something of value under that tarp, maybe a new RV, or a truck of some kind. I step closer when I hear Ben approaching, still naked, but revitalized and clean.

"Your get-away vehicle?" I ask.

He passes by me, heading to the rear of the building, glancing back to make sure I'm following.

I don't usually follow naked men, but in the apocalypse, sometimes you improvise.

CHAPTER 48

The inside of the building is a hoarder's dream, well stocked with provisions, food, water, tools, even a Harley Davidson Roadster stored among the clutter. Ben appears, dressed in clean jeans and a shirt, tossing me a package of crackers. I accept the food and tuck in, watching as he rummages through a tackle box. He removes five different phones, a Samsung, iPhone, others, replacing each one with a grunt, until he finds what he's looking for. He sits down opposite me on a stool and types into the phone. He finishes and looks up.

A robotic female voice—with an Australian accent, emanates from the phone. It's a text to speech application.

"You are the one they are looking for?"

Ben is annoyed, his fingers working the phone, making changes—Aussie female was not the voice he was after.

"That's me," I reply.

He's busy typing.

"Are you going for her? They will kill you. Do you think you are Rambo?"

He looks up at me, shaking his head at the French Canadian accent. It's obvious this phone is not his go-to device, likely the only one with juice.

I smile. "Something like that. I had a place, like this. Out of the way, safe, but she wanted to move on, had things to do. They nabbed her, came for me."

Ben glances up, then back to typing.

German accent this time, sexy in a Siri sort of way. He grimaces.

"Kept on the upper level. Master bedroom. Two guards inside, two at gate. Big mansion, know it?"

I nod.

Ben opens a pack of cigarettes, offering me one. I put the crackers aside and we both light up.

"The odds aren't good, but I have to try," I say.

The first inhale catches me off guard, not my usual brand. I look around the storage room, then to Ben who's examining another phone.

"Where were you heading—when you tried to leave?" I ask.

Furious typing. How those giant digits can navigate the tiny keyboard, baffles me.

"North to *Cindy*," says robotic, sexy Helga. Ben grimaces again; he meant *Sydney*.

"What's in Sydney?" I ask.

Ben shrugs. He points to his tattoo.

"I know about the dreams. You have a good setup here." I look around at his gear.

Typing.

"Temporary. I have a *boot* waiting at the *fiery*."

Ben shakes his head. 'Boat' and 'ferry', I got it.

He resumes typing.

"I leave soon. They will come looking, maybe already. They know this place."

He hesitates, then types.

"I can give you supplies, but I can't help you."

I shake my head.

"One of us has to live to tell about this," I say, smiling. Ben's cigarettes are the real deal, strong as fuck—I wonder if the yellow filter is for display purposes only.

Ben types.

"Generator at the rear. Fenced, locked. Kill it, they will be blind. Tonight is party at the Centre. Most passed out by *hen*." Ben sighs.

Ten, got it. I nod. He types.

"Can I ask you a question?" I tap the ash into an empty pop can.

He stops typing and looks up.

"When's your birthday?"

I regret the words as soon as I say them. Why would I ask that, what was I thinking?

He pushes the hair off his forehead, contemplates his cigarette for a moment, then picks up the phone and types.

"Today."

We look at one another for a long moment, each of us dragging on our cigarettes in silence, like a pair of aloof hipsters at a Jazz Club, introspective and distant.

I break the stalemate.

"How will you get to your boat, you have to go past the Manor?"

He types.

"I will get there."

"Have any others made it?" I ask.

He shakes his head and continues typing.

"Wait until sunset, walk in, stay off road."

I nod. A more bizarre conversation I have never had. It dawns on me that my journey is unfolding like an unscripted satire, an allusion of reality reminiscent of a Mel Brook's movie.

I put out my smoke in the pop can.

"I should get moving," I say, standing. Ben butts out his cigarette and rises.

He points to a five-gallon gas can beside the Harley.

"Thanks," I say.

I grab the can and head for the door.

CHAPTER 49

Replacing the gas cap, my eyes fall to the lake; distant, foreboding, the pathway to Sydney. I have half a tank now, plenty considering my odds of surviving the next eight hours are questionable. Ben emerges from the back, carrying a case of beer and a carton of cigarettes. He walks to the truck and drops the items in the back. Alexander Keith's India Pale Ale, of all things.

"You're a man of exceptional resources," I say. Ben almost cracks a smile, but not quite. He hands me two boxes of shells, ammunition for my Glock. He pauses to type into his phone.

It's a male voice this time, robotic, drab, but a better fit, none the less.

"Hope you get to enjoy a few." He pulls two bottles from his back pockets, handing me one. We both open and drink.

"Cold, beauty," I say.

Ben puts down his bottle a moment and types.

"Thank you. Come to Sydney when you're done playing Rambo."

I smile.

"Thanks for this, the supplies."

He waves off the thank you. I sense a tad of guilt, shame perhaps, from a man who probably never backed down from a fight in his life.

But this is not his fight. And I don't blame him.

We both pause to gaze out over the Bras d'Or, the waters calm, free of man, peaceful. I wonder what lies on the other side, what lies in wait. I wonder if I'll ever find out.

Ben types for what seems like a minute. I drink and watch him until he finishes. He hits enter, holding out the phone.

"Listen to your spirit guide, your inner voice. You have a purpose. This is a journey. The girl saw it in you. You are not Jack, not anymore. We have all changed, all of us. Something is happening, our meeting was not chance, it was fate. Wait for the *sigh*, you will know it when it comes. I will see you again."

Ben shakes his head, but I understood the meaning completely. I consider his words, thinking back to Allie, her beliefs, her fears. I look to my watch then gaze up at the sun. It's going on four, time to get moving.

"I don't think I'm that guy," I say, "but I'm happy we crossed paths. Give 'em hell in Sydney."

Ben nods. He types.

"Avoid Baddeck. Bad. Like the movies bad."

I nod. He types.

"Why did you ask me about my birthday?"

I shrug. "I don't know."

We finish our bottles, dropping the empties onto the grass. When we shake, I feel his power, his spirit, transferring strength into me.

"And Happy Birthday," I say, climbing into the truck.

A minute later, I'm barrelling down the laneway, Ben watching, the mountain of a man, with the gentle soul, my new found friend.

Funny, the people you meet in an apocalypse.

CHAPTER 50

Ben had his plan.

Take a boat north to Sydney.

Rene and I crossed at Little Narrows twice, once on our drive out to Sydney, and again on the drive back. The cable ferry ran vehicles back and forth across the narrow channel, twenty-four hours a day, seven days a week. If the ferry was ever out of service, or if someone didn't want to pay the fare, Orangedale Road was the alternate route, but that added forty minutes to the jaunt. An old Presbyterian Church with a cemetery in its backyard graced the shores of the Narrows, laden with aging crosses and crumbling tombstones, the dead keeping watch over the living. I never saw a sailboat or fisherman use the channel, but I knew the waterway led out towards the ocean, to the port of Sydney and beyond.

Ben stashed a boat there. He was cunning and knew the area. He could make his way north by water, or cross the channel, find a car, and drive up Highway 223, the scenic Bras d'Or route that followed the lake's east side all the way to Sydney. Not a lot up that way, the threat level would be low.

Sydney.

I uncap my fourth beer, promising myself this will be the last. I can't afford to get fucked up. Not tonight. My head is throbbing, the aspirins no match for my new found resistance to over-the-counter medication. To the west the sun is beginning to set, the winds picking up, the temperature cooling.

And I'm sweating. But I shouldn't be.

Either my wound is infected, or my illness is back. Maybe it never left. Tonight I can't afford either affliction.

I glance out to the highway. I'm parked atop an old farmer's road tucked into the hillside, the laneway overgrown and leading nowhere, an apt metaphor for my current lot in life. From this vantage point I can see vehicles coming or going, north or south; an ideal location to sit and wait.

I take a drink, wishing like hell the pounding in my head would subside. Tonight is Saturday the 21st, and according to Ben, party night. I'd driven by the Community Centre on past visits, it was a newer facility, unlike most of the run-down structures and shanties that lined that stretch of highway. The place was two kilometres from my position, far enough away to be out from under anyone's nose, close enough to walk. Ben said most would be lucid by ten, drug-induced comas, some wandering back to their motel rooms, others lying where they fall. Like a Stompin' Tom Sudbury Saturday Night, only Cape Breton style.

But Victor and his posse would not be among them. Not after ten anyhow. He and his trusted few won't partake in frivolity, at least not to excess, not with the peasants. Nobles don't dine with the serfs. They'd head back to the Manor, and Allie would be with them, or at least somewhere close by.

And that's when I make my move.

I spent the last hour going over my plan, in between cigarettes and beer, mapping out my road to victory, my path to heroism.

My Rambo moment.

But the more I consider it, the more a Brian Mill's moment is apropos, considering the circumstances. She was *Taken.*

In an hour I'll drive in close, leave the truck, and head out on foot. If patrols are about, I walk from here. No biggie. Either way, depending on who I encounter, my destination is the Manor. If the shit storm morphs into a hurricane, I'm on foot the entire way. Two guards I can handle, and if what Ben says is accurate, I have a chance. That is if the fever doesn't spike and drop me in my tracks.

I pop two more aspirin and grab the thermal goggles. I have an advantage with these, an unexpected one, especially if I can disable the generator. If I can kill their power, surprise is on my side, as long as I move quickly and don't shoot myself.

I set the goggles down and examine the rest of my gear; shotgun, ammunition, a few sticks of fireworks I kept in the bag since the RV, Bowie knife, multi-tool, binoculars, body armour, handcuffs.

I have plenty of ammo, thanks to Ben, but not knowing the layout of the property, not knowing what kind of crazy ass surveillance equipment they might have, I'm going in blind. I may need every bullet, every shell, or none of them. I may never get off a shot.

I light a cigarette and take a gulp. The beer is satisfying, not cold, but soothing, my body craving a dozen, maybe a chaser on the side. But I tell myself I have to earn my reward. Sew before I reap. After a job well done, no mortal wounds, mission accomplished, I can get shit-faced. I'll toast to Big Ben, the only sonofabitch who can get his hands on Keith's in the apocalypse.

Headlights approach from my left, down below the embankment. The vehicle passes by, not slowing, carrying on southbound.

Looks like the party's starting.

I unplug my phone from the charger and glance at the time. It's going on seven-thirty. Most of them are arriving or already there. This will be some party—Saturday night with the boys, no sports, no women, just a plethora of stoned creeps living *la Vida Loca*. Like a fucked up Ceilidh with a crew of backwoods fiddle players, distant cousins to the banjo playing retards in *Deliverance*. I wouldn't set foot in that place, not without a shotgun and a cork.

The sun's gone down, the darkness absolute; no streetlights, no lit up farmhouses, no flickering lights across the lake, just the moon and stars above. The moon hovers, like a beacon in the North, a signal for weary travellers, calling out to them in the night.

Only the north meant trouble.

Baddeck.

A once popular tourist destination, the quaint village was the gateway to the Cabot Trail, northern portion, a must-see for every visitor exploring the island. From its all-you-can-eat lobster suppers and world-class golf courses, to the Alexander Graham Bell Museum, I wonder what type of hell descended upon that town. I can only imagine the devastation.

Ben suggested I avoid it.

Allie mentioned it too. She'd overheard them talking; how it was off limits, home to the wanderers, killers, those beyond redemption. Orders were to stay away, the roads blockaded, warning signs erected. Rumour had it they hunted survivors, captured them, tortured them, ate them. That is real apocalyptic shit. Cannibalism. How can any self-respecting apocalypse exist without it?

Baddeck was to be my escape route. My Plan B.

How bad could it be?

I stop to refocus, my mind racing, my thoughts on hyper-drive. Ben's cigarette is making me ill and I toss it out the window. I glance at my reflection in the visor mirror, the tiny bulb illuminating the individual beads of sweat on my forehead. I pull back the bandage and examine the wound. It looks infected—infected as all fuck.

A car horn honks in the distance, then a blast from a siren.

I tap out two more aspirins and drink.

CHAPTER 51

I lean against the truck retching, my stomach muscles convulsing, dispelling the last of the crackers and bile. I've thrown up the beer; there's nothing left to vomit. My face is flushed, my ears are ringing, like I've picked up a high-pitched frequency, one that only dogs—or the terminally fucked, can hear.

I straighten up, hoping for the wave to pass. This is what a migraine must feel like, a headache so severe, vomiting is the only recourse. Fuck me.

What hero gets sick in the final act?

It doesn't happen, shouldn't happen, not in any movie I've seen. Stallone didn't abort his mission because of streptococcal pharyngitis. Arnold didn't disengage after a bad burrito. And Qui-Jon Jinn wouldn't let a little thing like a hundred and four degree temperature stop him. That shit makes for bad writing.

But this was real life—this was happening, now. I have no understudy, no one waiting in the wings should I falter.

The wave of nausea passes. I pop out more aspirin, convinced I'd thrown up my last four, swallowing them whole, resisting the urge to throw them back up.

Below me the search teams are out, vehicles travelling up and down the highway, looking for Big Ben—and his accomplice. I recognize the jeep with the roof lights, the asshole kangaroo hunters. They've been up and down the area, lighting up the darkness like a paving crew at midnight. Their wingman in the second vehicle has the handheld spotlight, shining the beacon into the ditches and up into the hillside. I'm hidden off the main road, elevated, but if one of those beams catches the truck's reflective lights, I'm fucked.

I take a deep breath as I adjust my backpack, letting the crisp night air clear my lungs. Satisfied my straps are tight enough, I sling the rifle and take a last look into my bag of toys. There's no room for the shotgun, not this trip, but I may need it again one day, God willing. It's the Glock and sniper rifle tonight, and a couple of surprises as backup. I pocket the truck's keys and quietly push the door closed.

Time for Plan C.

I crouch down as headlights come into view from below. I can make out voices, two-way radio talk, men barking updates. Every now and again tires screech and engines rev past, as if they found something, or someone.

I move into the bush, careful to watch my footing. I can't afford a spill, not now, not again. It's a twenty-minute trek on even ground to the Community Centre, but I can't chance stepping out into the open. I make my way down the hillside, pausing every now and again to listen. The pale moon shines through the canopy overhead, casting diffused light over the highway. I stop.

Headlights approach from the direction of the Centre. Two vehicles race past me, not interested in anything or anyone hiding in the tree line, not this time.

A steady stream of sweat finds its way into my eyes, causing me to pause and wipe them every few seconds. The vision in my right eye is blurry, but thankfully the aspirins are kicking in, lowering the pain in my skull to a dull throb. I no longer feel like vomiting, but the dizziness is concerning. It's like the early days on the island, gripped in a duality of sickness, body and mind, physical and mental, one feeding off the other. I'm due for a relapse, but even so, history suggests my instincts kick up a notch when my mental faculties go down for the count. For now, I plod on.

I err on the side of speed and leave the safety of the tree line, moving closer to the gravel shoulder. I can always hit the dirt, roll and find cover in the tall grass if I get cornered. My combat wear is night approved, black on black; I can blend in if I have to.

Up ahead, on the opposite side of the road is a red Ford Flex with a white roof. I recognize the licence plate—it's my vehicle. A corpse is secured atop the roof, struck in that familiar pose I've come to know. The only variation is the fireman's axe sticking out of its chest, recently put there no doubt, a grisly warning to others, and yours truly. They're taking no chances, not anymore. Crucifixion by conveyance takes too long, as they found out with Ben, a luxury they've come to regret. Fuckers.

The Community Centre is dead ahead. The place is lit up, an oddity in an apocalypse, like a single match flame in a world gone black. I watch as a car pulls into the lot. At least ten vehicles are parked out front with dark silhouettes milling about the driveway, talking, shouting, carousing.

Sorry to ruin the party fuck-wads.

I resume walking, picking up the pace, and when I get close enough, I slink back into the tree line. I remove the backpack and set the rifle down. The fever's holding but my adrenaline is countering, that and the aspirin, or so I figure. I'm thankful the migraine is backing off, keeping a low profile, cooperating for the time being. I pick up the binoculars.

Lights shine from inside the Centre, the windows emitting a warm amber hue, like a secluded farmhouse under a moonless sky. Silhouettes mill about the entrance doors.

I glance further up the highway as lights approach. Two vehicles pull into the parking lot in tandem. At once the group of men approach. One is a police SUV, the other, a black, BMW.

I switch the binoculars for the thermals, hoping to catch a glimpse of the occupants.

Hoping to see her.

I notice movement out of the corner of my eye and pan right. I thought I saw something move, but it could just be my brain failing, my visual acuity at the mercy of my rising core temperature. I strain to see what it was I missed, but I see nothing.

Then I pan up.

Two figures stand atop the expansive low-pitched roof, one on either side.

Snipers. Both wear dark jerseys, one looks to be a Bruins third jersey, the other I can't make out.

They're not partying, they're on watch. All business tonight. One looks out through a pair of binoculars while the other smokes a cigarette.

I shift my gaze back to the vehicles. Bull exits the BMW, Oakley's on, and steps towards the group. They disperse, allowing him a wide berth. He leans in and speaks with the other driver.

I can't tell if anyone else is in the car.

But where else would she be?

I have to wait. Without the element of surprise, my quest would be over faster than a Tai Chi student taking on UFC legend Georges St-Pierre. I have one shot. I need to think like Kato in the *Pink Panther* movies, surprise the shit out of them. I have to get creative—'hiding inside a fridge' creative—imaginative, bat-shit ingenious.

I wipe the sweat from my brow and put down the goggles, allowing my vision to readjust. The dizziness comes in waves, playing havoc with my senses. I think back to the motel, to waking up with no memory of recent days. It was as if my existence was compromised, my essence suspended, albeit temporarily, for some greater purpose I couldn't understand. It feels like someone or something up there just hit the repeat button.

A blast of a car horn catches my attention. A vehicle races past, pulling into the Community Centre, the tires screeching as the car skids to a halt. I grab the binoculars. Two figures emerge, agitated, excited, I hear voices and see arms pointing in all directions, others gathering around. Within a minute, two cars are squealing out of the lot, racing north, in my direction.

They found the truck.

Bull is barking orders, directing traffic. He leans back into the SUV.

I pan up. The snipers are on alert, rifles up, cigarette gone.

I reach for the backpack, knocking it over instead. I grasp at the earth, feeling around for any items that may have fallen out. I touch something cylindrical and snatch it up.

My finger inadvertently flicks on the flashlight.

I fumble for the off switch but in that instant, my fingers don't cooperate. I jam the light down the front of my pants and crouch down.

Someone is shouting.

They spotted the light.

Fuck me.

BANG!

The shot shatters the night, the bullet stray, but not by much. He can't see me, but he knows I'm here—and I'm not waiting around to be the third on a match, I know that analogy. It's time to go.

I jump up, grab the backpack and rifle, and start moving. The terrain becomes steep quickly as I struggle to grasp onto trees for leverage. I have no idea where I'm headed, no knowledge of the area, other than the highway below. If I keep going up, I may be able to lose them—or not, but my options are few.

Shouts echo into the night. Footsteps crash through the forest floor, an army of predators unleashed, frenzied hounds after a solitary fox. All in the name of a sport called *Kill Jack*.

I continue climbing, each step steeper, more treacherous. Branches scrape my forehead and I feel a trickle of blood seep into my eye, fucking with my vision, not that I can see much anyhow. I pause to wipe the blood from my face.

The voices are louder, war cries ringing out through the forest.

I soon reach an impasse, the terrain too steep to traverse. I look around for an alternate escape route, but there's nothing. I unsling the rifle and pull out the Glock, my hands shaking, my heart beating furiously, my energy tanking.

No choice left but to make my stand, here and now. I consider pulling out the thermals, but there's no time. They're too close, their primal war cries bating me, like predators encircling their prey.

Footsteps converge, within thirty feet, raspy breathing moves towards me. Then a voice.

"Come out, come out, wherever you are!"

The voice is jovial, comical almost, followed by a maniacal chuckle.

This asshole's getting it first.

I back myself against a tree, wipe the blood and sweat from my face, and raise the Glock. More shouting and yelling around me, branches and undergrowth snapping and crunching.

Footsteps, within twenty feet. The raspy breathing upon me.

"*Yoo, hoooo*—where are you?"

I'm reminded of a scene in *The Three Amigos*. I'd almost laugh, if I wasn't about to die.

The crunching sounds are closer, more distinct. The time for introductions has come. My finger spoons the trigger as I extend my arms, looking for movement, waiting for the first unfortunate asshole to show himself.

And then I hear it.

Quiet at first.

The footsteps stop.

Music.

I can't tell from where, but as it builds, I look down my belt line, not believing what is happening. I reach into my pocket.

My phone. The music is coming from my phone.

Fiddle music. The familiar ballad.

But the phone was turned off, set to a locked screen in case I inadvertently turned it on.

There's yelling, confusion, erratic flashlight beams shining in all directions.

And then I realize—it's not just my phone. The music is everywhere, in the air, the sky, hovering above the tree canopy, building to a haunting crescendo.

Allie was right.

The footsteps retreat. I stand frozen, holding my Glock in one hand, the phone in the other, no longer concerned the screen's glow will give away my location. I look to the screen saver, the photo of Rene and I at the Causeway. No App is engaged, no program active, yet the music plays.

Somewhere below me a car engine starts.

I pocket the phone and grab the rifle, navigating the hillside, looking for an opening in the dense brush. I find a cluster of smaller trees and stop. From here I can see the lake over the tip of the adjacent tree line. The music is emanating from the other side of the Bras d'Or, reverberating off the mountain behind me, consuming the forest with its foreboding refrain. I pull out the thermals and notice a low-hanging fog seeping across the water, magically almost, refracting the moonlight, as if embracing the ethereal accompaniment. Just like the Causeway.

I lower the goggles, looking around me, expecting reality to implode with another sign of rapid-fire dementia. But there is only darkness.

The ballad dissipates, diminuendo to single notes trailing in the wind. Soon the night is quiet again, save for the rustling of tree branches and the hum of insects. I make my way back down the hillside, careful and vigilant, pausing every few seconds to listen. I stumble upon my original camp and remove the binoculars, looking out across the highway.

Chaos consumes the predatory crackheads. Cars leave the Centre, tires screeching in the night. The BMW and SUV are gone.

A chill envelops me, as if someone just opened the island's freezer door. I look in astonishment as the fog creeps inland towards the Community Centre; a Bras d'Or mist, consuming all in its path, like a harbinger of fate, searching for weary souls.

CHAPTER 52

I embrace the chill in the air. Around me, the low-hanging mist hovers, a fog that was not here twenty minutes ago. I'd heard of strange weather phenomenon, extreme shifts, but I'd never witnessed anything quite like this. This was different.

I abandon the tree line and head towards the open road. I can see ten feet ahead and no more, everything beyond lost in a billion droplets of brackish water, the Bras d'Or's gift to the night. The only light visible is the amber glow from the Community Centre windows, the exterior lights now extinguished. All is silent, everyone gone, or hunkered down inside, laying low. For whatever reason, music tamed the savage beast and struck fear in the likes of man, Victor's men. The fog's musical accompaniment is bizarre, unexpected, a foreboding reminder that all is not as it once was. Whatever the explanation, the roadway is clear, barren, quiet, consumed in an ethereal cloud.

I walk down the centre of the two lanes, regenerated, my illness in hiatus, my confidence elevating. I fear no confrontation; my senses tell me there will be none, at least not here, not now. Every now and again I glance down to confirm the yellow lines are beneath my feet, ensuring I haven't wandered off towards the ditch, off course.

Follow the yellow brick road.

I chuckle to myself as I reach for a cigarette. I'm losing it. Whether it's the infection, withdrawal, or a combination therein, I can't shake the feeling my mind and body are no longer in sync, no longer working as a team. Reality and perception are indistinguishable, at a crossroads. It's like I've been removed from the equation, like I'm watching myself from afar, a doppelganger navigating the apocalypse; a game piece on a game board, awaiting the next roll. I've felt like this before.

Delusion or desire?

Perhaps I am at the mercy of some intuitive collective conscience after all, one that dictates behaviour, mapping out humankind's return to prowess—one bizarre twist at a time. Or maybe I'm victim of a transcendental mind fuck, a sanity loophole, a dish served frosty with a side of oblivion.

Where does the answer lie?

Allie.

I've not sensed her presence. The dreams have dissipated, the memory oblique.

I take a long drag and stop to gauge my bearings. I've been walking for half an hour, the fog relentless, the air heavy. I take out a water bottle and drink. Hydration is important; I can't afford to add muscle cramps to my growing list of afflictions. Not with a battle looming. I replace the bottle and pull out my binoculars.

Just around the bend is a faint glow, luminescence in an earthly cloud.

I've arrived.

The main entrance to the Manor sits a hundred metres ahead, illuminated. The generator must be running around the clock if they're keeping the gate lit at this hour. Maybe it's business as usual, or maybe they're expecting company.

Either way, the generator is my priority. As long as both my mind and body suit up, that is.

CHAPTER 53

BRAS d'OR MANOR

Twelve thousand square feet of luxury set back against the Cape Breton hillside. At least that's what Wikipedia says, the old world's all-knowing all-telling, portal of infinite wisdom. Victor would choose this palazzo to call home, absolutely. After all, it's a showpiece, an anomaly in a place where most lived in clapboard homes with curled shingles. Judging by its size, the Manor must have come with one hell of a backup generator.

A six-foot high wrought iron fence runs the expanse of property's frontage, a football field in length; Canadian field, not NFL. The main gate is lit by a pair of antique streetlamps, one on each side of the cement pillars. Beneath the glow of each lamp stands a sniper. They wear identical Edmonton Oiler jerseys, retro design, both with rifles slung across their backs. Watching the mist encircle them, their silhouettes aglow in the ominous fog, the image reminds me of a movie poster; the arrival of the old priest in *The Exorcist*, illuminated under the foggy glow of a streetlamp.

The battle of good versus evil, about to commence.

The driveway beyond the guards winds its way up the hillside, lit with low wattage bulbs lining the base of the laneway. The building is cloaked in fog, masked in a dark veil, save for a light in a second-floor bedroom window. The master suite.

I turn my gaze back to the snipers. They haven't sensed my presence. They don't know I'm stalking them, not a hundred feet from where they stand, close enough I can hear them fart. From this distance, even in the fog, I could take one out with little effort—Call of Duty camper style. But I'd not get my second shot off. It would be all for naught, counter-productive. One for the price of two is no deal, not an option except as a last resort. I have time on my side, patience as my ally, so long as my faculties don't let me down.

One of the two lights a smoke, the other shines a flashlight across the roadway. The powerful beam exposes the massive cloud of fog and nothing beyond. I remain still as he pans in my direction, confident he won't see me. The light switches off.

The two don't speak, a common trait amongst the greasy haired beanpoles, dedication to their profession perhaps. I reach for my thermals, but the fog is too thick. I replace them, gazing back up towards the Manor, to the second-floor window.

Is she in there?

Now would be a good time for a sign, an epiphany, a forerunner revisited, something, anything that might offer direction, sharpen my focus, validate my lunacy. Maybe a tune on the old phone for inspiration?

I pause to wipe my eyes, my vision still struggling. The bandage on my temple is soaked through, damp and slimy, like a sloppy sponge, the adhesive failing. No matter, I don't have time to worry about trivial things like whether or not I live beyond tonight. Surviving a gunfight but dying from sepsis is the devil's nightcap, last call at the bar of life, comic relief at an alcoholic's expense.

I rein in my thoughts and concentrate on my breathing, clearing my mind, focusing on what I'm doing and what needs to be done. I close my eyes, and in that moment I feel the moist air on my skin, the vapour in my lungs, the sounds of the night. I allow the island to infiltrate my soul, embrace my being, stoke my spirit, and revive my will.

And it hits me.

The island is my spirit guide.

It has been all along.

We have been one. With Sanctuary lost, the island guided me here.

Allie was right.

God works in mysterious ways.

My breathing slows, my heart rate lowers, I hear nothing but my own thoughts.

Then I open my eyes.

The island is my spirit guide?

Am I fucked?

I look around, convinced I've lost the sanity battle. Since when have I become a philosophical Zen-Master prophet?

Since I've lost my fucking mind.

I shake my head and look out towards the gates. Both snipers are pacing in a concentric circle, as if sensing something, or someone.

I remove Allie's jersey from the backpack.

Time for a costume change.

CHAPTER 54

A warm front overtakes the cold air, perpetuating the fog with revitalized gusto. The water density in the atmosphere is sublime, ridiculously thick, unrelenting. This must be what the Moors is like, on a full moon, only I don't envy being the unsuspecting backpacker.

I stand twenty-feet from the snipers, in between them. They don't know I'm here. Other than the occasional grunt from the sniper on my left—his primitive means of communication, the two don't speak. Why use words when a grunt will do? The thermals dangle from my neck and I raise them as I step closer. The two look barely out of their teens, brothers in arms, tall, lanky, unwashed bangs like strained spaghetti. The physical descriptors must be a prerequisite for the job, they've all looked identical, jerseys the only differentiating feature. But these two are matching, right down to the numbers on their backs.

Ninety-nine.

I lower the thermals and wipe the sweat from my eyes. Something in my backpack shifts.

The snipers react, their footsteps erratic. I keep still, sliding my hand to the Bowie knife on my belt. The blade is large enough to filet a moose, a cross between a Rambo and a Crocodile Dundee.

"You hear that?"

First one to speak, ever.

The flashlight beam comes on and I'm exposed. I have no idea if they'll spot me.

"It's bullshit," replies the other voice.

The light pans right over me. My knife is out. I wait for it. The beam dances past. They can't see me.

As if by some unforeseen cruel hand of fuck-with-Jack fate, I have to cough. Damn Ben's cancer sticks. I choke back the urge and wait until the flashlight beam has moved off, then walk between the two, like an archangel, sashaying my way through the Pearly Gates.

A minute later, I'm heading up the driveway, the low voltage garden lights illuminating my way.

As I reach the crest of the hillside, the enormity of the palazzo becomes apparent. Three stories tall, as wide as a sprawling villa, the grand entrance would impress a Saudi Prince. Above my head, the glow from the master suite illuminates the surrounding mist. The suite's balcony is enormous, enclosed in glass, looking out over the Bras d'Or, easily seating a dozen.

That's where she'll be.

I fight the urge to cough despite being out of earshot. Below me, the snipers remain on watch. I keep to the shadows, tromping through what once must have been flowerbeds and manicured gardens, keeping close to the outer wall, avoiding the windows. Raised voices echo from the roadway and I pause to look. A car's headlights illuminate the main gate. I crouch down and watch, but the vehicle does not approach, likely mobile patrols checking in with the gatekeepers.

I move quickly to the far side of the building, a stone walkway under my feet. The trickling of water catches my ear, no doubt the creek that traverses the property. I stick close to the building, feeling the brick as I move along, hoping not to step into a moat or goldfish pond. As I reach the corner, I take a wider berth around a garden of rose bushes and decaying perennials abutted against the wall, lining the entire length of the northern side.

The eastern sky lights up with a flash, followed by a distant rumble. The weather is onboard tonight, thunderstorms approaching, earthquakes and lightning on deck. I look to see if a bad moon is watching over me, but the fog is too thick.

But something more important lies ahead.

I hear the hum of the generator.

The sound is coming from the rear of the property, Bras d'Or Manor's back forty. Navigating my way around a six-foot hedge, I come upon a shed, attached to the rear of the structure. I pull out my flashlight. Beside the shed is a small fenced-in compound, the generator within, humming away quietly. She's a big deasil, mammoth, a backup to the main electrical grid, the envy of Nova Scotia Power. A place this size needed a second power source, and this bitch was the motherfucker of all generators.

I remove my backpack and pull out the bolt cutters. Snipping the padlock, I step inside and examine the unit. Heavy gauge wiring leads to the main panel. I flip the cover open, hoping to find an override or power switch, not sure what to expect, but wishing for the best. I figure turning this big bastard off can't require an engineering degree, but I've overestimated my abilities before. If I fuck this up, I won't have to worry about my escape plan.

As if on cue, the sky lights up in a brilliant flash, followed by another rumble. The storm is on tap.

I leave my tools and step out of the compound. No lights are visible, and it's just as well, the darker the better. Further up I can see large sliding glass doors leading out to the gardens. Benches and decorative urns surround the walkway; a tremendous water fountain splits the pathway, each section leading out to the pool and gazebo in the distance. Closer to me is what looks to be an enclave with a pair of doors, likely the servant's entrance. I approach and try the knob, but it's locked. Removing my knife, I wedge the blade between the frame and latch, gently applying pressure until I hear a click. I leave the door as is, just in case of perimeter alarms.

Seconds later, I'm back at the generator, my mind impressed with how quiet the machinery is, considering the size. I make a mental note, something to remember for the next apocalypse. I open my backpack and remove the essentials, extra magazines, thermals, flashlight. The rest stays here.

Lightning flashes overhead and I hear the first drops of rain hitting the pavement. The rain will obliterate the fog; I have to move now. I tuck the magazines into my pockets, contemplating whether the length of the jersey will impede my ability to reload under fire. I should tuck in but I won't. I want to look like them. I want them to know what it's like. Fashion takes precedence.

I shine the flashlight on the control panel, my finger hovering over the kill switch. The second I hit it, there is no turning back, the final battle begins, the countdown to extermination starts.

Am I ready?

Fuck no.

But they aren't either. I do a quick body check, ensuring I have everything I need, then punch the switch; the generator chugs to a halt. I grab the bolt cutters and count to sixty, not knowing how long an electrical charge remains in the main line but erring on the side of safety. On sixty, I sever the main cord. They won't start this bastard anytime soon.

Lightning flashes and the rain explodes into a downpour.

I hear yelling, voices calling out, distant, but the excitement is palpable.

Plan C underway.

CHAPTER 55

The door opens with a creak. I peer inside; all dark, no signs of life. As I step in, I notice a dim ambient light emanating beneath a doorway to my left, likely a main hallway or kitchen.

I consider emergency lighting but I doubt the place is rigged, at least I hope not. Battery backups should have drained the first few days after the grid when down. By the looks of things, I'm in a storage room, racks and shelves line the walls on three sides, an industrial-sized refrigerator sits in the corner. I flick on my flashlight for a second; the exit door is adjacent to the large fridge, a sign displaying the words 'Please wipe your feet before entering'. Yeah, I'll be fucking sure to do that.

Voices call out from above, at least two, maybe three. I have no way of knowing how many people are inside, how may adversaries I should expect. My hope is not a lot.

I follow the length of a long steel table laden with boxes of non-perishables and canned goods. Reaching the door, I listen. Footsteps, but distant, I can't tell if they're above me or on the same level. The place is huge, and the layout a mystery, especially in darkness. I push on the door, my other hand feeling for the comfort of my Glock.

The darkness is absolute, wherever the dim glow from under the door had come from, it's gone. Raising the thermals to my eyes, I see the hallway extends in three directions, right, left and straight. I decide to head straight, by my estimation I should be heading towards the front. Distant voices emanate through the wall. Someone calls out.

The reply is audible.

"Checking the generator. Jeez, Frankie Goes Hollywood—*relax*, cheesecake."

This person is on the same level as me and close. I step to the end of the hallway and push open the door.

It's a den or sitting room. A camping lantern sits on the floor across from the entrance, casting a dim glow throughout. An enormous fireplace anchors the elaborate room, the kind big enough to walk into, the mantle adorned with brass artifacts. Above the fireplace is taxidermy-reject moose head, one ugly specimen with bulbous, unnatural eyes and a questionable facial expression. Matching loveseats flank the fireplace and bookshelves line the outer walls. The ceiling above my head is two stories high, opening up into the upper level, a bannister lining the second-floor overlook.

Form outside I hear yelling, a car horn, an orchestra of chaos.

I pause to check my status. I'm still sweating, but my vision is okay, no dizziness, and that's a plus. Footsteps scurry past, outside the room, I can't make out the direction, and I can't afford to wait and find out. As I move across the room, I notice a black Yamaha upright tucked into an alcove beside a grand bay window draped in a violet curtain. I step up, careful to stay low, the lantern's light exposing my presence.

I look out from behind the curtain.

Rain is falling, steady but no longer a downpour. The fog has thinned, almost gone. I look past the entranceway, down towards the gate.

Fuck.

I bring up the thermals. Six people mill about the roadway, headlights from a pair of vehicles illuminating the area. A third car pulls up, then a fourth. One is the kangaroo poacher's jeep with the full array of blinding hunting lights, adding to the party.

They have an army.

Jesus Jack, what were you thinking?

What's my plan D?

I don't have one. I move from the window towards the door. Paintings of elderly old farts line the walls, but I don't stop to admire them, the irrelevant old coots scrutinizing me with pompous glares. I turn the knob and step through.

A door slams shut from somewhere.

"Update, what we got?"

The voice is from upstairs. There's no response. To my left is the foyer, massive, beyond that a double spiral staircase leading up to the second floor. Candlelight flickers from the second story. At least they don't have backup power, not yet anyway.

I hear footsteps.

More honking from outside, more assholes joining the party. Did I really expect things to go smoothly, according to plan?

I pause to reassess my next move when it hits me. Plan D.

A hostage situation. If I can grab fuck-nuts, I have a chance, slim as it might be.

Footsteps approach.

I hit the stairs three at a time until I reach the top. A pair of candles sit on the carpeted floor, creating elongated shadows throughout the corridor.

A trucker's air horn blares from outside, the blast long and powerful.

Shots ring out. Something is happening.

I hear the CRUNCH, the awful, wrenching sound of metal on metal, a high-speed impact, two unmovable objects, one catastrophic result.

Repeated shots, screams.

"What the fuck's going on?"

The voice came from behind one of the doors. The hallway extends left and right. To the left is the bannister that overlooks the sitting room below, the room I just left. The voice came from the right. I count four doors and a double door at the end, the only one lit from underneath. The master suite.

Footsteps rush by, beneath me, on the main floor.

"Who ordered beer delivery for fuck sakes?" The voice trails off.

More chaos outside, sporadic shots and screams.

"Deal with it." The voice came from the master. I step closer, pausing to listen at each door before moving on.

"Fucking gladly." The voice is below me. They're communicating with walkie-talkies.

I hear doors opening then slamming shut from the main floor.

Two chairs sit out front the master suite, likely for guards. Thankfully, my hydro interruption pressed them into service elsewhere, and with any luck, whatever's happening at the gate, will keep them occupied.

Above the doors is a Cape Breton Flag, recently placed there, sadly appropriate for the nouveau riche décor. Nothing like a little island pride.

I raise the thermals and survey the hallway. The candlelight is sufficient to navigate, but the thermals make it real, visual and gritty. I step up to the doors of the suite, pressing my ear close. I listen. There's movement inside, someone mumbles, only one voice, as far as I can tell.

I take out my Glock, wondering why the fuck I didn't already have it out. I reassess my combat technique, or lack thereof. Cops don't stand in front of a closed door when engaging a bad guy, so why am I? A surprise shotgun blast through the half-inch MDF is a game-ender. I contemplate my options. Rush in or stealth? The room is lit, at least by candlelight, so night vision won't help, my Seal Team tactical advantage, lost.

Time has slowed, like an unfolding nightmare in high definition. I can't afford to debate my options any longer.

I listen, then reach for the knob, knowing it will be locked.

But it opens.

My finger slides to the trigger as I push on the door.

A Coleman lantern sits on a table illuminating a king-size bed, draped in a blood red comforter. No one is around, but the glass doors leading to the balcony are open.

I step in.

The spray hits me between the eyes.

Like being hit with a sucker punch, I drop, blinded, clinging to my gun, unable to counter. My lungs seize as I struggle to take in air. Then I feel the crack, followed by that familiar flash of white.

CHAPTER 56

Each breath is torture, like being on a ventilator made in Taiwan. My eyes open, struggling to focus. I'm seated on the floor, my back against a wall, blood trickling down the side of my face, pooling at my feet. I can't see out of my right eye.

He stands on the balcony, back to me, wearing silk blue pyjamas, the kind privileged assholes wear, his bony frame peeking through at odd angles. I wipe my eye with the back of my hand, knowing I'm contaminated in residue spray. My head throbs with each heartbeat, the pain palpable. My temple's been split open—again, my jersey awash in red.

When I cough, I taste pepper spray, the residue tormenting my nasal passages, inflaming my mucous membranes, snot flowing with fervour. My breathing is laboured, raspy, like an asthmatic in a pollen factory.

"Welcome back. Thought we'd lost you there."

He approaches, holding my thermals in his hands.

"Nice jersey. You've got red on you."

I know the reference but ignore it.

He drops the thermals on the bed.

"High tech. Impressive. Something tells me I underestimated you Jack."

He pulls up a chair and sits down across from me, interrogation style. I struggle to focus, my left eye stinging, my right eye clocked out.

This guy is not your Alpha male. Not by a long shot. His receding hairline and weak chin pale in comparison to his bulging eyes; peepers that would make Marty Feldman envious. But what he lacks in physical appearance, he makes up for with his maniacal stare, yellow sclera the size of ping-pong balls, exuding malevolence, pure evil.

He removes a vape from his pocket. I watch as he fiddles with it for a minute, then inhales, savouring the experience, blowing the cloud of aromatic steam in my face.

"You fucked up my generator, huh?"

He reaches forward, tilting my head to the side, examining the injury.

"That's nasty. I appear to have reopened old wounds. How'd you get that one? One of my boys I hope."

His lip curls and he smiles, slyly.

"Are you still pissed at me?"

He puffs on his vape. I try to sit up, but my muscles won't cooperate. The vision in my left eye blurs, the dim lighting not helping.

Victor stands and walks back to the balcony, gazing out.

"Your cavalry arrived while you were having a nap. Damn, something I never thought I'd see in an apocalypse, but happier for the experience. The problem's been rectified, however."

He turns and faces me.

"I told them to be patient. That you'd come. They doubted

me, and yet here you are."

He sits back down.

"What's the matter, you don't approve of my methods for dealing with dissenters? A little mandatory fresh air and sunshine? Jesus died on the cross for our sins, I'm just a little more creative."

He leans closer.

"No one's breaking you out Jack. Certainly not that giant Injun. You know why we call him Juicy Fruit?"

Another reference that clicks. My mind is sharp for the irrelevant.

Victor removes a can of pepper spray from his pocket and sets it down at my feet.

"Did you know that Oleoresin Capsicum doesn't work on ten-percent of the population? They're immune, able to fight through it. It's not foolproof."

He snaps his fingers, making sure I'm paying attention.

"But for an even smaller percentage, people with severe asthma for instance, it can be fatal. Like a bee sting allergy, those unfortunate few can't tolerate it, stop breathing outright."

I look around the room, wondering where she is.

"For a minute there, I thought you were one of the unfortunate few. Then again, the whack to the melon might have exacerbated things."

He chuckles. My gun belt and rifle lie atop the bed, along with my knife and Glock. On the floor, beside the night table is an expandable baton, police issue. His whacking stick.

"Why are you here Jack?" he asks, getting down to business.

I try to reply, but I'm consumed in a coughing fit.

"Take your time. When you're ready."

He inhales, watching me keenly, like a curious child with a new plaything.

"You know why," I reply.

He stands and picks up the baton off the floor. He returns, cleaning the bloody tip on my already saturated jersey.

"All of this," he gestures to the room, "this place, the people, society—you know what's going on here? You have any idea?"

His demeanour darkens. Despite the pain and difficulty breathing, I force myself to sit upright.

"Rebuild. Re-establish. Start over. But better this time."

He holds the baton an inch from my temple, as if matching the weapon to the wound.

"Recruiting followers, protecting the herd, banishing dissenters. That's what's going on here Jack."

He hovers over me, his pale fingers grasping the baton like some psychotic maestro.

"And you're trying to fuck that up."

He swings and I duck, the baton narrowly missing my forehead, penetrating the drywall behind me.

He smiles and sits back down.

"Just kidding. What's your story Jack? Where'd you come from? How'd you manage to get past my boys?"

I swallow, the chemical taste still strong in my sinuses.

"No story. Surviving. Just like you," I reply.

He ponders my response as if calculating my cooperation level on a scale of one to zero.

"Well that's an absolutely useless fucking answer. Surviving. Ooh, how bloody original, how exquisitely informative. Please, do tell me more."

"Where's the girl?"

He stands.

"I was wondering when we'd get around to that. Tell me Jack, what drives the human spirit—what propels an individual to challenge convention, to risk it all in the face of danger, death even?"

He looks at me, as if expecting a response.

"Heroes and damsels, am I right? No story complete without a love interest, conflict, a showdown?"

He pauses at the balcony, picking up a two-way radio. I hear indistinct chatter on the other end. He holds the radio to his lips.

"Update."

The radio crackles, then a response.

"Beauty. You?"

"Ten-four," Victor replies, "just getting to know one another. Stand by for orders."

"Copy that."

He sets the radio down and turns.

"The girl's dead."

He stares, awaiting a reaction, his yellow eyes flat, listless. But I don't give him one. Because I know he's a liar.

After a moment, he bursts out laughing.

"Kidding. Well sort of. She did die, that's true, but through the miracle of pharmaceuticals, life found a way. Like I did with you when I thought you were checking out. I wasn't quite ready to let you off the hook, not just yet."

He snatches something off the bedside table and steps up, sliding the lantern closer to me.

"You needed all the help you could get, Jackie-boy."

He holds up a small canister.

"Know what this is? It's Naloxone, nasal spray. Miracle cure for drug addicts. Brings the dead back to life—most of the time."

He sits down.

"Pardon my bluntness, but I don't know how well the two of you got along, but I'm not ashamed to admit that the girl and I fight—like cunts and dogs."

He smiles.

"Well her, mostly. She doesn't like me much, go figure. Now I'm no Elvis, but you can't be so choosy in an apocalypse, am I right? So we make compromises, every relationship does."

He holds up the canister, rotating it, analyzing it.

"I don't allow my woman or deputies to partake in mood altering substances, normally. But with her, short of hogtying her twenty-four seven, well, let's just say intimacy is a challenge. You've seen what she's capable of. Feisty. She would not hesitate to gouge out my eye, if given half a chance."

He looks at my wound.

"No offence."

His eyes drop to the pool of blood at my feet.

"And as much as a little oral pleasure would not be unwelcomed, that's a risk I am not willing to take. Who the fuck's going to sew it back on, am I right?"

He smirks, tilting his head, like the ever curious puppy. His warped mind is in two different worlds, one, pontificating, the other, planning my death.

"So I keep her medicated. Just enough she doesn't try to bite anything off. Not so much that she's out, comatose, I don't get off on the whole 'lie still and think of Britain' thing—or necrophilia, although I'd speculate that little abnormality has regained some popularity lately. No shortage of willing participants, huh?"

A siren wails from outside. Victor picks up the lantern and steps onto the balcony. He waves, then comes back in, setting the lamp down. He tosses me a towel from atop the bed.

"Don't bleed on the rug. It's Persian."

I glance down. The red pool inches towards a monstrous carpet that covers half the room.

"Where was I? Right, her death. She did die, earlier, that part was true. I miscalculated, happens sometimes, it's not a perfect science. Luckily I was back in time."

He holds up the canister and mimics pressing the plunger.

"Two doses, and she's back amongst the living. A little groggy, but just as feisty as ever."

He takes out his vape again.

"Back in the day they called it Skydiving. Two shit-rats would get together, one would OD, the other would watch. Once the heart stopped beating, buddy would give him a dose or two, bring him back from the brink. Intercept him at the Pearly Gates. Then they'd switch, take turns, do it all night or until the drugs were gone. It was the ultimate high, kind of like autoerotic asphyxiation I imagine. The strange things people do, huh?"

I stretch my legs when his attention is off me, testing my strength, my ability to stand.

"W-where is she?" I ask.

He blows a cloud of steam towards the ceiling then slides the lantern closer and leans in, staring into my eye.

"You know you really do look like shit. I mean really. And it's not just the blood or the fucked-up eye—you got some serious deathbed shit going on here." He motions to my entire face. "Maybe you got the plague. A new variant, a phase two mutation?"

"Where's Allie?" I repeat.

He breathes in some steam, holds it for a long moment, then exhales.

"Not that you're in a position to demand information—or that it's any of your fucking business, but she's no damsel, nor is she in distress. Quite the opposite actually. You're fortunate she took a shine to you. She's not one to volunteer the information, no one ever does, but I can tell you first hand, people who get confined to the Forensic Hospital in Dartmouth—East Wing, aren't there for rehabilitation. They're the societal rejects, psychopaths, dangerous offenders, cuckoo-for-coco-puffs. You get where I'm going with this?"

He blows another cloud of steam in my face.

"Even with that Justin Bieber haircut and the baggy clothes, I recognized her straight off. Fugitive. On the run for months. Consider yourself lucky I relieved you of a very real threat. Thanks aren't necessary."

He takes a final puff then pockets the vape.

"I'm going to ask you once more. Where did you come from? Who's been helping you?"

I wipe the blood from my face.

"West. No one," I reply.

His expression darkens.

"You know what happens to people that get in the way of progress?" Spittle glistens on his thin bottom lip as he leans in.

I look past him to the weapons, wondering how I can get to them.

"I'll take a stab and bet you got a thing for fiddles and boats and haunting ballads and shit. Am I right?"

He stands and turns his back to me.

"You think this all just happened. Just materialized?"

I use the opportunity to pull my knees to my chest, testing my strength.

Victor turns. He holds a syringe in his hand.

"Fentanyl is fifty times more powerful than heroin, did you know that? And Carfentanil, is even more potent, it's the shit they use to sedate elephants. Elephants for fuck sakes! Yet druggies flock to it. The tiniest miscalculation in dosage is bye-bye. And yet this is what society embraced as a recreational drug."

He gazes at the syringe, transfixed.

"Patches and pill forms are unpredictable, the size of the dose too hard to determine accurately. That's why I prefer liquid. Fentanyl's absorbed through the skin, you don't even have to inject it. There's enough in this needle to silence a dozen dissenters."

I try to speak but I'm consumed in another coughing fit.

He breaks his trance.

"Fiddles and ships fiddles and ships fiddles and ships fiddles and ships." His voice trails off, sanity along with it. I sense the shift in his demeanour, his playtime ending. I maneuver my hand behind me, feeling around my rear cargo pocket for my multi-tool.

Victor pops the orange cap off the syringe and depresses the plunger, holding it towards the lantern, analyzing the tiny bead of liquid, lost in deranged thought.

"Did you ever dream your own death—prophesize your final moments? Wonder how it all ends?"

He sits back down in the chair, leaning forward, his yellow bug-eyes gazing into mine.

"Know what I did before the great purge? Where I came from, who I was?"

I don't respond. There are no right answers. I rest my hand over top the multi-tool.

"I was a sheepdog. A cop. Do you know the analogy? Wolves, sheep and sheepdogs? I won't bore you with the details, but I was a protector of the weak, that's what good men do."

"Where is she?" I repeat.

His cheeks burn red. He stands and turns away from me.

"If you hurt her…"

He cuts me off.

"Yes?"

"I'll kill you." My hand slips into my rear pocket.

He spins to face me and cocks his head in that curious puppy sort of way.

"That would be a neat trick."

He gazes at my hands, his eyes wide, aware.

"You weren't a cop," I say. "A wanna-be maybe. You're just a dirt-bag drug dealer."

His body posture changes, his breathing pronounced. He steps towards the bed and I pull the multi-tool out, fumbling for the blade.

"You're right you know. You're intuitive. I see that now. Sheepdog is old world. *Passé.* I've gotta get with the times."

He spins.

"I prefer wolf now."

He points the Glock and fires.

I hear the shot, and all goes dark.

CHAPTER 57

Playing possum is not a skill I possess. But then again, who's playing. The bullet hitting the vest at close range felt like a sledgehammer. I embraced death at that moment, certain I wouldn't survive a forty-calibre bullet to the chest at that range. Had he aimed higher, I'd be having a cold beer on the banks of Lake Ainslie with Cecil right now.

I open my left eye. It's been a bad week for shiners.

Victor is gone, the lantern gone with him. The balcony is vacant, but there's a light emanating from beneath the door to my right.

I hear talking, a back and forth, but only one voice, like they're on a phone or two-way radio. Something about 'not bothering to interrogate' and 'execute'.

I struggle to rise, my chest on fire, each breath worse than the last. Victor's in the next room. I hobble over to the bed, the rifle still there but the gun belt and knife are gone. I pick up the weapon, checking the chamber, when the sound of whistling rises from the other room; the familiar ballad, Cecil's tune, only an upbeat, remastered version. The bastard just shot me, and he's whistling a happy tune.

I move towards the doorway, staying in shadow. From outside the balcony, voices are arguing, car tires screeching, engines revving.

I press myself flat against the wall, pausing to wipe the blood from my face. A one-eyed king can't afford to contaminate his only working eye. The whistling grows louder as an elongated shadow appears across the carpeted floor. I watch as he steps past, the lantern in his hand, wearing my gun belt around his waist, accentuating his silk pyjama ensemble. He stops and turns.

I cross-check him in the face with the rifle, dropping him for a ten minute major and game misconduct. Teeth shatter, blood spews, the lantern drops from his hand.

He hits the floor with a thud and is still. I grab the lantern and inspect the damage. His mouth is a mess, lower front teeth missing; so much for those debonair looks. Sorry about your luck, Elvis.

I unclasp the gun belt and remove the handcuffs, latching one cuff to his right wrist. It takes all my strength, but I manage to drag his limp body to the bed, thankful he's bony as shit and not built like his counterpart. I raise the corner of the mattress and snap the other cuff onto the bedframe.

Time is a factor.

The others will be here, know something's gone awry. I pull the radio from the holder and check to see that it's on. Grabbing the lantern, I step into the adjoining room; it's a second bedroom, smaller than the suite with side-by-side double beds facing the window. The room is empty, but there's a new deadbolt on an adjoining door, hardware that doesn't quite match the décor. That's where they're keeping her. I drop the radio on the bed and unlatch the door. Candlelight flickers from within.

It's a small bedroom, unfurnished, only a cot and tray table. Allie lies atop the portable bed, covered in a thin blanket, naked, unconscious. Medical supplies, vials and syringes adorn the table beside her.

I step up, setting the lantern on the table. Her breathing is shallow, her skin pale. I touch her shoulder.

"Allie?"

No response. Her cheek is bandaged and bruised, her skin cool, clammy. I feel for her pulse, not knowing what the fuck it is I'm looking for. If she's breathing, she has a pulse, what the fuck am I thinking?

I shake her.

"Allie."

She doesn't react. I look over and see her clothes, folded neatly in the corner.

From outside the room, a voice comes over the radio.

"Boss?"

More talking, indistinguishable, the radio cutting in and out.

I rummage through the supplies and find a canister of Naloxone. The directions are illegible, the font so tiny even with a magnifying glass I wouldn't have a hope in hell. I pop the tab and test the plunger.

I check her again, placing my ear to her lips. She's breathing, as far as I can tell, but it's shallow. I try to rouse her again, but she doesn't react.

More radio jabber from the other room. I have to do this now.

I place the canister to her nostril and spray.

The radio crackles.

"You coming down or am I coming up? I need a thumbs up."

Allie remains still. I should administer another dose, but I don't know how soon is too soon. How the fuck would anyone know that? I consider going for the radio, pretending I'm Victor to buy some time, but that could backfire.

Allie opens her eyes.

The effect is immediate.

"It's okay, it's me," I lean in. "You're okay."

Her eyes dart back and forth as she tries to sit up. I hold her shoulders, keeping her secure, ensuring she doesn't rise too quickly.

She looks around the room, down at herself, then at me, realization creeping back slowly. I release her, and she sits up on her own, one hand behind her back, bracing herself.

"Why am I always naked around you?"

I smile.

"Your clothes are there." She grabs my chin, pulling me close.

"You look awful," she says, a look of sadness consumes her. "What have they done to you?"

"I'm okay."

"Where?" She gazes about the room.

I point to the doorway. "We have to move."

I help Allie to her feet.

"Get dressed, I'm next door. Move fast," I say, snatching the lantern and stepping into the second bedroom. I grab the radio off the bed and head into the suite.

Victor lies on his back, moaning quietly, his cuffed arm extended over his head awkwardly. I turn off the lantern and step onto the balcony, keeping low, staying in shadow. The night is dark, but a thin wisp of moonlight is visible, the storm moving off.

A large truck sits abandoned at an angle, halfway up the winding driveway. It's a beer truck—and not just any beer truck; it's an Alexander Keith's. The front tires are flat, the grill smashed, likely the impact I heard earlier. Four silhouettes stand out front of the disabled transporter of magic elixir, their bodies outlined by the still shining headlights. A fifth silhouette is on his knees, in front of the truck's steaming grill. I step back into the room and grab the thermals off the bed, then back to the balcony.

Ben is on his knees, hands bound behind his back, shirtless, his ponytail hanging down the front of his chest. Even from this distance, I can distinguish his tattoo.

He came back. Beer truck and all. His getaway vehicle—a beer truck.

The radio crackles in my hand.

"Waiting on you."

Bull appears at the truck, holding a long gun in one hand, a radio in the other. All eyes glance up towards the balcony, towards my location. I duck.

Victor is stirring from the other room, calling out. Allie has yet to appear and I glance to the sniper rifle, then back to Ben.

The radio crackles again.

"Tick tock boss."

I hold the radio arm's length from my face and press the button.

"Hold up. On my order," I say, releasing the button.

"Copy that."

I drop the radio and grab the rifle, taking a low position on the far left side of the balcony, staying close to the wall. Without the benefit of a tripod, I push a chair against the outer ledge and rest the barrel on the raised back. I just fucking hope they aren't watching with binoculars, or I'm fucked. I position the rifle barrel as best I can and lower to a half squat position, my muscles expressing their displeasure.

The radio crackles.

I press my eye to the scope. My hands are shaking, my leg muscles already struggling.

I focus the crosshairs on Ben's face a moment. He's cut up, bleeding. A hand holds his head up by his ponytail, another points up towards the balcony. Towards me. I duck.

Victor is calling out from the other room, whimpering.

I raise my head and press my eye to the scope.

The radio cuts in.

"Are we doing this?"

The crosshairs are on Bull, shaky, but more or less on him. I watch as he hands the radio off and takes the gun with both hands. The others step back, giving him plenty of room. Ben remains motionless, just like Cecil, resigned to his fate.

Bull raises the gun, pointing it down at a forty-five-degree angle, three feet from Ben's head.

Victor is yelling now, screaming.

I line up the crosshairs on Bull's chest, an ample target, but my aim is deteriorating, fatigue and blood loss overriding my coordination.

There's a high-pitched yelp from behind me. Victor is silent.

I know what that means.

I concentrate, holding my breath, steadying the crosshairs.

Bull slides the Oakley's to his forehead and looks up towards the balcony. He flashes the thumbs up sign, then leans in on Ben, the barrel less than a foot from his throat.

I start my trigger pull.

I hesitate.

"Do it."

Allie is behind me.

I pull the trigger.

The shot is low, but the results, adequate. Bull's groin is gone, a conglomeration of testicles and intestines covering the grill behind him. He's down and out. Roadkill.

No time to admire my handiwork, I line up a second shot, but everyone scatters. Except for Ben. He stands, bewildered, freeing his hands and picking up the shotgun. He looks to the bloodbath, then up in my direction. He can't see me, but waves then disappears into the shadows.

"Let's go." I turn, but Allie is gone.

I step in the room, slinging the rifle.

Allie stands over Victor, the Glock in her hand. He's bleeding profusely from the forehead, silenced by her wrath. He'd managed to drag the bed a few feet across the floor before being intercepted by Thelma, and her unpredictable temper.

"Ain't this a pickle?" he lisps through shattered teeth.

She stares through him, a look of unsettling calm on her face. A look I've seen before.

"What are the chances of a negotiation?" He sits up. "You both walk out of here, no one comes after you. Just pass me the radio. No harm, no foul. My word."

"Allie, leave him, let's move," I say, heading towards the main doors.

Victor coughs, spitting copious amounts of blood onto his Persian rug. "What he said." He wipes his mouth.

Allie doesn't budge.

"You may wanna relieve her of the weapon." His lisp is worse. "Remember our little chat?"

Desperation shows in his giant eyes, despite the insincere smile on his emaciated lips.

Voices erupt in the hallway, outside the door. I bolt the latch knowing it's futile, but worth the few seconds it may buy.

"Plan B?" Allie asks. Her gaze is still locked on Victor.

"Well past that," I say.

Knocking and pounding on the doors, voices overlapping.

"I can fix th-is," Victor continues, wiping his face with his lapel. "Let me t-talk to them."

More shouting.

"Boss?"

"Break it down!"

"Is there another way out?" I ask.

Allie shakes her head.

"Balcony?"

We're two stories up, but desperate times call for ingenuity, Spiderman tactics. What're a few broken bones to a dying man?

A boot crashes into the door. Allie spins, facing off with the pending intruders as I grab the rifle and step up beside her.

"The balcony," I say, "I'll hold them off." I raise the rifle.

And then I feel it.

I look down in time to see Allie stomp Victor's forearm, snapping it cleanly at the wrist. He shrieks as the bedroom doors splinter.

The room starts to spin.

In that moment I see Allie yelling but hear nothing. It's as if time has slowed, like some bastard unplugged the turntable, mid-song.

A hand reaches through the shattered door panel, grasping for the lock. Allie is on her knees, searching for something. My arms grow numb, my fingers tremble, the rifle slips from my grip. Allie pulls something from my ankle.

It's a syringe.

She looks up at me, our gaze locked for a brief moment, then she twists and jams the needle into Victor's eye socket. He screams, convulsing, his body twisting and flopping like a marlin on meth.

As my consciousness dissipates, my synapses misfire, colours bleed grey and black. I fall limp and Allie catches me, saying words I cannot comprehend. Her eyes evoke terror, but I'm at peace.

This is what dying feels like.

It's not that bad.

Flashes of light and blasts of gunfire envelop my senses.

Allie is pulling me across the floor as I watch Victor, lying motionless, the syringe dangling from his eye socket, his gaze frozen. We're on the same journey, him and I, the great reckoning, but all I can think of is how stupid he looks in those pyjamas.

I'm speaking but the words evaporate.

"I was born on the 21st," I say. It seems important now, but I no longer remember why.

Allie holds me, protecting me, my guardian angel. Her gaze shifts.

A figure stands over us, bathed in a haze of spiralling colours.

I reach out to touch her cheek. She takes my hand and leans in close. I feel her breath on my ear, her tears, as they trickle across my face.

I hear a shot.

Then nothing.

CHAPTER 58

Death comes for us all. Saints and sinners, preachers and parasites, no one gets a hall pass. Humanity is finite, one piece of a giant puzzle, a single drop in an ocean of tears, a grain of sand in a desert of forgotten moments. We live only to die and expire from conscious thought, from memory, obliterated from history, a forgotten blip in an infinite realm.

In our absence, life carries on. The sun will rise over Cape Breton, the cycle of life impervious to humankind. Amidst the valleys and mountains, the lakes and rivers, death has no lasting power, no influence beyond this single moment in time.

Faith is relinquished, mortality uncoiled.

In the presence of glory, we all expire to dust.

CHAPTER 59

I awaken to music—a hundred fiddles, playing in unison, the sound emanating from within. I feel movement, but I am lying still, wondering if I'm in heaven or hell, or somewhere in between.

My eyes open. Sunlight bleeds in from above, illuminating the narrow quarters that confine me. I sense the right side of my face is bandaged and I sit up. Beside me, a tray-table is awash with medications, bandages and washcloths. I'm in the hull of a ship, a watercraft of some sort, an interior adorned with intricate wood inlay, leather upholstery and brass fixtures. The boat sways, but we aren't moving, at least I don't get that sense. We're docked. But where? I search my mind, but the memory lapse is resolute; I remember only Bras d'Or Manor, finding Allie, but the rest is black.

To my left, the passage leads upwards to the deck. I'm dressed in grey sweatpants and a Jimmy Buffett t-shirt, the words 'A Pirate Looks at Forty' emblazoned on the front. Someone has a sense of humour in the apocalypse. Across from me is an envelope, taped to the side of the bunk, the name 'Jack', written on it in red ink.

I ease myself up and reach for the letter, sitting back down with a thump, my head foggy, my balance precarious. The envelope contains the photo of Rene and I at the Causeway, the same photo on our wine bottles, the glossy paper creased and worn, as if I'd been carrying it a lifetime, like some wandering fool traversing the apocalypse with nothing but a memory. Allie likely found the photo in that curious way she has of stumbling upon my most intimate possessions. I unfold the handwritten note, adorned with that familiar penmanship I've come to know.

Dear Jack,

Welcome back to the world of the living. I'm sorry I couldn't remain, but I hope to be back soon. You gave us a scare, clinically dead—twice, but you came through. You never gave up. We'll have to chat when I return, I am curious to know about those few minutes you left us, where you went, and what it was like.

If not for Ben, we would both be gone. We are safe. For now. But as you'll soon come to know, a greater threat has arisen. I've been asked to seek out another, someone of importance. I'm to bring her back to Sydney. Ben wanted to accompany me, but I've asked him to stay and care for you, to make sure you rest, and take your medication. We need the old Jack back, and soon.

We've tended to your wounds as best we could. Your fever worried us, but thankfully it broke before I had to leave. They have a medic here, but I'm sorry to tell you, you have lost your eye to infection.

You'll have questions, they'll be answered in time. Just know this Jack— you are here for a reason, whether you choose to believe or not. It wasn't me that was being led here. It was you. I was your guide. Not a very good one it turns out, but you're here now, and I count that as a win. Everyone we encountered, everything we experienced; the numerological signs, the dreams, the music, remains part of something much bigger. Something that began decades ago. Our birthdates were not random, nor were the choices we made, or the paths we followed.

In time you will come to understand and accept your purpose. Our paths converged as they were meant to, but the journey has only just begun. The location of the new life force, the energy we now adopt and embrace, is known. I will tell you more upon my return—and you'd better be sitting down.

These are good people, people like us. They are eager to meet Captain Jack, (that's your new nickname by the way). Fitting, don't you think?

If you still have doubts, I leave you with this;

These people dreamed of you, Jack. Every one of them.

And now you're here.

I never did thank you for what you did.

But know that I am deeply grateful, and forever indebted.

Be safe, I will see you soon.

Allie,

P.S. Check out the name of the boat, then we can debate the theory of coincidences.

I fold the paper and slip it back into the envelope along with the photo. I stand and step towards the ship's washroom, the head. The tiny space is pristine, sparkling and welcoming, like a five-star resort bathroom, micro-version. I study myself in the mirror, a clean gauze over my wound, my eyebrow shaved off. I don't recognize myself, my skin yellow and taught, like a heroin addict after a weeklong bender. I manage a weak smile and make my way to the ladder, allowing the sunshine to penetrate my core.

Emerging on deck, I gaze about my surroundings, the chilly ocean breeze duelling with the sun's warming rays. The boat is one of several docked alongside the pier at Sydney harbour. To my left, the great fiddle reaches upwards to the teal blue sky, sixty feet of polished mahogany, a symbol of hope and promise, guardian of humankind's future. People mill about the boardwalk, inspecting a goliath cruise ship that sits docked beside the Sydney Welcome Centre; the Norwegian Escape, likely the last ship to grace the harbour before the great cleansing.

I look to my left and Ben appears, wearing a Jimmy Buffett 'Changes in Attitudes, Changes in Latitudes' t-shirt, his cuts and bruises healed, a broad smile across his face. He nudges me and points.

The doors to the Welcome Centre open, people begin pouring out.

I watch as a steady stream of both men and women approach, different ethnicities, all ages, but no children. They look like an average cross-section of tourists visiting the island on any given day. Some are smiling, a few frowning, others wide-eyed and curious, as if Royalty has descended upon the shores.

Ben points towards an entourage of men approaching from the other direction. They walk in unison, in formation, six of them, all wearing dark suits and sunglasses; the Cape Breton version of *Men in Black*, or the *Blues Brothers*, whatever your preference.

The crowd of onlookers parts, allowing them passage. As they near the boat, the tallest of the group, an elderly black gentleman with vibrant salt and pepper hair, steps forward.

"Welcome Jack. You up for a chat?"

I look to Ben, who nods.

I nod.

"Wonderful."

They turn and head off towards the Welcome Centre.

Ben climbs down from the boat and I follow, taking his hand, careful not to ruin the moment by breaking a hip in front of a mesmerized audience. The bystanders watch intently as we walk along the pier, nodding and acknowledging each onlooker as we pass. I remember Allie's note, and pause to glance back at the boat.

It's there, centred above the outboard motors, the boat's namesake—*Blackjack*—an Ace of Spades and Jack of Hearts logo, emblazoned beneath.

I smile.

"I never did thank you," I say, looking to Ben. "So, thank you. And thanks for the shirt."

He nods, offering me a cigarette.

The thought of it makes me ill. I shake my head.

We walk, the ocean air revitalizing, the sunlight soothing, the eyes of strangers scrutinizing our every step. I tap Ben on the shoulder.

"Where has she gone?"

Ben's expression darkens. He types into his phone, an enormous new Samsung, and hands it to me.

It says one word.

Baddeck.

A bird cries overhead and I look. Two bald eagles, juveniles, hover above.

"Maybe I will have that smoke."

THE END

ABOUT THE AUTHOR

Mike Senczyszak is a Canadian author from Southern Ontario, occasionally hanging his hat in Cape Breton and Central Florida. A dabbler in screenwriting, horror fiction and children's books, Mike's been an aspiring author for more years than he'd care to admit.

And he finally got around to writing that book.

Stay tuned for Book Two in the series.

Visit www.senczyszak.com